REKIYA & Z

REKIYA & Z

Muti'ah Badruddeen

Copyright © 2020 by Muti'ah Badruddeen.

ISBN:	Softcover	978-1-6641-3143-9
	eBook	978-1-6641-3142-2

All rights reserved. No part of this book may be reproduced or transmitted in any form or by any means, electronic or mechanical, including photocopying, recording, or by any information storage and retrieval system, without permission in writing from the copyright owner.

This is a work of fiction. Names, characters, places and incidents either are the product of the author's imagination or are used fictitiously, and any resemblance to any actual persons, living or dead, events, or locales is entirely coincidental.

Any people depicted in stock imagery provided by Getty Images are models, and such images are being used for illustrative purposes only.
Certain stock imagery © Getty Images.

Print information available on the last page.

Rev. date: 09/28/2020

To order additional copies of this book, contact:
Xlibris
844-714-8691
www.Xlibris.com
Orders@Xlibris.com

DEDICATION

For My Daughters, S & A,
And My Sisters, My friends
The Women who bring Sense to Life.

And

For N.S.
And everyone I have lost in the course of my life.
The marks you have left remains.
Constant.
Indelible.

I

PROLOGUE

My eyes sweep over the room one more time as I walk back to my seat. The restrained smile on my face would be considered self-satisfied by most of the people present.

They would be wrong.

I, on the other hand, had no problem deciphering the somewhat-enthusiastic applause that accompanied the end of my presentation, part admiration, part amazement, mostly envious. No one seated in that room had any misconception about what the figures I had just gone through meant. My supposedly already-phenomenal, meteoric rise in the finance world just got shot to the stratosphere. In the cut-throat world of international business, this latest success translated to less space on the proverbial rung of the corporate ladder for many of the people clapping.

Stopping every few steps, I accept the reluctant congratulations of my colleagues, and the more effusive praise from the partners and directors who had flown in for this meeting. I had just made them more money, after all. Tons of it.

I sat through the last few minutes of the meeting with what has been termed, snidely I believe, my customary cool. No one looking would guess what I felt right then.

Nothing.

I recently closed a deal that would put my name on the list of *who is who* in international finance, making the firm – and myself - considerably richer. This was the elusive career-making deal, the stuff of legends. And since I have never been besieged by false modesty, I appreciate the enormity of what I have done.

I had just pulled off the improbable.

When I accepted the job of heading the start-up division eighteen months ago, I understood quite clearly the unstated risk. My entire career was riding on the success of the venture.

And it had been hard work; an audacious accomplishment made possible only by work of my dedicated but small staff of overachievers - all carefully selected, ruthlessly ambitious and mostly local. We had burned the midnight diesel – power outages being just one of the staples that doing business in Nigeria entailed – and it had paid off. Our hitherto experimental division would now become a fully functional branch, with three times the initial staff; all of whom were getting raises, added benefits and all sorts of promotions.

I, Rekiya Yusuf, at just thirty-two, had just been named Chief Financial Officer, Africa of a major international finance company.

In local parlance, *I don arrive.*

Yet I felt nothing.

It would be scary, this feeling, if it wasn't so familiar. But I have been here before. In truth, I lived in it – in this void of nothingness – for years. With the challenge of the past few months, I'd let myself hope, had let myself believe that I was – finally - past it.

Apparently, I had been wrong.

My cell phone rings just as I return to the office assigned to me. I root through my handbag for it, noting distractedly that the number was unregistered.

'Hello?'

'Ruqqayyah?'

I pause. I haven't been Ruqqayyah in a decade.

'Is this Ruqqayyah Gbadamosi?'

That voice. The emotion it bore. I know them, intimately. But not together.

'Yes?' Tentative, the response is out of character for the woman I have worked so hard to become.

A sigh breathed across the lines, poignant, and carrying its own weight of burdens.

'As-Salaam alayki warahmatullaah.'

CHAPTER ONE

Rekiya

I maneuver the car through the crowded road flanked on both sides by the boisterous Bodija Market and marvel at how little has changed in the years since I was here. The road, still chocked to almost a single lane on either side, was teeming with traders, street peddlers displaying their wares in innovative manners that had no regard for the traffic swirling about them. And their customers, haggling over the smallest bit of a bargain, they all paid no heed to whatever inconvenience they caused.

Bargaining is a time-honored tradition in this part of the world.

Pedestrians and commuters abound, coming, going, chasing or dropping off from the numerous buses. Buses – and surely, these, locally referred to as *danfo*, were the most ragged contraptions to bear that name - idled or drove by at snail speed. Hanging off the space for the usually absent doors, the conductors added their own lyrics to the cacophony of noise.

'*Agbowo. Yuu-ai. Ojooooo!*'

The scene held the distinctive bustle of an African city yet was less frenetic than would be expected of one this size. It was a welcome relief from the almost manic pace of Lagos, had a much slower and less desperate air to it. The place boasted a distinct something – a soul, if one was being prosaic – that I never noticed until now, was lacking in Abuja. This is the incongruous, seemingly irreconcilable oddity that is Ibadan, the largest city in West Africa.

A feeling of home-coming, as undeniable as it was fleeting, washes over me.

I lived in this city for a mere seven years as a girl. Most of it in the controlled environment of Noorah; the Girls-only Muslim boarding secondary school I attended. I haven't been back in ten years. It is disconcerting that I felt – even so briefly - as though this was home. It is something I never felt about any other place in my entire rootless existence – not in the city of my childhood and current residence, and definitely not in my country of birth and citizenship-by-default.

A few meters ahead, beyond the chaos of the market, I make a turn. The roads in this largely residential area are older. The tarred surface is always in a perpetual battle with the dirt path that would have – in a country where things like that mattered - been a sidewalk. Erosion from a high annual rainfall, the lack of an effective drainage system, and the endemic absence of a maintenance culture made it a losing fight. This road was nothing but a narrow strip of tar, which was fringed on both sides by large path of dirt, and generously dotted with potholes.

I pull into a side street and… stepped back in time.

Nothing, at least none that I could see, had changed here. If anyone ever ascribed a 'sub-urban' appellation to Ibadan, it would be to this neighborhood. The streets were somewhat planned – a throwback to an era before everyone that could, grabbed a piece of land to put down a structure with no thought to pesky details like drainage or even thorough-fare. The houses were old; bungalows or single-storied, with low fences and fenestrated gates. When I stayed here, most had been occupied by the owners – older, mostly retired folks, with long-empty nests who saw no need to hide behind six-foot walls and impenetrable fences. And though they lacked the elaborate ostentation of newly constructed structures, it was a serene environment, quite unexpectedly so, in such proximity to the mayhem of the market.

I park on the street in front of a nondescript single-story house and shove down emotions that threaten to overwhelm me. Since the phone call yesterday, I had gone from feeling nothing to feeling... everything. I can't handle my emotions, or so my former therapist always said. I do what she was forever accusing me of - I push them all away, take a deep breath and exit the car. The gate is not locked, something else that had not changed. If memory serves, finding it locked in daytime meant no one was home.

The door swings open inwardly before I get the chance to knock. Though I couldn't see into the shadowy interior of the house from my position in the blazing sun, I know there's someone behind the door. That door has been a hijab for the women of this house since long before I knew them. I step into the cool, dark house, and find myself automatically going through the motions borne from a lifetime ago - I move off to the side, toe off my shoes and turn to put them away. The shoe-rack is different, newer, but it occupied the same spot.

'*As-Salaam alayki warahmatullaah wabarakah.*' Zaynunah stood where I had envisioned her, in the space hitherto shielded by the now-closed door. 'I am so glad you could come.'

'*Wa alayki salaam warahmatullaah wabarakah.*' I am relieved – and maybe a bit saddened – that she did not try to hug me. 'I am so sorry about your...' I falter, briefly. 'Mummy. May Allaah forgive her, admit her into His Mercy, and grant you all the fortitude to bear the loss.'

'Aameen.'

I cringe inwardly at the stilted formality of my speech, and at the quiet distance in her reply.

Silence, short and uncomfortable, ensues. Then, 'Come into the kitchen. I'm alone in the house. Daddy went to the farm. I'm supposed to be going through Mummy's stuff but…' A small shrug, a wet smile. 'I'm baking. How long can you stay? I'm really sorry I pulled you away from your…whatever brought you to Lagos. When do you have to go back?'

There is so much I do not understand from what she said, but I do not ask. Her rambling, after all, sprung from the same place as my awkward condolence speech.

'It's no problem,' I wave away her concerns. 'I was already done. And it's a good thing I was in Lagos this week. So, I can, maybe, get a hotel… Stay a few days…'

'Oh, you can stay here!' she interrupts. 'You have to stay here! You know you are always welcome here.'

That assertion, the floodgates of memories and emotions carried in its wake, is too much. I bolt.

'Ok. Er…I'm just going to bring my bag in then,' I toss over my shoulder as I yank the door open and rush out.

Sitting in the car, I try to find some calm, some refuge from all the emotions that had been bludgeoning me since the fateful phone call yesterday. I had gone from my abyss of nothingness to this unfamiliar state of emotional overload. As someone who had spent the past decade or so of her life almost completely detached from her emotions, I am not sure how to handle this.

When Zaynunah called me out of the blue yesterday that her mum was dead, I had known this trip would be difficult. I just hadn't realized how much.

The first time I met Zaynunah's mum, I had been a wreck of teenage nervousness. Zaynunah talked about her mum a lot, and I was in awe of my mental image of her – a cross between an angel and Wonder Woman. That she had invited me, a strange girl she'd never met, into her home for the four days of a mid-term holiday just seemed to buttress this point.

I hadn't wanted to go to Abuja for the midterms. Even the two-hour bus ride to the airport in the air-conditioned school bus with other long-distance girls, drunk on freedom of being away from the strictures of Noorah was not enough to make the trip worth it. I would have been fine – kind of – to stay in school for those four days, along with any other girl whose parents did not make travel arrangements for the midterms. I had done that once, in my first year, when my mother and her husband had been away on their honeymoon. True, I had hated it then, but I am a big girl now – almost fifteen – I could do it.

After listening to me prose along these lines for days on end, Z invited me to stay with her for the holidays. I had demurred, she had persisted, the school had called my mum – who had agreed – and there I was. Squeezed into a commuter bus – a first for me – between Z and a woman whose hips should have been charged a double fare by default, I did not know what to expect.

'As-Salaam alaykum' Z called into the seemingly empty house as she removed her sandals, stuck her socks into them, and motioned for me to do the same.

'Mum, we're home' she continued, removing her hijab as she walked further into the house.

I mirrored her actions and followed, bemused. I had never seen Zaynunah without her hijab before. In our six months of after-school hanging out, it was my first time seeing my friend's hair. I would occasionally remove my regulation headscarf – as Z would call it – claiming the heat, or not wanting to get it dirty. Or pretty much any excuse I could find, really, to remove the head-cover. But not Z; she always sat there, calm as a clam in her bigger-than-mandated hijab, her ease and comfort long borne of familiarity and conviction.

Before I could process this new development, though, and possibly tease her about it, a woman appeared in one of the doorways ahead of us.

'Baby, you're back' she says, unnecessarily. 'Wa alaykumu salaam warahmatullah. How was school?'

She turned to me. 'You must be Ruqqayyah. Welcome to our home, dear.'

'Thank you, Ma, for having me' I put up the pretty airs I had not bothered to display for years. I very much want for Zaynunah's mum to like me.

She was older than I expected, her middle-age appearance probably more jarring due to my own mother's relative youth. She was also much shorter than her daughter, closer to my own rather middling height. I could not make out her features clearly in the dimly lit corridor we stood in, but the vibes I got from her were welcoming.

'Oh, no need for all of that,' she waved off my thanks. 'Baby, take your friend up to your room while I finish lunch. Ruqqayyah, I hope you like amala?' she called, heading back into the kitchen.

'Baby?' I teased as I followed Z up the stairs.

'Well, with ten years between my second brother and I, yes, I'm the baby' She ducked her head, embarrassed. 'I've asked her to stop calling me that but…'

'Hmm, I don't know' I sniggered. 'I think it's cute. And you are kind of a baby.'

She rolled her eyes at me; I had been lording our ten-month difference in age over her ever since we exchanged birthdays. We giggled as we made our way up the stairs….

Those four days would become a tradition – I never went to Abuja for midterms after that. I became a constant presence in the household. Zaynunah's family became my family, and her mother became 'Mummy'. At first, this was because that's what Nigerians – the Yoruba especially – do. Any woman old enough to be your mother was addressed thus, if your relationship with her – and not necessarily a familial one – was sufficiently close enough. It was the first time I had cause to use that form of address in years. Eventually, it was more than an appellation, she became to me the epitome of what a 'Mummy' is; this woman whose effect on me, from a mere four years of contact, ripples across my life in ways I am still discovering.

And now, she's dead.

Zaynunah

She came!

The thought kept echoing in my head as I returned to the kitchen, and the mess I had made in the guise of baking. Truth is, a day after my mum's burial, I am not sure I am up to the task of packing up her belongings. And as the sole daughter, the men – my dad and brothers – had left it to me. So far, I haven't ventured further into the house than this kitchen since Yusuf, my husband, dropped me off here this morning. I suppose if I'd asked them, Daddy, my brothers – or even their wives – could have helped me. Daddy did perform the *ghusl* – the ritual washing of a dead Muslim in preparation for burial – with me yesterday...

She came!

The thought intruded on my inner soliloquy, again. In fairness, my head has been a basket of disjointed thoughts in the two days since Mummy's death; some thoughts dropping in as others fell through – most of them unrelated.

When the men had returned from the burial yesterday – oh, was I glad that Islaam exempts women from that task – we had read Mummy's will, and I knew I had to call Ruqqayyah. For a woman with very little worldly possessions, my mother had been diligent in keeping a will. She updated it every few days, adding or removing debts, and occasionally making bequests. The document was a painfully simple summary of her life. She listed all those who owed her money and proceeded to forgive all debts. She was not, to her knowledge, owed to anyone but urged us to publicize her death so that anyone with a recorded debt from her might come forward. Then she left bequests, of mostly sentimental items, to her daughters-in-law.

And to Ruqqayyah.

Ruqqayyah – she had been Rekiya to everyone else, even then – and I met in my first term at Noorah Academy; an exclusive Girls-only Muslim Secondary school located on the outskirts of Ibadan. It had been an elite, predominantly boarding facility that rarely admitted new students beyond the first year. My admission – as a day student – and in the fourth year, had been a special concession from the proprietress for some never-disclosed favor owed to my mother.

I had been resentful that first term of being the new girl in a new school, although I had known the move was inevitable for some time. Mummy had explained to me after her last unsuccessful encounter with the principal of the government school I had attended for my Junior Secondary. I knew I would have to move after my middle school final J.S.C.E. exams were done. Public school officials in south-west Nigeria maintained the colonial tradition of repressing religious rights of Muslim students. Refusing to let girls wear hijab was just one of their tactics. They uphold frantically, the legacy of the not-so-distant past when the colonial masters mandated coerced conversion of Muslim children in exchange for basic education. Things were only marginally better, even in the 1990s. My parents had tried in the three years I was there to gain a concession to modify the uniform more modestly and allow me to wear my hijab but, in the end, they gave up.

Mummy had involved me in the search for a new school; I drafted mail enquiries, vetoed prospectus and went for on-site visits with her. I had agreed wholeheartedly with the choice of Noorah; it had boasted the best combination of academics, extra-curricular, and faith-based environment that I decided would compensate for the trauma of moving to a new school. In those days when the 'Muslim' in 'Muslim School' in Nigeria had been a euphemism for 'sub-standard', Noorah had been years ahead of its time, with its unapologetic emphasis on combining Islaam with high educational standard.

For a comparatively high fee, but still.

And starting a new school as a high school student has got to be one of my teenage life's most trying experiences.

It hadn't helped that most of the girls in Noorah had been there for the past three years, living together for the majority of that time. That they had settled into well-defined roles in the drama of high school social scene, which I had to navigate my way through, clueless. My status – or lack of one – as a day student, and one with evidently middle-class roots had made it obvious that I wasn't going to be a social success in my new school.

Not that I had been one in my previous school.

There, in the government-run single-sex school, I had been the Muslim Girl; a niche that had been carved for me before I appreciated that I was being labeled. Everyone seemed to know I donned my hijab as soon as I stepped out of the school gates, and that I didn't do boys, music and parties. And my mother, the fully veiled Muslim woman who never missed a school event, was just as well-known. I had been the de-facto girl called on to pray on the Friday assembly; the one day a week when the Muslim prayers were used for morning devotionals. And in Ramadhaan, which was about the one month a year when most Nigerian Muslims suddenly took cognizance of their religion, I had random girls walking up to me to ask, 'Can I do this in Ramadhaan?'

At Noorah, I found myself amid Muslim girls, all of whom were regulated to wear headscarves, pray five times a day and memorize the Qur'aan, at least in part. Yet I was bereft. I couldn't seem to fit in. An introvert by nature and nurture, making friends had never been my forte, and teenage girls are not known for being the nicest of the population. I had a particularly hard time, and one day it had all seemed too much.

Classes were over, and the other girls had gone to their hostels. I should have headed to the school gates, but I sat alone in my empty classroom. Crying. Over something so inconsequential, I do not remember what it was anymore. All I remember is I was crying my teenage angst out, and Rekiya walked in.

I'd seen her before, of course. She was the Hausa girl with the rich, Yoruba father. But our paths had never crossed. She was a commercial student; I was in the sciences. She had a horde of very popular friends; the girls who wore their regulated scarves with as minimal covering but as much fashion statement as they could get away with. Whose conversations revolved around boys, parties and celebrity gossip; they were the self-appointed top of the social ladder. I, on the other hand, was the friendless new girl who had not even merited a place on the metaphorical ladder.

I had been mortified when she walked in on my pity-party and, after an initial startled glance, I kept my head down; trying to control the sobs, if not the tears streaming down my face. Being found in such an ignominious condition only compounded my humiliation and I wept even harder. Quietly.

It was a while later before I realized that Rekiya had not left like I expected her to. She had been standing over me the entire time, silent. She did not ask what the matter was, did not offer any comfort; she just stood there with an eerily blank expression that was unfamiliar to me. In my world, consisting mainly of teenage girls, everyone felt everything and had no reason to hide said feelings from anyone. And growing up in Ibadan, where the average stranger was not shy to tell you exactly how they feel, when they feel it strongly enough, it was an unnerving expression to behold. It was yet another reminder of how different I was from this girl standing before me; all she was, all that I could never hope to be; and I felt myself morphing from self-pity and mortification, to anger and defensiveness.

'What?! You never just get the urge to cry?' I eyed her balefully.

'No.'

The quiet response was so unexpected; I did not know what to say. Majorly because my question had been rhetorical - I had expected returned bravado, mollifying platitudes, evasion or awkward silence, not an answer. But who on earth does not cry? I mean, obviously not in public places where you can make an embarrassing spectacle of yourself but… 'No.'? And if, by some super-power, that was true, who goes around saying that to the girl that just had a cringe-worthy cryfest witnessed by the much cooler, and-not-a-friend, girl?

'Crying is a luxury affordable only if you have someone to console you.'

Rekiya had settled into the seat across from me. I eyed her again. There was something vaguely sad about her words, though I couldn't put my finger on it. She met my eyes briefly, then looked away.

'My father left when I was eight' she said, her blank gaze settling somewhere above my head. 'I haven't seen him since. A year after he left, my mother sent me here and got married. So, no, I do not cry.'

'Something smells nice' Ruqqayyah's voice breaks into my reverie as she strolls in, pulling a small overnight case on wheels behind her. She stops inside the kitchen door and looks around. 'Well, this kitchen has changed.'

I follow her gaze, seeing it through her eyes. After a minor fire incidence a few years back, my eldest brother and his wife had insisted on re-vamping the kitchen. There had been a major intervention; Mummy probably never threw out anything since she moved into this house as a young mother of one. Eventually, though, Brother 'Isa got his way and, a few weeks later, Mummy had a modern kitchen with minimalist décor. A single, but huge, open shelf filled with shiny new devices was off to one side. That, the breakfast nook with gleaming granite top and the gas oven-top stove made up the entire kitchen furniture. Mummy had grumbled that she got lost in all the space, but I thought she had been secretly thrilled with her new kitchen, flitting about and experimenting with her new appliances with barely masked glee.

Shaking off the memories now, I turned to Ruqqayyah who had settled at the breakfast nook. 'I'm making meat-pies and beef rolls to bribe Yu and the kids. Since you are staying here, I plan to do so as well.'

'Oh, really, I don't mind getting a hotel—'

'Enough already, Ruqqayyah, with the hotel talk! It's fine. Plus, you know Mummy would smack me from the *barzaakh* – if she could – if I let you go to a hotel.'

'Ooookay.' The word was several syllables long – a throw back to our years of friendship. 'If you say so. I just don't want to be a bother.'

I gaze at her, silent.

'Er…. You?' She raised a single brow. She is the only person I know able to do that naturally, and without affectation. It is still infuriating.

'Yu. Yusuf. My husband.' I remind her. 'It was a joke, it stuck.'

'Ah.' Bland, non-committal.

The rumbling from her tummy saves us from another awkward silence. She looks at me, sheepish. 'I didn't take breakfast. Habit.'

'The pies should be done' I chuckled, turning to the oven. 'Mummy had a variation of tea, as always, and orange juice, of course – but I know you hate that.'

'Oh, orange juice is fine' I hear her say as she reached into the fridge.

I'm sure my gaze is incredulous – the Ruqqayyah I knew hated orange juice with a ferocity that was disproportionate to the subject matter.

I guess people do change.

She doesn't meet my gaze as she took a sip of the juice and smiled, serenely.

CHAPTER TWO

Rekiya

Soon after I suffered through my brunch of baked goodies and orange juice – which I still hate; I have no idea what contrary spirit made me claim otherwise – Zaynunah's husband and children showed up. I had only seen him once, at their wedding, and wondered vaguely what he makes of me. I am so different from that girl from over a decade ago, she seems like a forgotten dream, even to me.

Fortunately, or not, depending on how you choose to view it, the family etiquette mirrored what I had become accustomed to in this house years ago. So, after an offhand, 'You remember Ruqqayyah, right?!' from her, her husband had greeted me with the salaam, mumbled a few words on how much it meant to his wife that I came, and withdrew to the living room. Veteran of the Islamic principle of segregation of the sexes, Sanusi-family style, I was not perturbed. I stayed in the kitchen and watched Z's kids. I'd never met any of them before. Apparently, she was a now home-schooling mother of four.

'*Ummu*, Abdul-Ghaffar smacked me!' Abdul-Maalik, her four-year-old son started as soon as he saw that the adults' conversation was breaking up. 'And Abdul-Mateen climbed that place you told him not to ever climb again. Plus, Khawlah made *Abu* angry; he said she spent the whole morning in her room and didn't help him with ANYTHING!' His voice soared triumphantly over the last word.

His older brothers – nine and six - immediately launched into counter-offensive speech; trying to refute, justify or talk their way out of the maternal approbation that the little tattletale had coming to them. The sheer volume and rapidity of words was unexpected, and I tried to tune out the chaos. After spending seven years in Ibadan, I could hold a decent conversation in Yoruba, but it was a language that has ceased to be familiar to me, over time.

Their sister, though, was quiet; awkward in the way girls her age – she had to be about twelve, now – often were. She was tall, towering over my five-foot-five frame, almost as tall as her mother, and already had the markings of the beauty she would grow into as her body matures into womanhood. Her skin was fairer than her mother, favoring her father, as she hadn't in looks, in his light complexion, the latter rather enhanced by the flowing navy-blue hijab she wore.

'And what did you do?' I hear Zaynunah ask knowingly and tickling her youngest son, the ruckus having finally died down.

'Me?! Nothing! I was a good boy!' he declared piously and squealed in a burst of hearty giggles. 'Just like I promised, yesterday. Will Grandma come back now?'

I sat through an impromptu explanation of death and the afterlife, couched in language that a child that young could relate to. Listening to phrases like 'going back to Allaah' and 'now behind a curtain' and 'we will all meet again, someday, insha Allaah' I wondered how much the boy comprehended. I gathered it wasn't the first time they were having this conversation since Mummy died, but how did one explain ephemeral concepts, such as these, to children. Zaynunah appeared to be managing quite well, though. She was patient, and detailed, but somehow age-appropriate in her explanation. It was an insight into who she was now; someone I did not know at all but who reminded me of the girl I knew years ago.

Losing interest in their mother's talk, the boys soon started eyeing me with the innocent fascination of the very young.

'Are you really our Auntie?' Six-year-old Abdul-Mateen finally approached me. 'Because both Ummu and Abu do not have any sisters, and our only aunties are their brothers' wives. So, whose wife are you?!'

I looked at his mum, momentarily floored. For one, he addressed me in flawless English. I was not expecting that, given the fluency of their Yoruba and maybe some previously unrecognized misconception I must have about homeschooling. Secondly, I have had virtually no contact with children since being one myself. I have no idea how to deal with them; these aliens that, hitherto, only existed on very distant fringes of my life. And how, pray, was I supposed to answer that question?

'No, dearie, Auntie Ruqqayyah is not your aunt by marriage.' His mother comes to my rescue. 'The title is honorary because she was my closest friend growing up. We went to school together; remember I used to tell you the stories from my school days.'

'What's honor-y?' Abdul-Maalik piped in, sliding up beside his brother to examine me up close.

'It means she has the honor of being your aunt, because she was as close as a sister to me.'

I note the past tenses wryly.

'If she was so close' asked Abdul-Ghaffar, too cool at nine to get in my face but inching closer, nonetheless. 'How come we never saw her before?'

I decide this conversation about me had gone on around me for long enough. 'I had been living outside the country for several years. I only just returned to Nigeria recently.'

I was not lying to a child - three years was recent in the scheme of things!

'Where were you living?' This was Abdul-Mateen again, he must be the unofficial spokesperson.

'New York, America.'

This started off an impromptu review of their geography lessons, and the older boys spouted random facts that they knew about America, the country and the continents. Even their sister joined in this conversation, suddenly looking like the little girl she was in her glee to show up her younger brothers.

I am an only child in my mind – my parents and their families, nonetheless. This scene was unfamiliar to me; the care-free children, the sibling bantering, the parental bonding. The unconditional love. I had glimpsed it in the past, usually in this same house, it just was not a part of my life. Sitting alone and, for the moment, forgotten in that kitchen that resembled nothing from my tucked-away memories, I suddenly wondered what I was doing there. This family – whom I did not know, not anymore – were dealing with a loss, a difficult loss. How presumptuous of me to put myself in the midst of it all. They didn't need me. They probably don't even want me here—

A tug on my suit pant brought me down from the ledge I was mentally jumping off of.

'Auntie Ruqqayyah, if you're not *really* family, why didn't you wear your hijab before Abu?'

Out of the mouth of babes.

I had known – somewhere in my subconscious – that this topic was going to come up. The last time any one of them - the adults, at any rate - had seen me, I had been garbed in the islaamic covering, even if I had only donned it for their benefit by then. I had assumed I'd, maybe, have a discussion with Zaynunah at some point. I must admit that I had a faint hope that it wouldn't come up. She, at least, knew that I haven't donned the hijab in nearly a decade – and her mother had just died! What I never envisaged was having the conversation with a precocious four-year-old mite.

In my fourth year at Noorah, I went back to the classroom area just before the afternoon siesta to retrieve a book I'd left behind and walked in on a crying girl.

I knew her, of course – Noorah was exclusive enough that the entire student body knew itself. Besides, she was the only new girl admitted after the second year, so everyone noticed. Prior to that day, though, I did not pay much attention to her. Occasionally, some of my friends who were in the science class with her would pick on her – make snide comments, try to embarrass her and all – but I had since learnt to dissociate myself from such scenes. Not to say I was an angel – I didn't stand up for the girls being bullied or anything like that - I just never understood the need to put others down.

When I walked in and saw the new girl having some sort of melt-down, my initial reaction had been. "Turn around and walk away! You can get your book during evening prep." I had spent the last few years of my life avoiding any emotional drama. I didn't want to be dragged into one now, for a girl I didn't know. Then I remembered what it was like my first year at Noorah; alone, home-sick and miserable, with no one to comfort me.

No one should ever have to cry alone.

I stood there, frozen. My throat constricting around the words I wished someone had said to me.

It's okay. It will be okay. You will be okay. I know it all doesn't make sense now but someday it will. Go ahead and cry; I'm here.

The words did not come, though, and I did not try to force them. What did I know anyway? But when she turned on me in anger, all bravado and aching vulnerability, I could not stop the words. I found myself telling her about my father, something I never did.

I left abruptly afterwards; not waiting for her reaction to my revelation; then spent the next few days waiting for the other shoe to drop. I had no illusion about the role my father's name played in my social standing at school. As daughter of one of the wealthiest men in the country, I had been an instant social success. At first, my sheltered background and the recent upheaval that necessitated my coming to Noorah made me uncomfortable with all the attention I got. But now, four years on, that attention – my life as the Hausa daughter of Chief Sodiq Gbadamosi – was all I knew. And I had just jeopardized that for an unknown new girl who would probably use it to her own end.

Armed with the information of my estrangement from my father – well, my parents' estrangement but who's splitting hairs – she held immense power. Not only could she strip me of my life as I knew it, she could easily shoot herself up the social ladder. Everyone, including my current so-called friends, would want to befriend her. It would be easier to get the juicy tidbits, that way.

I waited on pins and needles for it all to unfold, this scenario I had envisioned of my downfall from high school social grace. I watched for snide and condescending comments from my friends, for whispers as I walked, and pitying glances from the goodie-two-shoes.

Except it never happened.

As the days rolled into a week, then two, I accepted that she had not told anyone. Against my experiences and expectations, I had – fortuitously - managed to confide in the only girl in school who didn't gossip. And had no social ambition. Or was too naïve, too stupid, to realize the power she held in that tidbit. Whatever the reason, I was thankful. And increasingly, intrigued.

Casually, in seemingly random moments of paths crossing, I tried to get closer to her, to find out about her. She fascinated me; this girl whose single act of inaction had turned my perception of the world – the world of teenage girls, at least - on its head.

I started to hang back after classes, spending time with Zaynunah till her father came to pick her, or she left by way of public transport. And that, the fact that she took public transportation AND admitted it, was the epitome of what fascinated me about her. She was sincere and unpretentious; open in a way I had no experience with. With her, what you saw was what you got. She did not assume airs, and did not mince her words, yet she was genuinely kinder than any of the girls I knew.

In hindsight, I think it was our glaring differences that compelled us together. Opposites attracting or some silly such. Raised in Abuja, I had always thought of myself as Yoruba. I identified as such, even though my grasp of the language was virtually non-existent. In Nigeria after all, a child belongs to the father- name, tribe, history and opportunity. Coming to Ibadan; this bastion of Yoruba culture; showed me how self-delusional I was. Not only did I not speak the language, I was unschooled in the complex nuances that made up the Yoruba culture and its people. I had been glad when the students and staff assumed my mother was Hausa, her Northern upbringing having colored her speech and dress. And the Yoruba, I soon found out, are more tolerant and indulgent to an 'outsider' in matters of cultural gaffes, so I saw no need to enlighten anyone about my murky origins.

Zaynunah on the other hand was the quintessential Yoruba girl. Born and raised in Ibadan, she had a huge family of older people – grandparents, aunts, uncles, and many more, of otherwise unspecified relationship. She could interpret a hiss, a huff, a 'pele' and the numerous eye-rolls that are deftly employed by the Yoruba in any given interaction. She peppered her speech with sage proverbs and presumably wise parables and was unapologetic of her local Ibadan-accented Yoruba. Or its distinct bleeding into her spoken English.

For Z, her language, her family, her roots were as much a part of her as her own sense of self. I had none of that.

She was also a Muslim.

This should not have been of note, as we were, after all, in a school for Muslim girls. However, until I came to Noorah, I had only a very superficial and ceremonial association with religion. I have vague memories of visiting the mosque a few times with my father as a little girl. And we used to dress up and celebrated 'eid – the two annual Muslim festivals – but that was the extent of it. Deen, as religion was referred to at Noorah, was something else I had to adjust to. Suddenly, I was expected to shape every aspect of my life by its rules. It had recommendations for any and every situation, and opinions on what I did or didn't do.

It had been overwhelming at first.

I had never given much thought to a Higher Power, other than the occasional 'insha Allahu' tossed into speech as people from Northern Nigeria – irrespective of religion - were wont to do. Now I was expected to live every minute of my life as though He was with me, watching me with the ever-present, all-seeing eye.

Suddenly, the sunnah was no longer a random word I learnt about in Islamic Religion Knowledge class, but this larger-than-life thing that had an view on how I dress, eat, sleep and spend my free time, for crying out loud!

Four years on, my friends and I had figured out how to appear as though we were growing into the mold the school was trying to shape us in. Even as we fought to retain what we termed our youthful lease on life. We did the basic minimum required to get by the staff's hawk-eyed notice unsuspected. And subsisted on contraband magazines and music, hours spent reliving parties we attended during the break, the boys we had met, and planning our L.A.N. – life after Noorah.

Zaynunah, on the other hand, lived the Deen. She was the most knowledgeable girl on islaam I ever met. And she truly believed in it, and actively studied it. She harbored none of the resentment and rebellion of most of the other girls who came from the deeply religious homes. All those things that seemed like fantasy to me – about Allaah, His Prophets, and living one's life according to His dictates – were her life's purpose. My initial interaction with her had been with the morbid fascination of the 'other'.

The more I got to know her, though; I began to realize that there was more to this girl than any label my friends and I slapped on her. Quite apart – were such separation possible - from her middle class, local Ibadan Muslim persona, she was a vibrant, smart and caring girl. Her sincerity and openness made her a welcome change I never realized I wanted. Then there was her very droll wit and adventurous spirit which, she liked to claim, was bounded by the limits of halaal and haraam.

By the end of that term, I felt like two persons. During the afterschool one-hour hanging out with Z, I could be myself. At least, the self I think I would have wanted to be if the course of my life had been different. She, this self, was more laidback and honest and had an opinion on things other than fashion, music, boys and celebrity gossip. The rest of the time, I was the girl whose skin I had occupied for the past three years; shallow, self-absorbed and shamelessly riding high on the popularity of a name she had no right to.

I kept my two personalities separate for the three years it took us to graduate. I met Z after school, went to her house for mid-terms but never invited her to my group of friends. When our paths would otherwise cross in school, I would give her the salaam – or reply hers – and move on. I never let on that the day-student girl had become my best friend, at least not to anyone in school. She didn't indicate if this bothered her, and we never talked about it. As for me, I didn't have the courage to try to find out if our friendship could survive in the real world. After all, what could someone like Zaynunah Sanusi gain from friendship with a girl like me?

Now, looking into the perplexed face of her little son, I marvel at how little the dynamics of our relationship had changed in almost two decades.

Zaynunah

It was *maghrib* before Ruqqayyah and I made it upstairs. Yusuf had errands to run after *zuhr* and did not return for the children until almost sunset. My husband had been understanding, and my children surprisingly accepting, of the fact that I wanted to spend a few days here packing up Mummy's things. I prayed in the living room, we shared a dinner of *eba* and left-over *efo riro* from the pot I brought my dad yesterday and headed up the stairs.

I had suggested Ruqqayyah go upstairs to my childhood room many times during the day, but she declined. She had joined us in the living room after Yusuf left and, at some point, pulled out a sleek notepad. I imagine that with a job like hers, you carried your work wherever you went. After the little embarrassing episode about the hijab question, which I diverted attention from by bringing out the products of my morning labors, the children more or less accepted her presence.

As we enter Mummy's room now, though, the truth I had tried to outrun all day – with all the baking, the traveling down memory lane, even while engaging my children – hit me again, like the bricks from a crumbling stone wall.

Mummy is Dead!

My thoughts once again took on the scattered quality they adopted since Brother 'Isa called with news of Mummy's death.

My earliest memories are of building with blocks in this room while Mummy folded the laundry, and they collide in a kaleidoscope of images with the most recent ones of seeing her stretched out on the bed where my dad had laid her that fateful day. He had come home from work and found her at the top of the staircase, collapsed. The emergency room doctor suspected it might have been a massive heart attack, that she might have been an undiagnosed hypertensive.

In Nigeria, routine health checks were almost unheard of. If one was not ill and tried a couple of home-made or self-prescribed therapy that failed, one did not visit a doctor. And apparently, hypertension could be potentially fatal while remaining completely symptom- free, so it was the best guess, according to the doctors. Not that we could ever know for sure, unless we had agreed to subject her body to an autopsy. We declined.

Standing here, in her room – and it had always been "Mummy's room" despite my parents sharing it my entire life – I am awash with memories. The ratty, old couch in the corner where she read to me as a little girl, where she still read to my kids during our last visit, was worn and shabby looking, had always been – in all my memories. The massive, old-fashioned four-poster bed where she had given me the mortifying you-are-now-a-woman talk when my menses started at twelve, still in the pristine form I left it yesterday after the men took her body away. My father had been sleeping in his home office since he found her.

Her knitting paraphernalia still waited by the couch in the corner, the various yarns and what-nots unaware that they were soon to change owners.

Mummy is Dead! Mummy is Dead!

I snap out of my daze abruptly, remembering Ruqqayyah's presence. She looked almost as dazed as I felt and, in that moment, the distance that the last few years wrought between us melted away. I hadn't dared, all day, to ask myself why I invited her to stay, why she accepted. Or why I insisted she stay here, knowing I'd have to stay with her. I had, in thoughts and deeds, carried on the farce that she was just someone I knew in my teens whom I was obligated, by my mother's bequest, to contact. Watching her stand dazedly in my mother's room, tears running silently down her face and all her irksome walls momentarily down, I am finally able to admit the truth – at least to myself. I called her, asked her to stay, and insisted the stay be here for the same reason my mother never forgot her – even in death. She is family. Time, distance and our own selves may have pushed us apart but in this moment, I know there's no one I'd rather have with me than this woman; so remote from the girl I had loved so long ago. I touch her hand, silent, taking and giving comfort.

'I always thought…' she faltered, her voice barely a whisper. 'I always thought, at the back of my mind, that someday I would be back here; to see her. Later, after I had gotten myself back under control, once I grew into a woman she could be proud of. Now, I… It's too late…'

Not sure if she even realized she was muttering aloud, I put my arms around her. It was penance, forgiveness, reassurance and seeking absolution in one gesture. I told her the only thing I could, the truth.

'She was always proud of you. Always.'

Ruqqayyah looked as though she did not hear me. Or maybe didn't believe me. She stood there forlorn, achingly similar to the Rekiya I knew in Noorah. Then she had hid her vulnerability behind superficial gaiety and her popularity. I didn't know her well enough, anymore, to know what she was hiding behind the aloof countenance she'd adopted for so long now. But I knew her well, once upon a time, to suspect that Mummy might have been right that day three years ago, the last time we had heard from Ruqqayyah before yesterday.

I had been visiting and we sat in Mummy's room; our usual rendezvous for serious mother-daughter talks. I remember being irritated when the phone rang and glancing at the mobile phone before passing it to her; it was an unregistered number.

'Hello? Ruqqayyah? Oh, salaam alayki dear. Are you in the country? When did you—Oh, really?! That's wonderful, barakallaahu feeki. Does Zaynunah know? Oh! - - .'

I walked away into the en-suite bathroom, thinking my mum had a way of sounding like an old, English lady when talking to Ruqqayyah. She had adopted the habit of speaking to her in English early after meeting her, when she found out Ruqqayyah was not fluent in Yoruba. Actually, that would have been an understatement then; the girl could understand virtually nothing of the language. Mummy herself was not a comfortable speaker of the English language, she spoke with the stilted formality of non-native speakers who had learnt a second language. This did not deter them, though; Mummy and Ruqqayyah never seemed to have any problems communicating. I was the one who had to pull a tooth to get her to talk to me. No, I wasn't going to think about her; not her last reply to my phone call almost a year ago, nor the fact that she called Mummy – not me – when she came into the country for the first time in years.

I returned to the room and found Mummy staring at the phone in her hand, pensive. She did not look at me as she sighed. 'That girl is lost.'

I pause, incredulous, then feigned nonchalance. 'Did she say that?'

Did she say anything? God knows she hasn't told me anything of import in years.

'No. All she said was she has moved back to Nigeria. She is going to head a new unit or something in Abuja. She just wanted to say salaam.'

'So why - -?'

'Because you can hear it in her voice' my mother answered my unfinished question. 'She is hurt, and lost, and does not know where to turn. When was the last time you spoke to her?'

I mumbled a few things, embarrassed. How was I to admit that I had no idea why my best friend and I drifted apart? That I looked up one day and our friendship had slipped away, unnoticed. How could I give words to the numerous emotions that assail me when I think of her; hurt, bewilderment, loss, confusion, guilt and a healthy dose of anger?

Who does that? To just pull away from someone who loves you, as though the relationship you shared was inconsequential - limited by time, distance, age and life's circumstances. And if it truly is so, if friendship – our friendship - was limited, why can't I move on? I allow myself to think I have. I don't think about her for so long, I believe I have. Then she does something like this, or I take a trip down memory lane, and I am right back where I was. Where I hate to be. Needy, and missing her, wishing I knew what went wrong. And how to make it better again.

Pathetic.

If she was going to pull away, the least I could do was not be an emotional wreck over it.

She was just a friend, I told myself. People make friends all the time.

What does it matter if I've never had another friend like her?

CHAPTER THREE

Rekiya

We slept in Mummy's room that night.

Zaynunah had pulled me down unto the bed, her arms still wrapped around me, and we cried. I know it had to be hard for her; she and her mother had always been close; but my own tears were of a far more convoluted nature. I had not even realized, until I came into the awareness of standing in that room, gazing into eyes shadowed by sadness, yet fiercely steeped in conviction – and the tears that shimmered in them – that I was crying.

I, who had not shed a single tear in over a decade.

Z's arms had been, symbolically, the first to offer me unconditional acceptance as a girl. With it had come the offer of friendship, and love, and a bonus family. Now, hers were the first arms to hold me in years; too many years than I ever want to recollect. Air-kisses from my mother did not count. In those arms, yesterday, I cried for all that I'd lost – friendship, love, family, my Faith, my Self, now Mummy. And so much more than anyone could ever know.

We sat there in each other's arms, sobbing through the emotions we could not give voice to. Eventually we crawled under the covers, spent. I heard Zaynunah get up at some point, while I drifted between sleep and wakefulness. I thought I heard her talking to someone just outside the bedroom door; probably her dad, as my consciousness drifted again….

Waking up before dawn was a habit I developed from circumstances. Insomnia often drove me from my bed, and I have come to find a measure of peace in those hours. It was then; while the mass of creation was unaware; that I called on, or prayed to, or raved at, whatever unseen force that shapes life – and sometimes, at myself.

It was in those hours that I healed. Somewhat.

Praying in the pre-dawn hours had started as an exercise my therapist came up with. She thought we weren't making any progress after two years of twice-weekly sessions, and suggested meditation. I had been skeptical, so I prayed.

Or raged.

And, later, I just cried. Huge dyspnea-inducing sobs, inexplicably devoid of tears.

The first couple of mornings, I just rolled out of bed, sat on the floor of my bedroom in my nightshirt, and mumbled halting, incoherent prayers.

Oh God… Ya Allaah…

It had been impossible to vocalize then, what even I did not know. And it would take some time; progressing through shame and anger, despair and despondency; to find some measure of lucidity.

Oh God. Ya Allaah. I want to live. Help me!

Those hours became my anchor, the affirmation that… I am. That I had yet to disappear into the nothingness of my own being.

I was alive.

It was the first time in a long time I found meaning in something, and I clung to it. Like driftwood in the ocean of my vast emptiness, flimsy and inconsequential as it may appear, it was all that kept me afloat. So, I woke up in the middle of the night, every night, and I prayed.

In time, I began to pray in the formal Muslim way, and *Tahajjud* – and the *Fajr salaah* – became my only link to this religion I was no longer sure I believed in and had long stopped laying claim to. The years did not seem to matter, though; the words, the motions, the routine all flowed from me as if I never stopped. The sense of peace that accompanied it took a while longer for me to find, but I did, eventually.

And I never want to give it up again.

Getting up now, I found my way gingerly to the bathroom, holding my mobile phone aloft to illuminate a path for my footsteps. As is typical of Ibadan, of Nigeria as a whole, the dark of the night is almost total, unchallenged by the presence of electricity and man-made illumination. I grimace at the coldness of the water trickling out of the tap, as I wash my hands, face and arms. I complete my *wudhu* –the ritual ablution for cleanliness that Muslims partake in before some prescribed acts of worship, posthaste, mindless, from years of habit, and feel the peace descend. It engulfs me.

Zaynunah must have brought my bag in last night. I found it sitting off to a side when I enter room again, as well as a rechargeable lamp that lit up the room quite effectively when I switched it on. I dug out my prayer garment from my bag, an old *abaya*-and-matching-scarf combo from a lifetime ago and walked to Mummy's designated *salaah* corner.

Her prayer mat was still laid out. Her trio of *Qur'an*s; the Arabic script, the English and Yoruba translations; and her *du'a* books sat on their low shelf beside the small folding chair she sometimes sat on in prayer. She would joke that her bones were getting so old; they'd started to forget that they had been created to bow to the Lord of the worlds.

It was surreal, standing there and knowing she never would again. As a girl, I had been in awe of the unquestioning certainty of her faith. The woman I am, now, still envied her that as I raised my hands in praise of a Deity, I wasn't sure existed.

'Allaahu akbar!'

When I finally got off the mat, daylight was in full splendor. I go through my morning routine, finding comfort in the norm. I, however, pause momentarily as I contemplated the meager contents of my carry-on case. I had packed for three days of mostly business functions, and my choices were severely limited. Not only were my clothes wrinkled from having been worn at least once in the last few days, wearing my work clothes – power-suits and business casuals – would be absurd in this house, under these circumstances.

Giving a mental shrug, I pull open Mummy's wardrobe. After all, I'd just slept in her bed, I reasoned. And it wouldn't be the first time I would raid her wardrobe. As long as I knew her, Mummy almost always wore a version of the same things; simple kaftans and *bubu*s made from local *Ankara* or *Adire* prints. She would cover them with her flowing black garments when leaving her house; or exchange them for the more ceremonial *iro* and *buba* in expensive, often imported, voile laces for occasions and parties; but these were her signature garments. She liked to say that at her age, a woman learns to dress for comfort. I pull out a comfortable looking one; the deep blue fabric muted and well-worn; dropped it over my head and went looking for Zaynunah.

I hear her in the kitchen, scolding her father about making sure to eat the lunch she packed for him, and I linger on the last stair. I didn't want to go in there and cut short their time together. Once again, I ask myself why I was here amidst this family, at such a trying time.

Zaynunah's father paused momentarily as he stepped into the corridor and saw me lounging on the bottom stair. We spend a few awkward moments exchanging pleasantries; salaams, and how long it's been and the well-being of my family. With his gaze lowered, mine catalogued his appearance – old and tired. His beard, grey since I'd known him, was now almost completely white. It looked listless, and much less dignified than it had appeared years ago. His face was lined and wan, and even his shoulders seemed stooped. He had been a giant of a man when I knew him, now he appeared shrunken. Either with age, or his recent bereavement I could not hazard a guess.

I never actually knew him well, the family's adherence to strict segregation of the sexes meant I spent my time mostly with Mummy and Zaynunah. Yet, there was a limit to which one could avoid the strange teenage girl that your wife and daughter had all but adopted. So, he had been there, too, solid and dependably present in the background. A part of this family that took me in and cared for me like one of its own. So, I squared my shoulders and beat back my doubts. If they need me now, even a little, the least I could do was be here.

In the kitchen, I found Zaynunah clearing up the last of her father's breakfast, furtively wiping tears off her face. I paused by the doorway to observe her, unseen, for a while. She had filled out significantly from the gangly girl of our teens. Her body was curvier, softer but not overweight. Her skin was uncommonly dark, and even more luminous than I remembered. And her hair, her one vanity, was woven into tiny cornrows of intricate, interlacing design that must have been beautiful when she first had the style made. Now the lines were blurred, and its ends were limp as they fell beyond her shoulders, its length unusual for its naturally kinky, unrelaxed state. She bustled about with the energy she'd always been known for, but I could discern sorrow in the slight drag to her step, the tension in her frame, the downturn of her lips.

She looks up and sees me. *'As-Salaam alayki.* How about some yam and eggs?'

I nod, return her greeting and perched on the chair at the breakfast nook. Living alone, I subsisted on cereal, and pastries off the daily coffee cart at the office, between business lunches and dinners. Although I can well cook enough to not starve – Mummy taught me a few things over the years I stayed in this house – it never seemed worth the effort to cook just for myself. As in times past, being here meant I would probably eat better than I am accustomed to.

'So,' I dig into the food she placed before me. 'You said Mummy has been buried, that you are here to sort through her stuff, and that she left me some things…'

I let my voice trail off, ending on a higher note that made it a question. It was all well and good to be emotional yesterday, but this is a new day. I need to focus on doing something; the earlier to return to my life as I knew it. The topsy-turvy state of my emotions since her unexpected phone call was draining. I did not want to deal with it anymore. I especially, most certainly, did not want to talk about it.

With a heartfelt sigh, Zaynunah pulls up the second chair and sits beside me. 'I'm sorry. My mind is so scattered. I just…' She takes a deep breath. 'She left you her knitting stuff. But… Will you stay and help my pack up her things? When do you have to get back?'

'I took the entire week off, so I guess I can stay until Sunday morning. My stepfather's driver will meet me at the airport to take the car, so I don't have to leave at first light.'

'Ya Allah! I have been so selfish,' Zaynunah exclaims in agitation. 'I never even asked about your mum! And the rest of your family. How are they?'

'She's fine. They're fine.'

She looks at me, as though expecting me to elaborate. I get up and carry the dishes to the sink, taking my time washing and drying them, then my hands. I don't talk about my mother, and I have no family. Not really. She knew this. Or at least, she did – a lifetime ago. Truth be told, I don't talk about much of anything nowadays either.

I square my shoulders before I faced her again, determinedly.

'So, where do we start?'

I lived with both my parents till I was almost eight. Yes, my father was prone to spells of absence but…we all lived together. We were happy. I was an only child. We lived in a huge house in one of the more exclusive neighbourhoods in the newly sprung city of Abuja, along with a couple of domestic staff. My parents weren't exactly hands-on with me, usually leaving me to the care of the maids and nannies, but I was well cared for and didn't know differently. The staff were rather indulgent in any case, letting me do –and eat – whatever I wanted.

My parents were very social; they gave and attended a lot of parties. I loved watching all the people, dressed up in their finery, at such parties – especially my mother – and I was dazzled by their beauty. As a little girl, I thought she was the most beautiful woman in the world. She spent a lot of time grooming daily, taking more care if she was going out or entertaining, and I spent most of that time with her, watching. I did not chatter at her as little girls were wont to do – even then, I recognised that my mother's tolerance for me waned when my dad was not around.

When she was done, and satisfied with her efforts, she would turn to me and ask, 'How do I look?'

'Beautiful, Mummy' I would enthuse. 'You are the most beautiful woman in the world!'

She would laugh and blow me a kiss on her way out.

My father had been on one of his usual jaunts when everything went haywire. My mother came to pick me from school, something she never did, looking more dishevelled than I had ever seen her, in a taxi. It drove us, not to our house, but to one of her friend's place. She told me we would be staying there for a while, and that my things were in that box, by the wall.

That was the extent of the information I was given about the crisis that would significantly change my life. My mother was too busy dealing with the fall out to bother with me. She spent her time crying and lamenting to her friends about how her life was over. And like any child, seemingly invincible to the adults, I learned to get the details from listening in on their conversation…

My mother had been born Esther Joseph to a low rank Ibo soldier, posted in Kaduna, and his wife. Her mother had died in childbirth when she was twelve, and she had lived alone in the barracks with her father afterwards. When he died during an ill-fated mission when she was sixteen, one of the neighbours who had been her mother's friends had taken her in. She attended school in the mornings and served in her benefactress' beer parlour in the evenings. And she had known early on that she wanted no part of that life. Since she had no options, however, she continued on in this manner till she earned her National Diploma from the polytechnic; and then, she *moved to Abuja. A new city was being planned and built there, and a friend's sister said there were jobs to be had if one was willing to hustle.*

She had been nineteen and just a few months in Abuja, when she met Chief Sodiq Gbadamosi. His company won several contracts from the various projects being carried out to build the proposed Federal Capital Territory, and he had come to oversee them. He had wooed her as only a man with almost limitless funds could – while he was not yet quite as wealthy then, he had appeared as Midas to a girl from her impoverished background. Within a year they were living together, and she was pregnant. She knew he had a family – wife and kids – in Lagos, of course. He was, after all, well into his forties when they met. But he and his wife had been practically separated for a long time, he'd said. They were just keeping up appearances for the sake of the children. And since his eldest son was almost as old as she was, it would not be long now before he could be free of his wife, in actuality. He made a show of wanting to go to her village to pay her bride-price, but she had never had much contact with her father's relatives back East, so the idea was temporarily shelved.

Then, one day eight years later, his second son overdosed – I did not understand this part until much later - on heroin in the US and my father left us. He decided his wife and children needed him, and his being with us harmed them. And that my mother, at twenty-seven, was still young enough to find another man to build a family with.

My mother had been devastated.

She wept and lamented, refusing to be consoled for months, during which I could have ceased to exist. I did not attend school as there was no driver to take me, and my mother was not functional enough to make alternative arrangements. I ate what I could lay my hands on in the kitchen; usually left over from whatever hostess fed herself. She was a single lady and, though kind to me in an off-hand manner, obviously did not want responsibility for a child – especially since the said child's mother was right there.

Ultimately, with some tough love from her friends, my mother pulled herself back together. She rented a small two-bedroom flat in a less exclusive neighbourhood and put me back in school. She made a lacklustre effort to look for work but, having not worked since her early days with my father, was not successful. She was unperturbed; my father had been generous in the amount of money he promised to send her for my upkeep. Increasingly, she spent her days lounging and her nights partying.

Leaving me in the care of the gate-man's teenaged daughter, my mother resumed her lifestyle of social indolence. But this time, she was accompanied by different men. And was solitary in her preparations. I was no longer fascinated by the glamour and superficial beauty of her life. I had gotten a first-hand lesson on just how fickle a life it was.

Then just as everything was settling into normal, or into a routine that could potentially become normal for us, my mother had news to share with me.

She was getting married.

And I was going to a boarding school in a place called Ibadan.

That was how I found myself at Noorah; twice removed from everything I knew within a span of two years.

It had been hard that first year, living with the knowledge that neither of my parents really wanted me. I had cried myself to sleep at night, and in the shower every morning, and in the daily deluge of the long Ibadan rainy season. The ambient environment of the school, the thoughtfulness and kindness of the staff and the interest of the senior girls just made it worse. I knew that I was there only because my father's money could afford it, and my mother's new marriage required the distance.

When I returned to Abuja at the end of my first term, I had missed my mother's wedding, and a midterm holiday – she had been abroad on her honeymoon, so I'd had to stay in school. I had also missed the move from our apartment to the spacious four-bedroom bungalow my stepfather called home. It was in an affluent neighbourhood, albeit built on a much smaller scale, as the one we quit almost two years before.

Oh, and Abuja was officially the Federal Capital Territory.

My stepfather was not an unkind man, just a disinterested one. He made no attempt to play a father's role in my life, or even to include me in the new one he was building with my mother. I learnt that I could have my mother's attention, but only if her husband was not around. I learnt to stay in my room, lonely despite all its amenities, so I did not feel like a third wheel. I learnt not to be hurt when they made plans, just the two of them, with no thought of including me.

In time, they had two children; a boy and a girl; arriving like clockwork three years after the wedding, and three years after that. Both were born while I was in Norah and were just two more half-siblings, I had no relationship with.

They were swept along into the life of their parents; celebrated from birth.

Their family was finally complete and, like my father's, did not include me.

Zaynunah

It had been another night of fitful sleep, and I tried to be quiet as I went into my childhood bedroom. I did not want to disturb Ruqqayyah and was grateful when she did not stir even as the door creaked loudly. My *Tahajjud* had taken a rather morose turn in the past few days, and I would rather she did not witness another meltdown of mine. Sure, she shed a few tears of her own yesternight, but I was feeling too vulnerable to face her special brand of inscrutability just yet.

I need to remember to oil that door…

Before long, I was weeping through my prostration; this grief, a weight I couldn't shake. And that only made me weep the more. I know, I believe, and accept that *To Allah we belong, and to Him is our return.* And I am sincerely hopeful that Mummy is in a better place – the promise of Allah is true – but I miss my mother. She was an integral part of my life, all of my life, and I have no idea how to go on. Being born a "surprise" so much later than my brothers, Mummy and I had a close relationship. She liked to say her job was to raise me, not be my friend, but she had been my friend. She got me, something I did not much appreciate until I was grown up and privy to many of my peers' relationships – or lack of – with their mothers. She raised me, supported me, and was always there for me. And now, I cannot wrap my head around the fact that she would no longer be here for all that, and the occasional babysitting duties.

I spent the night prayer asking Allaah for strength. And solace.

It was some time before it registered on my addled mind that the shuffling sounds coming from the next room must mean Ruqqayyah was up. The realisation surprised me. One never supposed that upwardly mobile executives got up before dawn. Although they probably had to, in order to effectively climb up the corporate ladder – especially if they were women. Or maybe it was the environment. She couldn't be accustomed to power outages anymore, I mused.

Then again, maybe she needs to use the bathroom, and is right now fumbling about; at risk of breaking something because she can't see. And, meanwhile, you are too busy speculating on her motives for getting up, to help her!

The last bit was in Mummy's voice, and I giggled at the absurdity of my thoughts, even as I wiped away the last of my tears and got up. I had placed a lamp in the room before leaving, and just needed to make sure Ruqqayyah sees it. When I pushed the door open – *I really need to oil these doors!* – I found the room brightly lit. Ruqqayyah was in Mummy's prayer corner, covered up in a manner reminiscent of the girl I used to know, her hands raised in *takbir*.

'Allah is the Greatest!'

Even now, hours later and knowing fully well how borderline judgemental it sounds, I admit to my surprise. I was not expecting that – to find Ruqqayyah, the woman she'd become, getting up before dawn to call upon Allaah. And I admit to only the 'borderline' bit because… well, she did not say any of the other four *salaah* that were due since she has been here. When *zuhr*, and later *'asr* rolled in, the boys, boisterous in their preparations, had gone to the nearby masjid, while Khawlah and I had prayed at home. Ruqqayyah had said nothing through it all, and

I hadn't asked. Maybe I had assumed, even then, that power brokers in the world of international finance did not make time for *salaah*.

Astagfirullaah. I seek Allaah's forgiveness for being a judgemental nitwit.

Looking at her now, standing before me dressed in Mummy's clothes and the prickly attitude I remember as a mask for her emotions from years ago, I admonish myself to be less quick to assume.

When we enter Mummy's room today, I did not- for the first time – feel overwhelmed by the loss. The room still felt like it exuded her presence, as though she was just behind the open wardrobe door. But somehow that just gives me a measure of comfort. Being there, amidst her things, I could almost bask in the warmth of her.

Mummy is dead.

Somehow, the thought doesn't hit me with the impact of a ton of bricks slamming into my chest, robbing me of breath. It sits heavy, like an anvil on my heart, but without the resultant will-I-survive-this panic almost crippling me. And for the first time since she died, I know – not just believe, I know – that everything is going to be okay.

I am going to be okay.

I glance at Ruqqayyah and think, apropos of nothing, that this room is the only place where I see in her a semblance of my friend. Since seeing her again yesterday, I startle at how remote she is. Like a stranger inhabiting the body of the girlhood friend I loved for so long and lost with no notice. In the years since I last saw her, the face she presents to the world – which I have, somehow unfortunately, become a part of – has become impenetrable. And the chunks of hardness I noticed during her last few visits to Nigeria before her relocation, have coalesced into a solid barrier that kept me from knowing who she has become.

In this room, however, she seemed… possible. Like the solidity that surrounds her being could have parts made of glass. Still hard, cold and difficult to penetrate, but here, in this room, those parts allow a faint passage of light to illuminate a vague hint of her person.

Realising she was waiting for my cue, I smile to cover my fanciful mental rambling, and motion her to the armchair where Mummy used to sit to knit, and the overflowing laundry basket of yarn, samples and unfinished projects beside it.

'Will you start there?'

Knitting was something Mummy shared exclusively with Ruqqayyah; I never understood the attraction. I had found it privately amusing that vivacious and outgoing Rekiya Gbadamosi, the star of student's social life at Norah, would spend hours practising patterns and be transported into raptures with Mummy over some yarn.

'Do you still knit?' I ask as I walked to what would have been Mummy's dresser if she had – like any other woman on the planet – bothered with a beauty regimen. As it were, she rubbed *adi agbon*, locally distilled coconut oil, on her skin after her twice-a-day shower, plaited her hair once a week; pomaded with the same stuff; and called it good.

'No. No time.'

Knowing she was not going to say more, I sat on a nearby stool and proceeded to go through the stuff on the non-dresser. Knick-knacks, old childhood craft projects and decades-old papers full of recipes and home-made remedy ideas all testifying to the fact that my mother had trouble throwing anything out.

'Daddy wants me – us – to put anything valuable aside for appraisal and distribution by the inheritance imam.' I tell Ruqqayyah without turning. 'Anything of sentimental; but not material; value, I –we - get to keep. Everything else will probably go to charity.'

'Ok' was the only reply I got.

It was like pulling a tooth!

Frowning in bemusement, I continue the task before me, and I had become lost in my head when I heard a gasp behind me.

'She kept this!' Ruqqayyah's voice wobbled beneath her sharp intake of breath.

This was a worn *oja*, a wide swath of material – traditionally made of the sturdy local handwoven fibre, *ofi* – which Yoruba women employed to strap babies on their backs, leaving the arms free for other chores. The one she was holding was made of wool, though; a knitted motley of colours, predominantly lemon green – which I had often found incredible to be Mummy's best colour. The other colours were chosen with no discernable consideration to pattern, or style, other than they had been available when Ruqqayyah was running out of the lime green yarn. It was one of the first completed knitting projects she undertook. She used to say, defensively, that it was made in a rainbow of colours. To which I teased that it was an insult to Allaah's rainbow. It was truly hideous to behold, but Mummy loved that piece of cloth.

'Yes,' I tell her presently. 'She kept it. And used it diligently to back all of the grandchildren.'

She paused in her examination of the *oja* and sent me a glance. 'Really?!'

That look, in that moment, was the Ruqqayyah I knew. The Rekiya of old. She always found it hard to believe that anything she did, that she herself, could mean much to anyone.

'Yes,' I repeated, careful to keep my manner careless and off-hand. 'Why do you think it's so ratty? Mummy would faithfully wash and pack this old thing whenever anyone of us had a new baby. And yes, she did use the *ofi* ones for outings or when there were guests present, but this was her go-to *oja*. It has practically become a Sanusi family heirloom.'

We snicker in surprising unison. The thing was so threadbare, the idea of its material value was hilarious. It used to drive my oldest brother crazy; he couldn't understand why Mummy would not discard it, or at least use the less ragged ones more often.

I tell Ruqqayyah that, and she chuckled. 'How is your rebel big brother?'

I turn away to mask my astonishment. This was the first personal question she'd asked since her arrival yesterday. The first time she acknowledged, even in an innocuous way, our history.

'Oh, he's fine,' I manage to say. 'He's settled some in his middle-age. He and Dad run a farm together now,' I volunteer. And because she didn't seem as shut off as she'd hitherto been, I continue, 'His wife died, did you know?'

She shook her head.

'It was a long time ago,' I said. *During those years when we drifted apart*, but I did not add that. 'He went through a phase, as Mummy calls – called – it. He packed little Juwairiyyah to stay here with the parents, and we did not hear from him for months.'

'I can't imagine how that must have felt. For him, for Mummy, for you all.' She mused.

'It was a trying time. But, Alhamdulillah, he came back home. Eventually, he met and married Jummai, and they have three kids together now, Nuh, Yunus and little Zaynah. Jummai has been really good for him, masha Allaah.'

'Nuh and Yunus. Are you serious?' Ruqqayyah snorted.

'Yup,' I answer, deadpanned.

There are a few seconds of eye contact, then our laughter rang across the room.

CHAPTER FOUR

Rekiya

Zaynunah's oldest brother, 'Isa, is almost thirteen years older than his sister. He had already graduated from the university and left home when I met her, yet I had come to think of him as the family rebel. As a young man, he had been respectful of his parents' way of life yet had made no secret that he was treading a different path. And while he had – nominally, at least – remained a Muslim, the religion did not seem to play much of a role in his lifestyle.

Personally, I had thought he was a cool guy. He had a good job in a multinational oil company, was respectful to his parents, kind to his sister – and to her stray of a friend. So, he did not live the details of his life in accordance with the detailed code of his religion, I'd thought. Neither did most of the Muslims I know.

In this family, though, he had stuck out.

And while no one – except Z and I, in private – talked about it, I knew they all worried. And prayed for him, afraid for his soul, hoping he would not stray too far from the path, that he may someday find his way back. It had almost been comical when he brought his intended home.

Tope had been everything that the women of this family were not. On the surface, at least. She had been voluptuous, with an abundance of curves and a shockingly fair complexion I always suspected may have been chemically enhanced. Playing to her assets, she had been… obvious, is the only word that comes to mind. With her rather heavy make-up, perfumes and unrealistic hair weaves, 'Isa could not have chosen a woman more unlike his mother and sister, had he tried.

Oh, she tried to tone it down around her conservative and deeply religious prospective in-laws, but it had been almost painful to watch Z's parents trying to be graciously accept her as a bride for their first-born son. Mummy had come around first, treating her with the same welcoming lack of artifice she had shown me. The same way she treated everyone she knew. Her husband, too, had initially been gruff and stiff. The poor man could not even look at her, as Tope pushed the bounds of modest dressing most days – so there was no talk of the hijab. He kept his interaction with her to a bare minimum, displaying a stilted formal manner I had not witnessed from him since my first days of crashing his family's hospitality.

Musa, the second brother, had been furious.

Everything about the proposed marriage irked him. 'Isa had not courted the bride-to-be properly; going through her father, meeting her only under the supervision of her male kin, maintaining proper distance and decorum till they were legally wed. They travelled alone all the way from Ogbomosho, where Tope was posted for her National Youth Service Corps, to Ibadan in his car. Alone! And she didn't even wear hijab. How could his parents even consider the match?!

Z, on the other hand, was resigned. Islamically, she'd pointed out, Brother 'Isa did not really need the consent of his family to wed. They could put up a fuss, and risk alienating him, or they could accept that this was his choice. Truthfully, had anyone of them ever really thought that Musa would do things the traditional way? Or pick a bride that remotely resembled what would be acceptable to his family?! He had been buckling against what he saw as the restrictions of their lifestyle since he came into his own. At least, his intended was Muslim. And she did seem like a nice enough lady who genuinely appeared to care about her fiancé...

The marriage had gone on, and the Sanusi family did their best to adapt to the family of the bride. The extent of their concession would only be apparent to someone who attended Zaynunah's wedding several years later – a simple and sedate ceremony, nevertheless beautiful in its execution. By contrast, 'Isa and Tope's had been a carnival. Being an accessory to the groom's sister, I had attended the traditional Ilorin wedding that the bride and her family had insisted on; seven days of revelry that culminated in a lavish wedding reception that must have been the talk of attendees for months to come.

'What happened? To Tope?' I clarified into the silence that followed our mirth.

'Kerosene explosion,' Zaynunah said quietly. 'The neighbors saw the flames, and tried to help, but she died of the burns she sustained a week later. Alhamdulillah, Baby Juwairiyyah was in another room and was unharmed.'

That was something I suppose. Sadly, there were numerous stories of people unknowingly purchasing adulterated petroleum products, often with devastating end results. It was just another of the country's dubious legacy from its oil-producing status.

My thoughts returned to her again, Tope. Normally she would be 'Auntie Tope' to me, being a couple of years older, but since I was not really family, I had avoided that Yoruba affectation by studiously not addressing her by name, and by speaking to her only in English.

She had been so young, vibrant and yes, obvious but also a genuinely pleasant young lady. And despite their initial misgivings, her in-laws had accepted her unreservedly within a few months of the marriage – her zest for life, and the joy she brought 'Isa, being undeniable.

'I still can't believe that Brother 'Isa continued your father's legacy of naming his sons after the prophets,' I say now.

Yes, I call him 'Brother', what can I say? He's eleven – almost twelve - years older than me, and practically became my brother in the years I stayed in this house. And did I mention that Z's family had a streak of Yoruba-ness that was only secondary to their islaamic values?!

'I know, right?!' Zaynunah chuckles. 'We were all surprised, too, when he asked Daddy to name his first son.' She nods at my raised eyebrow and continues. 'Then again, he was much older – he must have worked through his issues. And Jummai; she's Hausa. They met in the months he disappeared on us. She seems to have a calming effect on him. Some years back, he bought this huge expanse of land in the village, well it belongs to the village but borders the city limits. Anyway, he asked Daddy to consult for him on a farm venture. I thought it was his way of giving Daddy the farm; you know, something to do after he retired; but last year he quit his job in Port Harcourt and moved back to run the farm together.'

'He quit his job?'

I don't know who it was speaking with my voice, but hours passed, and we talked through packing up Mummy's stuff. Zaynunah filled me in on all that happened with her family in the last decade. And I heard her; this person who was not me, asking questions, interested, lapping up the details of the lives that had gone on in my absence… of this family I had emotionally exiled myself from years ago. And who had yet claimed me, once more, in this, their most vulnerable moment.

When Zaynunah broke off mid-sentence, it took me a moment to register why.

The *adhaan*.

After years of living in New York City, years which I distanced myself from islaam – except my therapeutic exercise of pre-dawn meditation-turned-*Tahajjud* – it was a sound that was almost alien to me.

When I moved back to Nigeria, I had wanted a place of my own as an investment, but also somewhere with the conveniences I had become accustomed to – security, constant power, hassle-free parking, and home maintenance – without having to deal with all the pesky details myself. So, my apartment in Abuja is in a serviced complex in an estate full of similar units, catering predominantly to expatriate workers of multinational firms. This means I only catch a faint echo of the Muslim call to prayer on the rare mornings peaceful enough for the sound to travel from a mosque in the distant neighborhood.

It was like a blast – or a frigid wind blowing in from the arctic –from the past. I had been here; in this house, hearing this call; so many times, I almost feel like I was back there.

In the then.

And like any glimpse of my past, I was uncertain and uncomfortable with the feeling. It had taken me years of therapy, and even more hours of pre-dawn soul-cleansing exercises to get where I am now. In this place in my life where I was... not happy, precisely, but content.

Or, at least, not discontented.

And while my former therapist might have believed I did not make significant progress, it was better than what I had clawed my way out of. I did not want to be back there, ever, and looking in the past threatened just that – to hurl me back to the despair I thought I had left behind.

I am fighting to regulate my breathing when I see Zaynunah get up, mutter something and head out the door. The door I saw closing, though, was in another continent, three years ago…

I had known, going in, that I was using him.

But I was tired of my therapist asking if I had met anyone, been on any dates. In the heart of Manhattan, I had no life beyond work, and more work. And in her world of singles hook-ups and bar traipsing, my lack of a love-life seemed the yardstick for emotional progress.

Plus, I was lonely.

I had no friends, had formed no new attachments, having severed old links. At work, I was the brilliant rising star no one liked, but everyone envied. And I was fine with that. For a while.

But with passage of time, I was aware of a niggling loneliness that grew increasingly hard to ignore, and an ache for all that I had lost.

Zeke had been there; the only friendly colleague I had; and somehow the business lunches became dinners and I had to decide if I wanted to take it further.

My therapist had been encouraging, so I went on a few dates with him. Casual dating, he must have realized I was skittish. And when, after the third date, on my doorstep, he leaned into me, I very consciously did not stop him. I wanted to know if I had a chance, if it was possible that I could still have what I'd always dreamed of – a family of my own.

Quite abruptly, and probably way too soon as far as he was concerned, I pulled away and beat a hasty retreat.

At work the next day, I had my story lined up when he caught me in the break room during lunch. As I was the only executive who never went out to lunch unless I had a business meeting, the room was blessedly empty.

'Er... So, Rekiya, about last night...' he started.

'Look, Zeke, I'm sorry. I thought we were just hanging out as friends.' I lied.

His look was quizzical. 'Sure. I mean, I like to think we are friends, Rekiya. But you've got to know I like you. I didn't think I was being too subtle, was I?'

I lowered my gaze. No, he hadn't really been, but most guys would have backtracked after I threw out the friend bit. I hadn't really expected him to put it all out there quite like that.

His hand on me forced me to raise my chin, and I flinched.

It was reflex, I hadn't been expecting the contact. I had become skilled at masking my reaction to physical touch enough to endure handshakes during meetings, but I had almost no other reason for another person to touch me. The night before had been my way of assessing myself, the extent of my damage. So, I had been ready for it. This, though...

He crouched before me where I was sitting till our eyes were level.

'What's going on, Rekiya. Talk to me. I thought we had something, was I wrong?'

I didn't want to do it, but he left me no choice. 'Zeke, I can't... I don't date.'

I hold off again, hoping he'd let it go.

He didn't. 'I hear you. I just don't get why. You're single, smart, ambitious and gorgeous. Help me understand here.'

I sigh and tell him, 'It's a religious thing. I don't do the whole dating and intimacy thing.'

He rears back and corks his head at me. 'Are you Amish? Cos you don't look like any Amish person I know,' his smile was teasing but his eyes, wary.

'No, I'm Muslim. Or I was, back home. And I know I don't look like what you expect a Muslim woman to, but... I can't...'

'Wait, what? You're Muslim? And what do you mean back home, I thought you're American?'

His shock was understandable, I had never mentioned a religion, or a root different from American, before. It never came up since I pretty much kept to myself, and most people had assumed the same thing about me – I was a Black American girl from Houston. I had seen no need to inform them that I had been in Texas only for college and grad school, by way of Qatar before it, and that home was somewhere in Nigeria. Allegedly. Or that my American passport was a product of maternity tourism. All my father's children had been born in the US; the pregnant mother having flown there weeks before the blessed event was anticipated. In that at least, I was very much his daughter.

I explain all that to Zeke, minus the murky family history, embellishing a little on religion being my motivation for not wanting to be with him. Truth is, I was mortified. I had used him to find out if I could, maybe, have a shot at a future. And now, I had my answer. Physically, it was a possibility. Emotionally, though, I was still too much of a mess. I was numb, a gaping void of emptiness that I could not imagine letting anyone into.

And I definitely had no business getting involved with anyone.

Fortunately, Zeke was very understanding, having believed the version of my story I told him. We remained platonic friends, the first friend I made in a long while. I knew he still hoped for more, and he very subtly dropped hints, but he did not try to touch me afterwards, and I was fine with that.

Two years later, he invited me to his local masjid to witness his Shahada.

I almost did not make it out of there before I broke down. Being in the Masjid, like echoes of my past life, reminded of all that I had lost or given up, and that was a torment I never wanted to go through again. My uneasiness over what I presumed would be Zeke's expectations of our relationship —in light of his conversion came a very distant second to it.

That single visit into my past life set me back some. Maybe my therapist was right when she said I was running away when I told her of my plans, sudden plans that I had not given serious thoughts before.

A week after he took his Shahada, Zeke discovered that the firm had offered me the start-up Nigerian division, and that I was taking it.

If all went well, I had confirmed it when confronted, it meant I was moving back to Nigeria, possibly permanently.

His look had been sad, resigned and pitying all at once. 'I don't really know what your deal is, Rekiya. And God – Allaah – knows you never told me in all the years I've known you. But I hope you'll one day find happiness. You are a lovely woman, and you deserve to be happy. To be loved. And while I had hoped you would let me be the one to do it, I've known for a long time that you weren't quite ready. And that's fine. I'm glad I met you and developed these feelings for you. It brought me to Islaam. I just hope you can find your way back to it, too. Maybe you'll find what you seek then.'

I hadn't said anything, just watched my office door as it swung close behind him...

Zaynunah

When I heard the *adhaan* being called from the masjid down the road, signifying the time of *zuhr*, I paused in my recollections. By now, I had moved on to tales of Musa, my second brother, and his family of two wives and six children. He had followed my father's footsteps, becoming a lecturer at the University. And, since he had always been kind of a stick in the mud, his stories were not as colorful as Brother 'Isa's.

Now, though, I stopped; and repeated the phrases of the call to prayer as the Prophet had enjoined us to.

Allaah is the Greatest
Allaah is the Greatest
I testify that there is nothing worthy of worship except Allaah
I testify that there is nothing worthy of worship except Allaah
I testify that Muhammad is the messenger of Allah
I testify that Muhammad is the messenger of Allah

Come to Salaah
Come to Salaah

Come to Success
Come to Success

Allaah is the Greatest
Allaah is the Greatest

There is no one worthy of worship except Allaah.

I finished the recommended supplication afterwards before I noticed Ruqqayyah had gone silent. And unlike the lapses that occasionally interspersed our reminiscences all day, it was an uncomfortable quiet. I could see that her guard was back up and, not knowing how to deal with this stranger who had re-emerged, I rose abruptly.

'I'm going to say Zuhr in my room, then start lunch.'

She had not answered, and I was pensive as I prepared lunch. I didn't know how to deal with this Ruqqayyah. Even as girls, with all our apparent differences, our relationship had been easy, uncomplicated. We had unwittingly opened up to each other after my crying jag and her astonishing revelation, and we saw no need to dissemble with afterwards.

Till this moment, I have no idea why she chose to tell me about her family situation on that long-ago afternoon. As far as I knew, her place at Noorah among her circle of friends had been due in a large part to who her father was. As a business mogul, he had made a name for himself as one of the wealthiest men in the country, prior to the current era of pilfering politicians and show-biz celebrities, with their gauche flaunting of wealth. It was one of the things that defined her to the other girls.

She's Sodiq Gbadamosi's daughter, you know!

It had meant nothing to me, beyond a vague curiosity of what her life would be like having such a rich and well-known father. But even I could surmise that much of that awe and adulation would wane if it got out that she was not in contact, was effectively unacknowledged, by said father. I realized then that sharing that piece of information with me was her way of making herself as equally vulnerable as I had been when she walked in on me crying. And those words had formed the basis of our relationship; open, and fully trusting that the other would not take advantage of that vulnerability.

This new Ruqqayyah, though, I had met six years ago. Then, it had been easy to let our friendship slip, unnoticed, away. Especially after my ill-fated call to her a few years later. She had been so closed off, so cold.

Now, I wonder if I should have tried harder to hold unto what we had. And if there was anything left to fight for, even now…

After a solitary lunch of leftovers, I call my husband to check in on the kids. He was full of good-natured, mostly exaggerated, laments of woes concerning how their day went. I feel the tension dissipating as we hoot over our children's antics.

'Are you ok, though?' he asked into one of the lulls in our laughing conversation.

'Yes. I guess,' I temporized. 'With Ruqqayyah here, it's not quite as bad having to pack up Mummy's life. But…'

He waited, and I am grateful for how far we've come. We've hit a rough patch or two in our twelve years of marriage, but there was a closeness in our relationship now that we had lacked before, even as newly-weds.

'It's just that I don't really know her anymore,' I started.

I tell him how remote I found Ruqqayyah. And how, for a few hours, I had glimpsed a semblance of her old self beneath the barrier. How her guard had gone up suddenly, once again. With the *adhaan*?

'I think she doesn't want to be here. With me.'

I cringe at how the last statement came out; low and needy. Which was not what I liked to think of myself. One of the reasons I had let our friendship slide then was how needy I appeared, even to myself. She had been pulling away, and I had been trying so hard to hold on. There was something incredibly desperate, pathetic really, about trying to keep someone who had emotionally moved on from you. Did I really want to go back there?

'She's here, though,' my husband's voice was calming, reminding. 'That she was the one you wanted with you at such a time means something. As does the fact that she came when you asked. Whether these 'something's are an echo of a long-lost friendship, or a new beginning of a different relationship, you'll both have to figure out. But she came, for you. Don't forget that.'

'When did you get so smart?' I teased.

'Oh, years of being married to a near-genius tends to rub off on a person,' he returned.

Years ago, I would have bristled at that near-genius comment, totally missing the point. Back when I thought everything he did was from resentment – of my education, of my work, of my apparent success. Alhamdulillah, I was now generally more secure in my own sense of worth, and in my husband's feelings for me, to recognize his words for the affectionate banter it was.

There was a knock on the front door as we said our goodbyes, and I spent the rest of the day receiving condolence calls.

It never really occurred to me, and I have paid a number of them myself, but there is something inherently cruel about a condolence call. Or maybe it was the Yoruba way of paying condolences. We expect the grieving party to sit through endless clichés, platitudes and prayers of varying sincerity, while displaying the appropriate demeanor of what we consider to be grief. Or needless recollections, and lamentations of '*if only*' s that must surely burden the family with more sadness, remorse, and maybe even guilt. And we expect them to be gracious, and ever available, while we fulfil this social contract, irrespective of their own feelings at the time, their own way of dealing with their loss.

I wish I could just say to people, 'Please, do not visit us after the third day. Do pray for my mother's soul – but in private; I do not have to be a witness to it. Please stop asking me how she died, or if we knew before-hand that she had a medical condition. No, I do not really want to go through all your memories of my mother with you – I am still reeling under the weight of mine. Can you please go somewhere else to continue your conversations on the ephemeral, and fleeting nature of life, the eventuality of death and all sundry matters you all seem to think it is okay to keep me prisoner for? What can you do for me? How about please leaving me alone – for now – with my grief?'

But of course, I don't say all that.

For one thing, I knew that – for the most part – it all came from a good place. For another, my mother – that veteran of condolence calls herself – had raised me better than that.

CHAPTER FIVE

Zaynunah

My mother, Munirat Abeke Raufu was born the thirteenth child, and eighth daughter, of a traditional Muslim-clerical family. The Raufu-Agbenle family of Ibadan prided themselves on the legacy of an illustrious ancestor that was supposedly one of the first people to accept islaam in Ibadan, sometime in the 1800s. He was said to have travelled for a while in pursuit of knowledge about his new religion; going as far as Kano to learn Arabic and other Islamic disciplines. Upon his return, he had settled into the life of an Alfa, a legacy that most male children of the family continued.

Munirat's father, Imam Bashiru Raufu, was a respected and influential man in certain quarters in the 1950s Ibadan. While not exactly wealthy, his influence as a well-known alfa brought him certain privileges. He owned a large compound in Oje with a sprawling structure to which he added as his family – of three wives, their motley of children, and an assortment of dependent female relatives – grew. He was the imam of the mosque adjacent to his house, allegedly built by a grateful wealthy benefactor in appreciation to his grandfather for prayers rendered, and subsequently answered. It was *a single-story and, by the time of Munirat's childhood, an ageing structure with rickety stairs, gloomy interior, and walls held together by the multiple coats of paints applied over the succeeding years of its existence.*

Like most of his contemporaries, Imam Bashiru had no other source of income than his clerical-related duties. He led the faithful in prayer and enjoined them to donate generously to the 'mosque's' coffers. He officiated their ceremonies – weddings, burials, naming ceremonies, dedication of a new house, and a multitude of other reasons that the Yoruba had for celebrating – and milked even more generosity from them. He listened to the woes and problems confided in him, prayed for them or prescribed certain supplications, and received appreciation in tangible forms.

He had several boys and young men whom he taught the Arabic texts that he had learnt from his father. And though typically not from well-to-do families, thus did not pay any standard tuition, they aided his labors – copying phrases by their thousands unto wooden slabs which would later be washed off for specific purposes, among other things – and added to his prestige as an alfa. Indeed, he liked to play up this prestige when he attended ceremonies; his flowing agbada trailing behind him, his bulky turban wrapped around his head and face, surrounded by a dozen ole-n-tele-alfa who alternated between repeating his utterances at deafening decibels for the enlightenment of his listeners, and singing his praises at comparable volume.

Unlike some, however, Imam Bashiru was very strict with his womenfolk. Not for his womenfolk the quintessential eleha of Ibadan in the indifferent black outer garments that left her shins uncovered. Such women who sold eko, the slightly-firmer-than-jelly local staple dish made from corn starch, via the curtains of their dwellings and with increasing boldness until they were found on the streets, and in the marketplaces. Some even flipped back their garments, exposing their faces to all and sundry!

In keeping with their legacy as the self-appointed vanguards of Islaam in Ibadan, the Raufu-Agbenle women were known to practice total isolation. Traditionally, it was an accepted norm in Yoruba land that the wives of an alfa would be an eleha – a woman who wore loose garments that veiled her completely, face included, in presence of non-related males. The women of this family, though, took it a step – or a million steps - further. In a practice called "Ipade di alujono" in local parlance, the women did not emerge from her marital home, for any reason, from the day she enters it as a – usually, teenage – bride, except as a corpse. No males, most times not even the legitimate mahram of the women – brother, father, uncle – were permitted access to the recess of the dwellings.

Someone unaccustomed to such tradition would be forgiven for concluding that the women effectively disappear from the moment they are married until their death. Especially, if one believed that the measure of a person's life was her visible contribution to the society. Growing up however, Munirat's life did not appear any different from a child her age – she spent time playing and squabbling with her siblings, running errands for her mother and stepmothers, and very occasionally sitting with her much stricter, and usually absent, father.

When she was eight years old, her father enrolled her and two of her half-brothers in school. Prior to that, he had been among the most vocal against the enrollment of Muslim children in schools. The missionaries had lured many a child from the religion of his family that way. However, it was becoming increasingly obvious that this tactic was counterproductive. The Muslims needed to be well-grounded in their religion, but also pursue the western style education that was fast becoming the prerequisite for influence of any kind in the society. There was now a general clamor to register Muslim children in schools, and Munirat and her brothers benefitted from it.

Munirat excelled in school. From the moment she'd donned the checkered uniform and clutched her wooden slate, it was as though a door opened for her. A hitherto-unknown world where she could just be – undefined by the limitations of her gender. She loved learning new things at school and put all her efforts into it. Her academic brilliance paid off. It prompted numerous visits to her father from her teachers when he tried to stop her schooling after grade six.

Then at age fifteen, she had been in form two of secondary school, when her period started. It was the first time she appreciated wanting something so bad, you would do whatever to have it. And the reasons why children lie.

She had previously watched as a small girl, with mixed fascination and longing, when her sisters had been fussed over when their 'time' came. There was an informal rite of passage that involved the killing of a chicken, a secret talk that the young girls were invariably ushered away from, and the announcement of a groom within a few weeks. It was an almost instantaneous transition from girlhood to womanhood, and Munirat had longed for her own 'time'. To be the central focus of the women of the family, and even her father – for just a little while.

The irony was not lost on her on that fateful day. Hiding in the tin building that housed the pit latrines at the back of the compound, she stared at the streaks of blood covering her inner garments. What a double-edged sword it was. This event she had waited for most of her life would hinder her from what she hoped would be her future.

Her father held the position that a girl must be married before, or soon after, her third menstrual cycle. Then, she had not been aware that there could be a differing opinion; or imagined that everything her father held onto could be less than the islaamic ideal. Not that her teenage self had possessed any awareness of Islaamic legalities, all that mattered to her was not stopping her education.

So, she'd lied – by omission, subterfuge, withheld the truth. She told no one of her physiologic milestone. She cut up old dresses rather than have specially designed rags her mother would have given her. She discarded her clumsily made, used rags in the pit latrine; unable to wash and hang it up like the others did. In a compound as large, and with as many inhabitants as theirs, it had been fairly easy to mask the days she did not pray. It helped that her first cycles were few and far between. The same irregularity was what ousted her, almost a year after she'd seen her first blood.

When she had got up that early morning, there was no hiding the evidence from her sisters, with whom she shared a room, or her youngest stepmother, who had come to wake them all for prayer. She kept quiet about her previous deception and allowed herself to be fussed over; all the while waiting for the other shoe to drop.

She listened gravely as the women imparted age-long secrets of womanhood, like the significance of the blood – 'You are now a woman. If you let a man touch you, you will become pregnant!' And what was expected of her as a woman – 'You have to be meek and obedient, serve your husband with all your heart, and protect his honor and dignity.' They shared with her the hygiene of this delicate issue; how to make her rags and keep them clean, how to prevent soiling her clothes and how to prevent offensive smell. They told her which household remedies helped with the pain; assuring her that it would reduce significantly once she had children. They impressed upon her the importance of record keeping – and that problems with her flow may affect her ability to get pregnant.

It would have been impressive, the amount of knowledge these women – deemed uneducated by societal standards – had to pass along to her, if Munirat had not been listening with trepidation. That all their points alluded to marriage, a husband and childbirth did not escape her notice. She understood their reasoning. Her body bled, ergo it was ready to fulfil the destiny for which it was created. And while she wanted that too; marriage, a husband, babies; she wasn't ready.

Fortunately, it was ileya a few weeks after that and she went off with the rest of her male and younger female siblings to visit her grandmother, as had been the norm all her life. Because she was stuck in the limbo between girlhood and womanhood – until he found her a husband, at least – her father had relented and let her go. Munirat had no intentions of coming back.

In the months during which she had concealed her status, she had decided that Mama, her grandmother, was her most likely ally. Spry and lean, she was still an active and very vocal woman, despite her age and previous status as a Raufu-Agbenle wife. When she had broken her isolation after the death of her husband to move back to her long-dead parents' village, it had caused a furor. But she had been the oldest person – male or female – in the extended family, and no one could stop her. Her eldest son, Munirat's father, was vehement in his opposition but they had maintained an uneasy truce; his children were permitted to visit her once a year.

Mama never visited his household.

It took Munirat the entire three days of their annual visit to convince Mama to let her stay in the village. When she relented, all she had said laconically was, 'a girl should be able to choose when, if not whom, to marry.'

Predictably, Imam Bashiru had been incensed. Munirat had been awed to witness the ferocity that had allowed her grandmother to defy age-long tradition, and her husband's entire family, to choose her own course, albeit much later in life. She fought for Munirat, insisting that if an old woman wanted a granddaughter to stay with her to comfort her in her old age, she was entitled.

And while Munirat had been elated that she got to stay behind, and finish her secondary school in the village, she had been cognizant of the toll that had been paid. Her father's relationship with his mother was further strained. Munirat herself would not step into her father's compound for another three years. And Imam Bashiru stopped his daughters from attending school beyond grade six afterwards. Unfailingly.

When Mama died two years and eight months after Munirat came to live with her, she had assured her granddaughter that she had no regrets for anything she had done, urging her to live her life. Her words were, 'Never let anyone tell you what you can, or cannot, do. You find what you want to do, what brings your heart peace, and you do it.'

Those words resonated with Munirat all of her life, especially in the months following her return to her father's compound. He had loathed to take her back in, but she was his daughter and it was becoming an embarrassment to him that she was living unchaperoned in the old woman's house.

It had been hard to find herself a pariah in a place she'd always called home. But it was a world where you were either a young girl or a married woman, and there had been no place for her. She herself had had time to consider what she wanted, and realized that much as she appreciated her education, there was not much she could do to pursue it without losing her family totally. In the 1960s South-Western Nigeria, higher education would have meant casting off her hijab – if not her religion – and she simply was not willing to do that.

In the end, it had been surprisingly easy a choice to make.

She could not, would not, further her education at the expense of other things and people that mattered to her. That it was her choice, made the months following her return to her childhood home bearable. She threw herself into studying Arabic texts with her brothers, something that had hitherto been the prerogative of the males in her family. It was in those months, while studying demanding texts to keep herself occupied, that she found her faith in the religion she had been raised with. And by the time her father finally informed her that he had a suitor for her, she had made peace with herself, and what she'd assumed was her lot in life.

Abd-Razaaq Sanusi had been a neighbor to her grandmother in the village, his parents' modest house being the closest structure to Mama's. Munirat never had much contact with him in her years living there, as Mama did not break the habits of a lifetime just because she had forgone her isolation. Hers had still been an eleha household, and their contact had been largely limited to the women of the village. Yet, Munirat recalled the quiet young man, humble despite his being a student at the university, who occasionally came to help Mama with handiwork about the house.

The marriage had been very simple, even by the usually austere Raufu-Agbenle standards. The groom, and a couple of his male relatives had met with her father, presented the idana gifts, and a few hours later they had left with Munirat in tow.

Munirat would recall the first few years of marriage with a survivor's gratefulness. She had been a nineteen-year-old bride, rather old by her family's standard, but wholly unprepared – given her sheltered upbringing – to face life as the wife of an educated man, in what passed then for cosmopolitan Ibadan. For one thing, her husband was rarely home. Though he had a government scholarship that covered his tuition, books and a small stipend, he worked weekends and evenings to support them. Munirat, who'd had no previous experience living in such proximity with anyone who was not closely related to her, had been on her own, trying to cope in their rented apartment in a building that housed five other families. In addition, she had bought into the innuendoes of the women of her family that she was marrying an alakowe and had spent the first few years trying – in her opinion – not to embarrass him with her 'bush' habits. So, while she did not remove her hijab; he had married her knowing her family's history after all; she did not don the full veil that had characterized the women of her family either. In his absence she continued her study of the texts she had started with her brother, and even began committing the Qur'an to memory, but when he was around, she felt the need to be – or play at being - the educated and sophisticated wife.

This had gone on for three years until she had felt stifled in the 'liberated' lifestyle her family had scoffed about. It did not help that she had no one to talk to, no one to reassure that it was okay to be herself; not what her family thought she ought to, nor what she imagined her husband expected her to be.

Finally, in her third year of marriage, she had become pregnant – allaying another fear of hers – and heeded her grandmother's words. She realized that with motherhood imminent, she had to define, for herself, who she was and who she wanted to be. She shared her concerns with her husband one quiet moon-lit night; she would try to be the best wife she knew how, and support him in his goals, but she needed to be true to herself too.

It turned out her husband had no alakowe notions. He said he had first taken notice of her because she never let her love for education rob her of her religion. No, he had no objections to her adopting the fully veiled dressing of her family. In fact, could she make it her intention to emulate the wives of the Prophet, and the illustrious women-companions, rather than just the women of her family? And yes, he was proud of her studies and memorization of the Qur'an.

Munirat liked to think that was when her marriage really started. Her relationship with her husband grew deep. And her family became more accepting; whether because her father died shortly afterward, or because she adopted what had been the familial mode of dressing for generations, she would never know. Certainly, her having a son helped.

In the subsequent years, her husband graduated and got a job on the faculty of the university, while pursuing his postgraduate studies. They moved to another home – a semi-detached single-story structure in Bodija – and she had another son. The next few years were marked by a series of miscarriages, followed by a pregnancy that ended with a difficult preterm caesarean section, grim predictions from the university hospital doctors about future conception, and a baby girl that died two days after she was born.

It had been the dark time in her history but with patience and prayers, Munirat and her family thrived. She accepted her lot as a mother of two sons, with gratitude, and did her best to nurture her home.

Then, in her seventeenth year of marriage, unexpectedly and amidst life-threatening conditions, Munirat was delivered of another baby girl.

Me.

CHAPTER SIX

Rekiya

The next few days passed uneventfully. Zaynunah and I developed a routine of sorts. She slept in her old room while I used Mummy's. We met in the kitchen for breakfast, then went back upstairs to sort through more of Mummy's life. Zaynunah left, presumably to pray, by *Zuhr* and often had to receive visitors after *'asr*. I tried to do some work during those times, but I found that the numbness that work afforded me waned in direct proportion to the length of time I spent in this house. I joined Zaynunah once in receiving condolence calls but left a few minutes later. It was not really my scene, my Yoruba was not up to the challenges of the proverbs and prayers being offered and, frankly, I felt it was carrying my presumptuousness - in being here at all - too far.

Afterwards, we huddled in Mummy's room until her dad returned from the *'Isha'* prayers. We chatted like strangers; superficially, cautiously, politely. Too many years have passed, too much has been left unsaid between us, to presume upon the ghost of the friendship past. She told me about her children, her husband, and her work - apparently, she was something of an IT guru and had a flexible consultancy she ran from home. I mostly listened. Or talked about work – it was all I had done for years now.

We did not dredge up the past. Zaynunah was, as she'd always been, open, warm and accepting, without alluding to our previous history. I was, well, I suppose I am as I'll always be – cautious and slightly offhand. By some tacit, unspoken agreement, we were getting to know each other again, ignoring any baggage.

At night, when she bade me goodnight before going to spend time with her father, I felt a surprising sense of possibility. I wasn't the girl who'd been friends with her so many years ago, but maybe the women we had become could find a common ground. I wasn't even sure how feel at that thought.

Today, my fourth morning in the Sanusi house, I came out of the bathroom and found her waiting for me.

'What's going on?'

'Yusuf just called. It's all over the news… Ruqqayyah, your father died last night.'

She eyed me warily, probably expecting some form of reaction. After all, her own grief over the recent loss of her mother was still vivid.

I, on the other hand, felt nothing. Not for this, in any case.

I turned away from the look in her eye, a mixture of empathy and pity, and began rummaging through my handbag.

'I'm going to need to charge my phone. Could we, maybe, switch on the generator for a few hours?'

As usual, there was no power.

I had let the phone power down two days before. Any urgent issue at work would have found its way to my email, and there simply wasn't any other reason to stay connected.

Zaynunah nodded, started to head out, then pauses at the doorway. 'Ruqqayyah, I'm really sorry about your dad…'

I sigh.

'Z,' the affectionate diminutive slipped out without my awareness, 'the man walked out on me when I was eight, and I only saw him twice afterwards. He's not my dad.'

I listen to her footsteps as she walked away, hearing it fade before I allow my shoulders sag. This is *so* not something I wanted to deal with today – or any other day, if I was being scrupulous with honesty.

I go through the motions of dressing, plug in my phone when I hear the roar of the generator and, decisively, pull up the papers online. Z was right. Sodiq Gbadamosi's death, in Germany, was the headline on every local news outlet. He had been ill for a while; speculations were rife about the exact nature of the illness; and had 'passed away, peacefully, in the early hours of this morning'.

I snorted. *Who writes these obituary things anyway?*

Why Zaynunah expected me to feel anything was beyond me, seeing as I was just one of the numerous Nigerians reading about this in the papers.

I heaved another sigh and called my mother.

'Rekiya!' My mother had never called me anything but the Hausa version of my name. 'Where have you been?! I've been trying to call you all morning, why did you switch off your phone? Have you heard? Your father is dead!'

I was momentarily taken aback. I hadn't encountered this shrilly, highly excitable part of my mother in over twenty years. Since her funk after my father left us, to be precise. I suppose the death of one's youthful love could erode the veneer of cultivated control.

'Yes, Ma, I know. It's all over the news.'

She doesn't acknowledge the dig in my response, probably did not hear it.

'Where are you? Your brother called this morning, from Germany, to inform me. The body should arrive in the country this afternoon, and they plan to bury him immediately. He says they'd understand if you can't make the burial, but the reading of the will is to be just before the eighth-day prayers, and your father expressly asked that you be there.'

I'm shaking my head incredulously, forgetting that she could not see me.

'Who…? My…? What brother?'

'What do you mean "what brother?"?! Tunde Gbadamosi, of course! Are you paying attention to me at all?' my mother shrieked down the line.

Tunde Gbadamosi. My father's oldest – and legitimate – child. The heir apparent. We had met before, once. I shudder now, remembering.

'Tunde Gbadamosi is *not* my brother.'

My mother must have heard something in my voice. She was quiet for a while, then the poised woman she'd become since my father left spoke up. 'Where are you?'

'Ibadan. Zaynunah's mother died.'

It was all the explanation I gave. It was all she needed. She sighed. 'What should I tell him if he calls back?'

Her voice, its sad dignity, stop me from asking since when she'd been in contact with her estranged ex-lover's family. Or since when they wanted me, acknowledged me, involved in their affairs.

Understand if I could not make the burial, indeed! More like, do not come and make a scene with your illegitimate self.

'Tell him I'm busy.'

It had been a Friday.

I remember this because Mummy had been cooking up a storm. Both her sons were coming home for the weekend and there was nothing that gave that woman quite as much joy as having her entire family under her roof. Having a number of people to feed came a very close second, though.

Z and I sat downstairs, flitting between occasional dashes to snatch goodies from the kitchen and working on our entry forms in the living room. It was midterms holidays of the first term, our final year at Noorah, and we were filling out our University Matriculation examination forms.

It was a forgone conclusion that we were both applying to the University of Ibadan – for first AND second choices. Neither of us had any plans to go elsewhere. We were having a harder time deciding on our courses of study. Z wanted architecture, computer science or engineering – she was a whiz at maths. I shuddered theatrically at her options; maths was the bane of my academic existence. I could muddle through it enough, though, to get by in business administration, banking and finance, or accountancy. In truth, I did not really want accountancy – it sounded boring! However, I felt the need to at least be seen to consider one 'serious' career option. Everyone in this family; and they were the only people who knew I was at a career-deciding phase of my life; was in the sciences. Accountancy was my way of saving face.

Z was trying to talk me out of banking; the evils of riba and all that when the phone rang. It took us a minute to fathom the source of the shrilly sound, as it had jolted us out of a silly laughing bout.

Z had still been giggling from my snarky comments when she picked up the receiver. 'Hello?'

She muttered a few greetings, flagging me down as I made to leave – Mummy had some delicious dried shrimps she was planning to use for efo riro, maybe I could snag some…

'It's your mother,' Z mouths to me as she shoved the receiver into my hands.

My mother rarely called me when I stay over at Z's. After that first midterms, she had given a blanket permission at Noorah allowing Mummy to act for me in pretty much every capacity. Which was telling, as she'd never even met the woman. Phone calls didn't count in my opinion.

Not that I was complaining, since – for the first time, ever – I had visitors on visiting days, someone came to see my teachers and my schoolwork on open day, Mummy cheered loudly for me at prize-giving and any other school function that required it. For the first time, I had a parent show up for me, too.

'Hello, Ma.' I was cautious. I didn't like surprises, or deviations from the norm. The few I had gotten in life so far had not been pleasant.

'Rekiya, how are you?' she opened.

My mother and I only ever speak to each other in English. Maybe that was partly responsible for the distance between us. I snorted inwardly, wondering how she'd respond if I ever answered her perfunctory query by telling her how I really was.

'Fine, Ma. How is everyone?'

I cared only about as much as she had with her question, did not expect her to tell me any more than I had told her. We were just going through the motions. This was a dance I had mastered very early on.

'Fine. Look, your father called me a while ago. He's in Ibadan and wants to see you. He said he went to the school, and found out you were on midterms, but someone mentioned you were staying with your friend in Ibadan. Anyway, so I gave him the address and he said he'd be stopping by this afternoon.'

My mother's words ran into each other; the only indication she gave that she, also, realized how bizarre this was.

My father?! I hadn't seen him in almost eight years. She hadn't mentioned him in almost as long. And now he wanted to see me? Whatever for?

I was dazed, incoherent as she rang off, seemingly oblivious to the boulder she just dropped on me. I gazed blankly back at Zaynunah who was looking at me in concern.

'What is it? What happened?!' she prodded impatiently when I took too long to say anything.

'My father.' I tell her. I am trying, even as I said the words, to understand them myself. 'He's coming here. To see me.'

I passed the next few hours in the same daze, swinging through a myriad of emotions I could not name even if I had wanted to. Application forms forgotten, I sat and stared. Z must have told her family what was happening, and just like that, their family reunion became about me. Mummy fussed over me, carefully chattering about everything except my complex family situation. And Mummy, the woman I had known in the last two years, never chattered. Z stayed close to me; holding my hands, but not saying much; the worry in her gaze plenty eloquent. The men, her father and brothers, also kept to the house – Musa, especially, was rarely at home except at mealtimes and to sleep, at least when I was there.

On this day, they left only to pray in the masjid and returned rather promptly.

They alerted us to my father's presence as they were heading out for maghrib. The expensive, air-conditioned car stood out even before the driver slowed to ask them for directions. And no one could mistake the man sitting impatiently in the back seat.

Z came downstairs with me to see him. The men had already let him into the house, and we found him standing, looking around in the dusk-induced darkness of the room, his expression hard to read. I heard Mummy fiddling with the generator in the backyard, grateful when the lights flickered on.

He looked almost as I remembered him; tall, dark, and rather running to fat. The deep groove on his cheek, his ila - the tribal mark from the increasingly unpopular Yoruba custom - seemed to be thrown into even greater relief as he gained more weight. He was in his trademark guinea brocade agbada, its edges just touching the floor as he stood, and ofi cap that he almost always wore. Suddenly, I wondered how much I remembered of him was truly memory, and how much was superimposed from magazine pictures and TV images gleaned over the years.

I stood there, immobilized, as he turned towards me; this man who I'd thought loved me as a child, who'd walked away from me without a backward glance.

'As-Salaam alaykum, sir. Welcome. I'm Zaynunah, Ruqqayyah's friend from school. Won't you please sit down?'

Thank God for Z!

I sank gratefully into the nearest sofa, watching as my father did the same. Although I had a few hours' notice – a few years, really, if I had ever let myself think of meeting him again – I did not know what to say to him, or how I'd have survived this if she hadn't taken charge. She sat next to me, drawing him out in polite conversation, allowing me to collect myself without seeming to notice that I'd needed to.

My father, on the other hand, was not so tactful or subtle. He conversed with Z easily enough but made no bones that his attention was reverted on me. I could feel his eyes on me as I brought in the refreshments Mummy had laid out in the dining room. I served him without meeting his eyes, not saying a word.

The men came in just as I had poured out the home-made fruit squashes, and Z's father took charge. As he introduced himself and his sons, I saw a glimpse of the University professor he was, an intellectual secure in his place in the world. The confident, almost worldly air he presented was an image almost incompatible with the quiet and unassuming man he was in his home. I guess I had fallen into the mistake people make; supposing that religious people would be socially awkward.

Having lived with his name all my life, I knew how a man like my father could be intimidating to a lot of people – his wealth, his fame, his power. And I guess I'd expected them to be intimidated, too; this humble, middle-class family. Around me though, I saw a graciously polite, but decidedly cool family who made it clear that they were doing this – hosting this stranger, irrespective of his worth – only for my sake. Professor Sanusi was affable but not particularly differential. 'Isa was his usual social self, as though millionaires were guests of his parents ever so often. And Musa was as taciturn as ever.

Z made to excuse us, saying we had yet to pray, and I gratefully went to follow her out of the room. My father's voice stopped me.

'Rukayat.'

That name, the Yoruba connotation it held, was so strange despite it being the official name on my birth certificate. No one else called me that.

'I was hoping you would have dinner with me,' my father said. 'I am staying at the Premier Hotel,' he explained to Zaynunah's dad.

'Can...' I swallowed. 'Can Zaynunah come?'

He was quiet, and Zaynunah's dad quickly stepped in. 'Maybe another time, Ruqqayyah. I'm sure your father has a lot to say to you, after all this time.'

My father looked taken aback by the rather casual reference to his family circumstances, but I just nodded and escaped.

I did not actually have to pray so I just sat watching Z as she prayed, then proceeded to find me something to wear. Since we were in regulation clothing most of the time at school, I did not have much by way of clothes. Usually, Mummy let me wear a few of hers for the few days I stayed with them. She and I, rather ironically, shared a much shorter stature than Z's five-foot, nine inches. However, I had drawn a line at appearing in public in her 'old woman's clothes' about two midterms ago. Fortunately, I had my own limited supply of clothes I brought from Abuja for Noorah's biennial Cultural Day. They tend to be fussier than I'd normally prefer but were dressy enough for dinner at the city's most expensive hotel.

The ride had been painfully silent. My father had asked a couple of 'How have you been?', 'How is school going?'-type questions to which I had replied quietly, 'Fine.'

I watched the city lights through the window as we were driven past, not wanting to meet his unwavering gaze.

'Is this part of your school uniform, this head-covering? I noticed your friend was wearing one too.'

I glanced at him briefly then turned back again. 'I guess,' *I shrugged.*

I certainly was not about to delve into my confusion about the hijab with him.

'Hmmn. I was not introduced to Mrs Sanusi. There is a Mrs Sanusi, I presume?'

'Yes. There is.'

Again, I was not about to delve into the social etiquettes of the Sanusi family.

'Has your mother met her?'

'No, but they talk on the telephone.'

'Interesting' *was all he said.*

Unperturbed, I watched as the hotel's entrance came in view. I just wanted all of this, whatever it was, to be over. The table we were ushered toward was already occupied, and I sensed the confusion of the young man that stood up when we drew near. He was tall, likely in his late twenties and dressed in a business suit. I had no time to wonder about his presence for my father had already reached him. He clasped the young man on his shoulder and motioned to me.

'Tunde meet your sister, Rukayat. Rukayat, Tunde is my elder son, your biggest brother.'

Tunde's confusion cleared, the anger took its place, and his scowl grew exponentially ferocious. I wondered what he'd first thought when he saw me, and why finding out the truth was even worse.

'I am your only son now. I hope'

That stark, somewhat snide, reminder seemed to jolt my father out of his blasé unconcern. He seated me solicitously then rounded on his son.

'Do you think I don't know that? That every day, I don't re-live the loss? Yes, he's gone but we are here. And you wanted me to retire – you and your mother. You wanted me to hand the reins of my affairs to you. Well, this is one of them. And I know you must have heard of her. She's your sister, Tunde, and you have now acquired the responsibility for her. It comes along with my other obligations.'

I watched the heated, whispered exchange in fascinated horror before I realized what was amiss. He was speaking in Yoruba. At Z's, I had spoken to him in English – in contrast to everyone else. And Z's dad addressed me similarly, something that stemmed from the formality he tried to maintain with me as a non-related female. And our subsequent conversation, such as it was, in the car had been conducted in the same language.

He must have assumed that I did not understand his native tongue.

Tunde, apparently chastised but still fuming, sat down. He did not address me or acknowledge me in any manner. The fury poured off him in waves, almost tangible in its force.

Our father sat down a moment later and, blithely, summoned the waiter.

Zaynunah

When Yusuf called that morning, I had just seen Daddy out of the door, worrying that he was doing too much, and immersing himself in the farm to avoid facing Mummy's death. I decided to call Brother 'Isa to discuss it. He spent more time with Daddy daily, he should be able to tell if there was a cause to worry.

My phone vibrated just as I picked it up.

I smiled in anticipation as I walked into the kitchen. I missed my husband, and the kids of course, and the twice daily calls were not enough.

'This is a pleasant surprise,' I say. 'As-Salaam alaykum warahmatullah.'

The pause was infinitesimal. 'Wa alaykumu salaam warahmatullah wabarakah. *Zaynunah*, is Daddy still home?'

'No,' I answered, puzzled. 'He just left. Did you try his phone? Oh, did he leave his phone behind again?'

In many ways, my father did not fit the stereotype of a university professor. Except for his disdain for mobile phones and habitual – and I'm almost convinced, deliberate - misplacement of them.

'I did not try his phone. I just… Did he get the papers, listen to the news, before leaving?'

That was something else to worry about. Daddy used to be so tuned into the news, always read the papers, before heading out. Since Mummy died, though…

'No. What's going on, Yusuf? Should I be worried about Daddy?'

His reassurance was swift and hurried. 'No, no, it's nothing like that. It's just… Well, all over the news today, there are reports of Sodiq Gbadamosi's death. Didn't you say he was your friend's father?'

Ya Allaah! *'Inna lillaahi wa inna ilayhi raji'uun.'*

'Na'am,' my husband corroborated. *From Allah we've come, and to Him is our return.* 'I just wanted to see if you, if she, was aware.'

'No, we hadn't… I don't think she has… I must go and…'

Breaking the news to Ruqqayyah had gone about as well as expected. Knowing her, and her history with her father, I was not sure how she'd take the news. On the one hand, he had abandoned her, seemingly without a care. On the other hand, he – the time he had been with Ruqqayyah and her mother – represented the last time she had a home, a family. And Ruqqayyah; the girl I knew, the woman I have glimpsed these last few days; did not deal well with the murkiness of emotions.

When she finally came downstairs, it was almost noon and she was in full amour – impeccable make-up and a virtually visible *keep out* vibe.

'Do you mind if I take off for some time today?' she asks, not making eye contact. 'I'm feeling like *amala* and *abula* from the *buka*.'

While at Noorah, Ruqqayyah and her friends had somehow gotten some of the support staff to buy them the highly contraband local delicacy for which Ibadan was well-known. She had developed a taste for it, and never passed up an opportunity to have it. Mummy had been aghast at the thought of eating food prepared under the usually unsanitary conditions that prevailed in the *buka*s. But, in time, Ruqqayyah had won her over. Memories of laughing with Mummy and Ruqqayyah over the decadent pleasure of buka-prepared amala with abula, topped with goat-meat or cow-tail laced soup, flashed before my eyes.

'Do you mind if I come with you? After all, your being in Ibadan for four days without indulging must be something of a record.'

My tone is decidedly light. She gives a tight smile and shrugs, and I turn away to get ready. I know she does not want to talk about her father's death, but I was not letting her drive away all worked up either. She was upset, and in a city which she had not visited in over a decade – to my knowledge, anyway.

She relaxed as the day wore on. We spent the day driving through familiar places – the buka in the stadium was still there, and the food as superb as always – noting the changes in the city. She did not say much but her silences grew progressively less broody. She waited in the car while I prayed zuhr at the University central mosque, and then 'asr at the Teaching Hospital mosque. I tried, so hard, to hold off the questions; why don't you pray anymore? Why did you remove your hijab? Why did you shut me out all those years ago?

Ultimately, I had to say something.

I blurt out the first thing that came to my mind, as I got back into the car after praying 'asr.

'I did ask Yusuf for a divorce, you know.'

She slanted her gaze at me and started the car. 'You did?'

'Yes.'

Though she did not enquire further, I continued. 'We had been married seven years, and had three kids, but I was feeling restless. I had started taking some contracts by then. It started by accident really. I helped a friend who was starting her business, and she told someone else, and soon I had people willing to pay me for a skill I took for granted. And I was home-schooling, handling the female section of the madrassah, along with my home keeping duties… I guess I just burned out. I was short-tempered with the kids and nagged my husband non-stop. He didn't help out at home, did not support my own vocation, he wanted to use me as free labour in his madrassah… Oh, the things I said! And when he said my out-of-town commissions were disrupting his schedule at the madrassah, and he couldn't accompany me on those trips anymore, I just… Well, that was about the time I called you.'

She didn't say anything now, and I pushed through. Pushed away the remembered feeling of crushing loss I felt that day. What she'd said to me, this woman I considered my best friend despite the distance that had been growing between us, her voice very clear and obviously detached over the line.

It was the day I acknowledged to myself that our friendship was over. That for whatever reasons, known only to herself, Ruqqayyah had ceased to consider herself my friend. And that I needed to do the same. It had been nauseatingly easy. We lost all contact once I stopped making the overtures.

'I was still vacillating over this, whether to ask for a divorce, when it all came to a head. We were fighting all the time. Or at least, I was. He was just stoically silent. Or he'd walk away. And that just made me madder… Anyway, we were trying to work through this – he found a sister who was a haafidhah to help in the madrassah, I tried to schedule out-of-town jobs for when he was free or when one of my brothers could go with me. It appeared on the surface that things were getting better. And then, I found out I was pregnant! I was so resentful of him, I felt trapped. To make matters worse, he told me that he wanted to marry a subsequent wife.'

Another glance. This one wasn't so blank; I could almost read sympathy in it.

'Ah, Ruqqayyah, it was a trying time. I moved out and insisted on a divorce. He relented enough to give me one *talaq*, rather than the *khul'* I wanted. On the condition that I observed my *iddah* at my parents' and spent one hour, three days a week talking to him – trying to work out our problems. It took months, but we eventually made it through. I moved back home just a week before Abdul-Malik was born.'

Ruqqayyah was quiet, and I suddenly notice that she had parked the car in front of the house.

There was a moment, she did not alight. 'And the subsequent wife?'

'Oh, he did not marry her.' I said, grateful that my *niqab* meant she could not read my expression just then.

CHAPTER SEVEN

Zaynunah

I met my husband through the machinations of my father and my second brother, Musa.

Unlike most of my university friends, who were often the only practising Muslims in their family, I never had to navigate the scene of whatever process passed for spousal searching amidst the undergraduate Nigerian Muslim population. With a professor, and member of the University Muslim community board of trustees, for a father and my very stern-faced PhD student of a brother, most of the M.S.S.N. brothers stayed clear of me. Not for Prof. Sanusi's daughter any of the numerous offers of courtship by brothers who were in no way ready for marriage, for some years at least. I always thought it amusing and just a tad bit disheartening; the JAMBite rush, M.S.S-style that goes on among the Muslim students at the various universities. Deluging the newly admitted, or newly reconnected with Deen, female students with proposals of dubious relationships, often termed as courtship, well before they've had time to grow into themselves, as students, as women, as Muslims.

For me, life went on unencumbered and unconcerned, with the blithe certainty that – when the time was right – my family would figure largely in the process of finding me a spouse.

When Mummy finally raised the topic, I was twenty and in my third year at the University. I remember my puzzlement when she asked if I had given any thoughts to getting married.

'Not really,' I said. It wasn't exactly a lie.

There was a twinkle of amusement in her eyes. 'So, no brothers have caught your eye, not even among those who've been visiting Daddy and Musa recently?'

Understanding had dawned then, bringing mortification in its wake. 'Subhanallah! Is that what they have been doing?'

Mummy nodded, laughing outright.

I cringed, suddenly remembering the increased amount of young men that have visited the house recently. It had been odd to me that the men had taken to entertaining inside the living room. The patio had always been the place where they hosted non-family male visitors in the past. But I had attributed the new turn of events to the heat wave we were currently experiencing.

'What did they do?' I wailed, embarrassed by the thoughts of all those men. 'Announce that they had a sister, a daughter to marry off?!'

Mummy was still smiling. Should mothers enjoy their daughters' discomfiture this much?

'I don't think so. I think they just invited eligible men over, hoping one would catch your fancy.'

I couldn't believe it. 'Why didn't they say something?!'

'They are men, baby,' *Mummy shrugged, as though that explained everything. Anything.* 'And I'm saying it now…'

'Yeah, after Daddy asked you to have the embarrassing talk with your clueless daughter, I'm sure,' *I grumbled.*

She did not deny it, just watched me with the steady, unnerving gaze that mothers have used to keep their children in line since time began.

I closed my eyes. Partly to escape said gaze, and partly to marshal my thoughts. I knew how my parents operated. This was a negotiation, and I needed to make my terms clear and unambiguous. As for Musa, I would deal with the high-handed traitor later.

'I want prior knowledge. I want to be told something about the man before he comes, and to be informed of when he's expected.'

Mummy nodded solemnly, eyes still twinkling.

'I want to be in the room. Not,' *I quickly clarified as she moved to cut in.* 'Not in the living room. But if they leave the door open – and the curtains *drawn – I can listen in on the conversations from the dining room. To get an idea what kind of man...'*

'Anything else?' Mummy asked. I shake my head. 'You would not ask to see them?'

'Oh, I plan to be by my window,' I replied saucily. 'You know, the one that overlooks the gate!'

Even as an undergraduate, I lived at home. I could have lived in one of the student hostels – at least for some of my years of study. But the idea of sharing cramped living quarters with any number of strange girls, from all works of life, held no appeal for me. Even the supposed freedom to be away from parental cynosure did not offer a temptation. I was from that minuscule portion among the youth whose ideals meshed almost seamlessly with their parents'. It helped that we lived just a bus drop away from the university campus and commuting with my father on most days saved me the hassle of braving the Ibadan public transportation.

The first day he came to our house, Yusuf Alimi had not come as a potential suitor. Nor had my menfolk set him up with a spurious excuse of an invitation, for me to look him over. He had been newly returned to the country from Cairo, where he had studied at al-Azhar, and was looking for my brother, Musa. They had spent some months together in Egypt a few years before, while my brother was obtaining his ijaza certification for memorizing the Qur'aan.

I had been the one to receive him, and that first encounter, short and barely memorable, had me intrigued whenever my brother would mention him.

Months went by, Yusuf and my brother grew closer, their friendship solidified when my father's influence helped to get them both Assistant Lecturer positions at the University. One day Musa let it slip that Yusuf saw his lecturing job as a means to his dream of opening a madrasah. His goal was to help people study the Deen of Allaah, not to play the politics of an academic career in the Arabic and Islaamic studies department. That day, I admitted the truth to myself.

I wanted to marry Yusuf Alimi.

He was everything I wanted in a man. His knowledge and passion about the Deen were obvious, as was his sincerity, when he made decisions such as these – to give up the security of a lecturing job to teach about Allaah's Deen. Musa – and my brother could be voluble despite his stern and boorish nature – was full of stories that showed his kindness, honour, patience and general good manners in all circumstances. His father had died when he was seven years old, and his mother had done her best to raise him, and her own two, much younger sisters. To hear Musa tell it, Yusuf Alimi thought the world of his womenfolk.

It did not matter to me that he was not educated in the typical western style. Placed in the madrasah route from childhood; he had spent most of his life learning the various branches of Islaamic studies. It was only after he was awarded a scholarship to study at al-Azar that he'd learnt English through self-study. He then pushed himself to read widely on what he considered beneficial knowledge. Personally, this only made me admire him more, for his tenaciousness in acquiring what he saw as a useful life-skill, especially if he wanted a more secure future for himself than his antecedents as son of a humble widow with no formal education.

And honestly, that incidental meeting with him was the first time I had an inkling to what all those Victorian novels I devoured in my teenage years alluded to. I actually felt the butterflies-in-the-tummy, fluttering sensations I had hitherto been sure was just a marketing gimmick to sell their tales to gullible and unsuspecting females. It had been hard to keep my gaze lowered in the niqab I had just lately donned, and my voice firm and steady, in those few moments it took to answer the door and inform him of my brother's absence.

It was even harder feigning disinterest in my brother's friend as Musa and Daddy helped him settle into his life back in the country. Because, in time, he slowly became entrenched in my family's life.

As a girl, I considered the story of Khadijah's proposal to the Prophet Muhammad incredibly romantic. I sigh over it in a way the Georgette Heywrer novels I devoured from my teens were never able to make me do. But in real life, as the young woman now – discreetly – mooning over her brother's friend, the idea of being the one to initiate a marriage enquiry did not hold much appeal for me. What if he did not want me? Would he be too shy, of my father and brother, to say no? And would he then resent me after the marriage. And what if he did say no? Oh, the mortification! And how would that affect his relationship with my brother, my father? What if he already had someone else in mind? What if he did not want me?

Eventually I did not have to do anything. Mummy guessed my mind and put her husband to work. And when Daddy told me he had found a groom – not suitor - for me, it was all I could do to smile demurely when he mentioned Yusuf's name.

Our official sit-down had been more of a formality. We were supposed to discuss any issues we deemed important, with the aim of ascertaining compatibility, but neither of us raised any serious topics. We spent the barely half hour in loaded silence, broken by the occasional desultory question and answer, trading shy glances with smiling eyes. It was apparent both our mind was made up, long before that meeting. He never even asked to see my face.

For several honeymoon years, I thought that had been incredibly romantic, too.

***

I stared at the lines on the home pregnancy kit mocking me from its perch on the bathroom sink. At the two lines that meant the lateness of my otherwise clockwork cycle was not due to stress or anything else I'd been telling myself over the past week. And I burst into tears.

I couldn't do this. How was I supposed to bring another child into this life, this house; this marriage that I wasn't sure I wanted to be in, myself? Just seven years of marriage, and I was pondering the wisdom of, maybe, throwing in the towel.

It was almost surreal how our relationship had soured. All those things that had seemed so great in Yusuf as a suitor, I could no longer stomach in him as my husband. I had tried to be supportive when he left his lecturing job to start the madrasah. Brother 'Isa, my eldest brother had been generous with an interest-free start-up loan, and I had put in almost as much hours as Yusuf. Serving as cleaner, receptionist, moderator of the female beginner's class, and all-around general-purpose worker, I had slaved for his dream too. We barely scraped by financially, but we were happy. But then the children had come, one after the other, and I could not keep up that pace. Not with three children under the age of five.

And I wouldn't have to, if my husband had listened to – and implemented – any of the ideas I had about improving the madrasah and making it into more of a success, commercially. But he shut me down every time, content with the meagre income he was making. He claimed he was doing what he wanted; teaching the Book, and Deen, of Allaah; so, he was content. And while that had been swoon-worthy to the wide-eyed romance-seeking me as a young woman, the reality of living so close to poverty line grated.

Especially since I knew we could do much better. But all my nagging had done was drive a wedge between Yusuf and me, slow and inexorable. When I found I could make some money with my computer savvy, I jumped at it. And what first started as a bit of side hustle, soon turned into a thriving business.

Rather than make things better, though, my success made things worse. Yusuf did not share my excitement at how my paltry money-making venture had morphed into a consultancy, virtually overnight and almost entirely from word of mouth referral by satisfied clients. He seemed to resent that I was making so much money, and was adamantly opposed any changes I tried to make in our lives – a new car, a move to a larger apartment, money - even as a loan - to purchase a property to house the madrasah permanently.

He had not been pleased that I stopped putting so much time at the madrasah and was not shy to let me know it; so much so that I stopped going there altogether. He voiced concerns - about the kids; maybe my being so busy meant I wouldn't have so much time for them, should we consider regular schools for them, rather than the home-schooling we'd decided on? That hurt me more than everything else – his suggestion that the welfare of my kids had somehow become less important to me.

In turn, I lashed out at him, needing to make him feel some of my hurt, becoming a shrew of a wife that I myself did not recognise, or even like. The more he resisted acknowledging what I had built with my business, the more I saw it as a rejection of me. I struggled, in the face of that, to remember the husband that loved me, the relationship that we had built to nourish that love.

It all seemed hopeless.

These past few weeks I had tried to rein myself in, to make more of an effort to be something of the wife he, too, might remember from our early days of marriage. He must have come to the same conclusion. He was politer; less critical of what he perceived as my faults. But rather than remind me of the man I married, I felt like I was living with a stranger – congenial but detached. It makes me wonder if I had failed as spectacularly in my own masquerading of better times.

And now this. How was I supposed to, how could we possibly, deal with a baby now?

Yet, even with all that between us, I had been lamentably unprepared when my husband came home after Fajr the next day, waited calmly while I finished my morning adkaar, and announced rather baldly that-

'Zaynunah, I want to marry a subsequent wife.'

Whoever coined the term 'heartbreak' knew exactly what she was talking about. Because that was what I felt that day – like my heart was literally breaking into pieces, while my world imploded in sympathy. I knew I had to get up, get out, before I did anything drastic.

Patience, I reminded myself quietly, is at the first strike of adversity.

I picked up my niqab from the side of the dresser, tying it over my face. I walked out, dressed in the faded jilbaab I'd relegated to a prayer garment.

I was almost at the door before I realised my husband had followed me, his voice having lost its calmness, frantically asking where I was headed.

'To my parents. Please bring the children over when they are awake,' I told him as I got into my car. The same one he had made every excuse known to man to avoid driving. I had gone against his expressed opinions to buy it, just a few weeks ago.

By the time I finally pulled up at my parents, it was mid-morning. I had spent hours driving aimlessly around the city, absently glad for the morning commuters' traffic that provided me a mindless distraction. But now, I was tired, heart-sore, and not up to talking.

'Zaynunah?' Mummy's puzzled gaze peeked at me from behind the curtains, where she'd come to investigate who was driving into her compound.

'Yes, Mummy. It's me,' I replied, dragging my weary self through the backdoor and flipping my niqab back.

'What…Are you okay? What's going on? Where are the children?'

'The children are fine, still sleeping. I'm going to do the same…I'm so tired. I just -'

Peering intently into my face, Mummy nodded. 'Ok, baby. You go ahead and rest a while. Have you eaten; do you want some breakfast?'

I shook my head, mumbling thanks, and went up to my old room. Apart from the absence of my clothes and personal effects, it looked just like it did when I lived at home, unmarried.

Afraid to analyse this thought, I crawled unto the unmade bed, niqab and all.

***

'Why did you marry me?'

It was after 'isha and we were in the backyard of my parents' house. It was a balmy night, the gentle breeze just strong enough to keep the mosquitoes away. Moonless, but with a smattering of stars, the temperature of the cloudless night was just right. There had been a lull in the rains, but harmattan had yet to descend, with its cold, biting winds.

Mummy was always quick to point out that the backyard was the main reason they had rented this house all those years ago, even though it had been a bit too big for the then one-child family and Daddy's fledging academician budget. Enclosed on three sides by a six-foot fence attached to the house, and bordered on both sides by bungalows, it had been the ideal yard for a fully veiled Muslim woman. While she had not wanted to practise total isolation of her maternal ancestry, Mummy said she had felt claustrophobic in the apartment complex they had lived in before. In this yard, however, she could hang out her laundry without first covering in layers, she could sit and sip tea while feeling the rays of the sun on her face, and she could chase her kids about with abandon. When the house had come up for sale a few years before, the children of the original owners had been given my parents the first option to buy it. As far as I know, it was the only property they owned.

Yusuf looked at me now, the steady light of his gaze letting me know he was considering his answer carefully.

It was my third month back at my parents, and into our official separation.

After the initial three days of covering for me as I dodged my husband's visits, Mummy had put her feet down. She insisted I go down and talk with my husband and sort out whatever mess we'd made of ourselves. Her words.

I had gone down and asked for a divorce.

Once he had realised that I had no intention of returning to our matrimonial home, Yusuf had involved my parents. I would not go back home, and he would not divorce me. It was finally agreed that he would utter a single talaq, I would spend my iddah at my parents, and we would spend one hour three times a week talking – trying to work things out.

Neither of us mentioned his plan to re-marry.

His visits had somehow become daily, and often began before maghrib and extended into well after 'isha. I did not mind so much. I was seeing more of my husband than I'd seen in the past few years. And without the pressures that had piled on us in recent times, we were getting to know each other again. The sharp edges of my pain had blunted, and I was seeking to discover the joy I had once found in being joined to this man.

'Because I wanted to build a home with you,' his voice had risen on the last word. The voice of a wise man, threading carefully around verbal traps that women lay.

It was the same answer he had given me seven years ago when, as a bride, I had been fishing for his declaration of affection.

It was not as gratifying now.

'Yes, I know that. But you could have built a life – a solid life with foundations based on the Qur' an and sunnah – with any number of

women.' I say, pre-empting the second part of his reply from all those years ago. This time, I refuse to be placated. 'Why me?'

My husband is what you would picture when you imagine a typical African, Muslim man. Stoic and silent, he does not do sensitivity, or talking about feelings. I see him squirming, uncomfortable with examining his emotions – much less putting it in words for my elocution.

'I don't know what you want me to say…'

I look him in the eye steadily, waiting out his masculine floundering. It was a technique I learnt from the master – my mother – and it did not fail me, even now.

'I wanted you, okay?' I heard the exasperation in his voice. 'Yes, I could have found someone else to build a home with. Someone I was more suited to, probably. You would definitely have found someone better – I never expected that you would accept me, an uneducated fellow like myself. But the more I got to know your family… The more I heard Musa speak of you… I couldn't help myself – I wanted you. And when he began to drop hints—'

'What?!'

How had I not known this? Seven years of marriage, and I was only just finding out that my brother had 'dropped hints' to Yusuf?

He chuckled at my obvious discomfiture. 'Yes, and I am glad he did. Because I would never have presumed to ask for your hand otherwise.'

'Why not?' I mumbled, unable to meet his eye just yet. He had known – they had all known – that I had been pinning for him back then.

I felt his hand beneath my chin, bringing my eyes to meet his, the tenderness in his gaze reminding me of all that we shared.

'Because you were everything I was not – brilliant, beautiful, with a bright future ahead of you – and you could do so much better than me. But your father got me the lecturing job – imagine, me, a lecturer at University of Ibadan! And Musa dropped all these hints… And I thought maybe my dream could be obtainable after all…'

It was the first time I saw how deeply it cut him that he had no formal western education. It eroded his confidence, making him alternatively insecure and defensive. It was a realization that put a lot of our issues into perspective for me.

One thing I have learnt, being apart from my husband is how much I still loved him. I had let myself forget that in the multitudes of issues that had grown between us over the years. And now, contrary to my feelings when I first moved back to my parents' home, I had come to realize that I wanted to remain married to him. But only in truth – a real joining of two people in Love and Affection, being each other's refuge, as Allaah had described it in the Qur'an.

'If you wanted me so much, why have you been trying so hard to change me, to make me into someone else – maybe your subconscious idea of an ideal Muslim wife?'

'Why would you - -' he spluttered.

'You said it yourself, Yusuf,' I interrupted. 'I am brilliant, or I was when you met me. I had a bright future ahead. And now, I am working on that future, Yusuf. I am very good at what I do. But you act as though it's an effrontery to you, a disservice to my family, when I do it.'

He was quiet, so I continued. Years of suppressed emotions bubbled up with the heat and strength akin to an active volcano. 'Remember what I told you when we just got married. That I wanted you to call me by my name. Zaynunah. Irrespective of where we were, who we were with, and how many kids we had; I always want you to call me Zaynunah. You never asked why. Well, it's because I want you to remember who I am. Me. Not some generic Muslim woman, who happened to be your wife and mother of your children. It is important to me that you see me. And I did not want some other man but you; the so-called uneducated, not-so beautiful, and with-uncertain-prospects you. I chose you, and you chose me. Why, then, are you trying to make me into someone I'm not?'

He was quiet a long while, as was his way. It was another thing I rediscovered over this break of ours- how much I appreciated my husband's thoughtful silences. They probably saved us from doing irreparable damage to our marriage in those months when we seemed to only hurt each other. That I found those silences irksome then…well, what can I say? Apparently, I'm a woman!

'I did not realize I was doing that… That you would think of it as that, me trying to change you. I just… I guess you are right – I do believe that it's my place as the husband to provide for you. It makes me feel unworthy of you that I can't do that, and that you have to work…' His voice trailed away.

It was my turn to lift his chin. He looks up, surprised. I have not voluntarily touched him since I left our home.

'In an ideal world, maybe even decades ago, you would have had to provide for me. Now, in this age, I can help with the finances. Fortunately for me, I have skills to do that without compromising on my ideals – my Deen, my hijab, my family. And I love what I do, especially the fact that I'm so good at it, that I'm actually succeeding at it -'

'But if I made enough that we didn't have to worry about money, if I hadn't left my job at the university for instance, you would not have to work.'

'Don't ever say that again! You left that job because it was the best thing for you to do, and I supported you in that. The madrasah was your dream, and I will always support you. But it was not making enough to sustain us, and Allaah blessed us with this other means. Would I have pursued this work if we hadn't needed the money? I'd like to think, probably not – that I would be too immersed in life as your wife, in raising our kids the best way I can, in improving my knowledge and practice of the Deen… But the truth is, I don't know. We won't ever know. Maybe I would have become bored, maybe I would feel the need to challenge myself or put all I learnt in school to use, or maybe I would have felt the need to earn my own money. I don't know, and we can't really know anymore. Fact is, we needed the money, and I did start working, and now I love it. Even if you were to become a wealthy man tomorrow, I know – now – that I'd still want to continue my work. Or at least, to have the option to continue my work. And you need to understand, and accept, that.'

I took a deep breath, feeling as though someone had lifted a boulder off my chest. I never took the time to explain to him before how I felt about working, and the fact that he did not support me in this. And while I'm beginning to realize that his attitude was more about him – his insecurity, his feeling of inadequacy – than me, it still hurt remembering his demeanor over the past few months.

As a Muslim girl, then woman; especially in niqaab; there are already too many things – and people - to hold you back. Schools we had to leave because they wouldn't accept a piece of cloth on a fourteen-year-old girl's head. Hassles we had to go through; to drive, to go to the bank, or travel by air. Ignorant people whose perceptions we had to overcome or deal with every day – even when you take your ill child to the E.R. Too many choices that are taken away from us, or thrust upon us, because of other people's fear, ignorance, close-mindedness, and misguided notions that our faith – or our dressing – made us somehow incompetent to live our lives as we deem.

And I know that I had it relatively easy. There were no immediate familial or societal pressures that dictated what I had to, or not, do. I have parents that supported me and, having lived that lifestyle themselves, paved the way for me. I had no constraining financial concerns mitigating against me. I have skills I could employ, marketable skills that enable me to dictate my own terms. I knew I had it easy compared to most women the world over, Muslim or not, niqaabi or not. Yet, the fact that I had to justify this choice, even in the face of my assumed ease, hurt as much as it grated.

With so many factors against us, and so many people ready to dismiss us, victimize us, condescend to us, was it really too much to ask that our menfolk – those with whom we supposedly shared a faith, an ideal, and our very lives - support us?

Why does a woman's success have to be a blight on a man's masculinity? He promised to love and care for me, why can't he do that even if he does not necessarily need to provide for me?

'Okay.'

I looked at him in puzzlement. 'Okay?!'

What does that even mean?

'Okay, I'm sorry. Ok, you're right. Okay, you can work if it's what you want-' *He stopped, and raised his hands in a gesture of surrender, grinning.* 'Okay you have my support. Okay, I have been a boorish male over this, and I'd probably need you to remind me from time to time, but I'd try harder to be supportive from here on. Okay?'

I smiled. 'Okay.'

CHAPTER EIGHT

Ruqqayyah

That night, Zaynunah and I were alone in the house. Her dad was spending the night with his aged mother in the village. We opted not to switch on the generator; the three rechargeable lamps should get us through the night if we stayed together, using them sequentially. Zaynunah still avoided Mummy's room unless absolutely necessary, so we were in her old room. Having spent the better part of the day reminiscing on Ibadan scenery, and visiting three *buka*s, neither of us was hungry. I felt like something had changed during the course of the day. There was an undeniable thread binding us together – old friendship, new discovery, loss of a parent, who knew? I did not want any serious issues marring the languid atmosphere around us, so I avoided that thought and where it could lead. I had become deft at pushing aside emotions over the years.

We sprawled carelessly on the bed, already in what passed for our sleepwear, and I was still too stuffed from our earlier escapades, even to talk.

'I missed this.' Z's sigh was soft, mellow.

I grunted in content agreement, recalling several similar scenes – without the preceding binge *buka*-feasting – from a lifetime ago.

'The freedom to just be.' She continued. 'No husband, no kids, no chores. Nothing that needs my attention, otherwise the earth may stop spinning. You know, even when Yusuf and I were separated, the kids were here with me…' Her voice trailed off, and she sighed again. 'I love my family, but I have missed this!'

It could have been that she mentioned it again. Or that I was too sated with good food to be my usual, guarded self. Of course, it may have been the guilt that washed over me as she told me about her marital issues – again – this afternoon. Or the fact that I'd known, even as I was doing it then, that it was a horrid thing to do to a friend. Maybe it was this thing I felt building between us; a glimpse of friendship, the recognition of a kindred soul, the loss of a parent – hers more than mine. Hadn't I spent the entire day avoiding the reality that my father was dead, that there was no reconciliation with him in my future? I, more than anyone, know what it's like to feel that someone you cared about did not want to have anything to do with you. And I never got over the fact that I did that to her. She who was, had always been, most accepting of me, despite all of my posturing.

'I'm sorry,' I say now, quietly. 'For what I said then.'

She raised herself up, reclining on her elbows and peered into my face, her gaze steady. That gaze, the steady unwavering regard that stopped time while you fumbled to put words to your heart's echo, was Mummy at her most.

'You called me. Told me about the problems you were having. That you were considering a divorce. Asked my opinion. And I said… what I said.'

I don't know you well enough anymore to give you advice on divorce.

'It was a crappy thing to say to a friend. To anyone.' I finally admit aloud what my heart has nagged about, incessantly.

She burst out laughing. 'That's such an American thing to say! Who says "crappy"?'

I forced a chuckle, equal parts glad and mortified that she did not make a fuss. Maybe she did not think it a big deal. Could it really be this easy to put it behind us?

'Yeah, it was pretty horrible to hear you say that, and be so disinterested. I…' She looked away. 'It was the day I realized you did not consider yourself my friend anymore.'

Ok, so maybe a big deal after all.

'I didn't.' She turned back with a startled, hurt look and I rushed to continue, 'I didn't consider myself worthy of being your friend anymore.'

'What…? Why…? Okay, you know what, I've been sensitive, and considerate, and haven't asked questions but… What on earth?! What happened to you? I mean yeah, you were always sort of very complex and hiding within your layers but… You just shut me out! You shut everyone out – even Mummy. You just disappeared from our lives, what happened to you?'

She was a beautiful soul in righteous indignation. And she was so wrapped up in everything good that had ever happened to me; my friendship with her, her mother's role in my life, her family's acceptance of the lonely orphan with living parents, the nugget of faith that saved me at my lowest ebb.

I smile.

It was an absurd reaction, as evidenced by Z's expression, but I couldn't help it. I did not want to help it. Not this time. I revel in the emotion that was slowly suffusing me, of love and a sense of worth, warming the long-frozen parts of me that I had refused to thaw out for so long.

'Quite a bit happened to me, Z,' I finally tell her, wearing a lingering smile. 'And I'm not ready to go there. Maybe I never will go there again. But I am sorry I shut you out, that I was a bad friend, that I was not there for you when you needed me.'

She narrowed her eyes and pinned me with that gaze of hers for several more heartbeats, then nodded once. 'Okay.'

Huh? 'Okay?!'

Her smile was at the same time radiant and mysterious. 'Okay, I accept your apology. Okay, because I know that you must have been going through a lot then. Okay, you don't want to talk about it, and I get that you may never want to talk about it. And just… Okay!'

I was quiet again, enjoying this unfamiliar feeling. It had been an age, a lifetime even, since I felt like this.

Whole.

'Tell me about Yusuf. How you met, what happened, how you worked it out… Everything.'

Hours later, I drift off to sleep with Z's voice in my ear, soothing and gentle like its owner, admitting me back into her life.

*

It is a dream.

I know it is a dream – I have had this dream several times over the past decade or so. Yet even knowing this, I can't wake up and the terror grips me.

I see myself – the girl on the cusp of womanhood that I was twelve years ago; happy, unsuspecting, naïve.

There are no sounds in this dream; everything passes like a collage of silent movie reels. Scenes flash past at the speed of light, then slowing down with agonizing taunting. Speeding then slowing down, then speeding up and slowing down, with no discernable pattern.

There I am, the clueless Nigerian girl amidst the unbelievably opulent American college in a middle eastern country. Adrift without the friend and family that had been my crutch for five years; alone, lonely, wistful.

Next, I'm in the parent college in Houston, Texas. My American passport had made me a shoo-in for the US elective semester. Yet I was as alone as ever, even surrounded by the legion of Nigerians in Texas. Even at the MSA mixer…

Then I'm laughing, chatting with my friends. I finally found some; a superficial connection reminiscent of my Noorah days before Z, but still…

I see my new friends standing by while I entered the Vortex. They were busy; laughing, making merry, and no one saw me. Maybe they did not care. Even I was laughing blithely, as the force sucked me in…

Then there is nothing. I am in the nothingness. It is pitch-black. There is not a sound. I am weightless. I do not struggle. I float in the emptiness…

I burst out.

There is light, so much light, blinding in its brightness. And the sound, sudden and jarring. Deafening.

Pain! The pain…

I jerk awake.

Years of waking to debilitating, almost physical, pain has taught me how to muffle the scream – even in my sleep.

I look around, glad that Zaynunah had slept through it, undisturbed.

Heaving a sigh of relief, I tiptoe my way through the darkness. Minutes later, I'm in Mummy's prayer corner, going through the motions of the coping mechanisms that have become almost instinctive by now. I was donning my prayer garment before I recalled my period started last night.

I sit, bewildered. I have not had that dream in years.

Initially, when it first began, I would get up drenched in sweat. I would sit out the rest of the night, unable to sleep, cowering in a corner, until the fear subsided – the pain, however, was enduring and felt physical.

In time and with therapy, I have taught myself the futility of being held hostage by my mind, my feelings. And while I baulked at my therapist's suggestion that I examine the dream, I learnt to get up and do, rather than wallow. To channel what I was feeling into something, hopefully healing. For me that something had been, unbelievably, *tahajjud*.

In recent times, and without the dream to contend with, the days of my period became the days I exercised. As someone who actively hates to exercise, it seemed fitting to do so on those days when I hate my body most, with its cramping, bloating and general *urgh*-factor at its peak. And since I only ate cereal, and whatever food was expediently available from work, those few days a month on my ridiculously top-of-the-line home exercise gadget was enough to keep me fit. Or so I tell myself.

Knowing that exercise wouldn't cut it, even if there were somehow to be gadgets in this house, I settle in for meditation. But I couldn't do it. Today, I cannot seem to clear my mind of the lingering anguish, I cannot pray. My mind keeps straying, I can't find words… I don't know what I want.

Too much was happening all at once; Mummy died, I came here, my father died, I'm reconnecting with Z…

And the dream.

Maybe my therapist had a point after all, and I need to examine this dream, confront my past. For years, I have leapt straight from that dream into coping mechanisms, suppressing even a tiny bit of its recollection. I had buried it for so long, unwilling to risk it that remembering would return me to that abyss…

These last few days, though, of being in this house, re-living the past when I had people who loved me, of finding my stride in this new relationship with Z… It made me want to fight, to claim at least a portion of all that I had lost. Everything else seems so pointless now; all that I had crawled my way out of the abyss for; without this one person – one family – I ever had. And maybe it was the passage of time, but I want the life, or a semblance of it, that I could have had if events of the past had not torn me away from this. A friend, a Mummy, a family; that loved and accepted me.

When my mother told me the plan for my life on my Graduation day from Noorah – the only time she stepped inside the school – I was livid. My father had decreed that he did not want me attending the University of Ibadan. I could either enroll in the University of Abuja, or he would send me to the US. I couldn't believe the nerve of the man; he had abandoned me as a child but felt it within his rights to dictate my future! Z and Mummy had to talk me out of letting this news ruin my day. It helped that my mother left immediately after the school ceremony – her husband was in Lagos on business, and she had to go prepare for a stake-holder's dinner that night. Or some such.

I would have disregarded my parents wish when my admission to UI on merit came through, but Mummy won't have it. Since she was responsible for me – sort of – she could not knowingly let me go against their expressed commands. She reminded me how hard it had been convincing them – well my mother really, but I'm sure my father was pulling the strings behind the scene – to let me stay on in Ibadan after graduation. A-levels and SAT classes had been my proffered reasons, as there were a couple of places recommended by Noorah for any of the girls planning to travel abroad for university. But they – again I'm sure it was he – insisted that I live on the campus of the educational consultancy service. I chose my battles, though, and did not tell Mummy that bit of it. Since he was unlikely to come check on me, and she was content with my bi-monthly desultory calls from the NITEL phone booth, I stayed at Z's, added the boarding fees to my savings, and no one was the wiser.

But university was a big step, and I grudgingly conceded that it might not be in my best interest to be that defiant. I also did not share my suspicions; that my father's sudden interest in my education was just a ploy to separate me from the influence of the Sanusi family; with Z or Mummy. Like most people, especially educated Nigerian Yoruba Muslims, he probably took one look at people whose faith was vibrant enough to manifest in every sphere of their lives – most visibly, in their dressing -and jumped to the most preposterous of conclusions.

I watched wistfully as Z started orientation and then classes. I went to my A-levels classes as if that was what I wanted. And I nodded in pretend agreement when mummy said things like –

'Obedience is part of the good behavior towards parents that Allaah commands us. Even if we feel they have been remiss in their duties to us, it doesn't lift this obligation off us.'

I did however draw the line at going to the US. I had vague memories of visiting once with my parents when I was five or six, back in the then. Now, after spending the past six years cloistered at Noorah, and the Sanusi's, the thought did not appeal to me. I had been mentally distancing myself from my group of friends at Noorah for months, and pretty much broke off all contact after graduation. I was praying my salaah regularly, and of my own volition. My wardrobe – never particularly racy – had also undergone a subtle change over the past years. They seemed to tend toward long and loose, with scarves secured by pins and brooches – as opposed to tossed indifferently – over my head. I was not sure the life of a college girl in the West – and I'd gleaned something from the ubiquitous books and movies – was for me.

It was sheer happenstance that I saw the advert for the newly launched middle eastern campus of an American college. I could not believe it when I was offered provisional admissions based on my O-level results and written essay. Convincing my parents was insultingly easy, and far earlier than I *was prepared for, I was on the plane – heading out to a future I had not envisaged and did not really want.*

The first few months were hellish. I was alone – truly alone – for the first time in my life. In a strange country, with an unfamiliar language, and a people so different they might have been aliens. Or maybe I was the alien. I was the only Nigerian, the only African, in the entire school. Granted it was a new school, I was in the second group of students admitted, but still…

I was a social failure.

It seemed all the bravado that made me one of the popular girls at Noorah deserted me. Or maybe it was like that Yoruba proverb, finding that your father's largest-in-the-village farm was just vegetable garden size by someone else's standards. Compared with the collective wealth apparent at the school, with the students, in the country, I – the unacknowledged daughter of a Nigerian millionaire – was seriously out of my depths.

I persevered, though. Because that is what I do. The most consistent lesson life has taught me is that I must endure. I tend to find myself in these situations, often due to no action of mine, and there was nothing to do but endure. So, I did. I withdrew into myself and tried to concentrate on my studies. I sent emails to Z every other day, called her and Mummy twice weekly, and my mother monthly. That first year, I spent only the first and last week of my summer holiday at my mother's in Abuja. Returning to Ibadan, the Sanusis' unconditional welcome; being with Z and Mummy; was a lifeline.

In second year, I applied – and got in - for an elective posting to the parent campus in the US. Since our course structure was based on theirs, I would take all the same courses, and earn extra credit for being an international exchange student. It seemed like a good idea; I was not happy where I was, anyway, the US could surely not be any worse. And since I had to go over the spring break, it was a viable excuse to avoid returning to my mother's or staying back on campus.

The US campus was a blast.

I met a group of girls from other African countries who shared some of my classes, and they were really cool. We hung out together, and I started to feel like myself again. The self I was at Noorah, before. But that wasn't necessarily a bad thing, was it? Maybe that self was me, who I really was, and I had just spent the last few years submersing her under the weight of gratitude to the family that accepted me. Of course, they never forced me to do anything, but maybe I had begun to dress more and more modestly out of deference to the men's sensibilities and in solidarity to the women's convictions. I could not have brought my music and movies lifestyle into the house, knowing no one condoned it, but I never really made any conscious decision to give up anything. It just seemed to happen. What if I was just responding to the environment? What did I really know, or believe, about Islaam anyway? Maybe I was just a product of norm, Sanusi-household style.

I told myself all these as I became more entrenched in my life of a college girl in the West. Oh, I tried hanging out with the Muslims at first. I even attended the MSA mixer at the beginning of the semester. And a couple of

Jumah at the MSA center. Mainly because Zaynunah kept going on about it, but it felt flat and I stopped.

I let things slide.

First, it was my salaah. Coming from a country where virtually everything shut down for salaah to this one where the adhaan could not even be proclaimed aloud, it was the first thing to go. I couldn't schedule all my classes around salaah. It wasn't convenient to race back to my dorm to pray before meeting up with my friends. I did not even want to deal with the looks I got from my dorm roommate when I was praying…

After that, it was pretty much a landslide.

By the end of the semester, I had decided to stay in the US. My friends and I were going to pull funds together and rent a modest house just ten minutes' drive from school. I had also gotten a full scholarship and bought a car. I had taken to wearing form-fitting tops, snug pants and the indifferent scarf.

I did not want to return to Nigeria for summer that year, but Z was getting married. I flew in for a brief three weeks, most of which passed in a whirlwind of wedding preparations. I unearthed my middle eastern styled abayas for the trip, so that I did not have to deal with any uncomfortable conversations. My mother had her family and did not notice my wardrobe change, but Z and Mummy would have. It was just easier for everyone this way. Of course, Z was preoccupied with plans and daydreams about her future, making the charade easy to pull off.

The night of the wedding, though, after the bride had gone with the groom and his family, Mummy came to me. I was in Z's room, trying to unearth my belongings from the mess of tsunami-like proportions that was bridal preparation, and pack for my return to Abuja the next day.

'Ruqqayyah, darling. We did not get a chance to catch up before. How are you? How has school been?'

I ramble at length. Telling her about my electives and how it went. About my decision to remain in the US. About the scholarship that I won, and what it would mean for my future. It was a sponsorship from a firm, and I had an assured internship upon graduation that could mean a permanent position if I did well. I regaled her with anecdotes of my experiences trying to fit into the American culture and psyche.

Mummy listened carefully as I went on, she let me prattle on inconsequential things till I ran out of steam. Then she touched my arm, and said –

'Alhamdulillah that things are working out for you. I was worried that you might be having difficulty adjusting. You've had two major moves in three years, that can't have been easy. So, if there's anything, anything at all-'

I squirmed. She waited. Then, 'Is there?'

I thought of the doubts, the lapses, and the company I kept, and...shook my head.

'I'm fine, Mummy. I mean, yeah, it's taken some adjustment but I'm fine. Really.'

She looked like she wanted to believe me. I sighed in relief when she hugged me, got up and started to leave. At the door, she turned to me.

'I hope you are really okay, Ruqqayyah. But if you ever want to talk, I'll be here. For you, always. And don't forget that Allaah responds to du'a. Always. As long as you call on Him.'

That was the last time I saw Mummy.

CHAPTER NINE

Ruqqayyah

I returned to the US three days after Zaynunah's wedding. I still had a couple of weeks left of my holidays, but there was nothing to keep me in Nigeria. Most of my friends had stayed behind in the US, anyway, avoiding the airline fare back home and in need of the income from summer jobs. It was the one good thing that could be said for my father – I never lacked for money. He had set up an account in my name when he abandoned us, to which my mother had been signatory. She signed it over to me on my eighteenth birthday.

I spent the next few weeks hanging out with my friends when they were not working. The girls had met a couple of British guys, just graduated university and vacationing in the US, while I was in Nigeria and they made a seamless addition to our already-boisterous group. It was the most fun I'd had in a long time.

Soon, the girls started teasing me that the scarf I still insisted on throwing over my head did not seem to hinder my flirting. To hear them say it, I needed to lose the scarf along with the last bit of inhibition I clung to. Indeed, it was obvious that at least one of the guys was feeling me. I just had to let myself go all the way…

Taking a critical look at my conduct, I was aghast at how far from my comfort zone I had strayed. I had somehow allowed myself to adopt the norms of the place and the people around me. Yes, I still clung to my scarf but little good it did; slipping off my head as often as it was pulled back. My form-fitting clothes could barely be termed modest, covering less and less of me with the passage of time.

No, I did not do the club route with them, but I had lost the battle to keep our place alcohol-free. In fact, I was so de-sensitized to it by then that I sat with them all as they drank, hugging my sobriety tightly like a worn blanket, too flimsy to offer anything other than cold comfort. And while I did not have any boyfriend, had not committed actual zina, their teasing drove home the point that my conduct made that fact somewhat redundant. I had flirted heavily, exhilarated at the innuendo-laden exchange.

If I was being honest, while I could still lay a tenuous claim to chastity, I had long given up on modesty.

It was a sobering thought. And maybe it would have been enough to propel me to change my life, go try find the path I had somehow wondered from. I would never know, though, because a few days afterward my life did change.

Horrendously.

I had spent the next few days at home, keeping to myself and trying to evaluate my life. Pulling back from my friends and their activities. And more importantly, from the guys with whom my indiscretion had been pointed out to me. In truth, I had nothing against any of them; they were living the life they wanted. I was the one who had compromised her principles, the beliefs I had held dear – no matter how I had recently taken to pretending that I hadn't.

I decided I needed some space and time to find myself, again. To figure out what, actually, mattered to me. To define, for myself, what was important to me. And it could not just be a reflection of my environment or the people around me, as it had apparently been all my life.

I knew my friends were bemused as to why I was suddenly quiet and unavailable. I needed to reassure them that all was well with me, with us, several times. So, when they trooped in from yet another club that fateful night, I chose to remain in the living room with them. Someone got me a cola - no one bothered to tease me about my sobriety anymore - and I pretended to be interested in what was being said. It was the guys' last night in Texas, the longest they had stayed in any of the US states during this trip of theirs. Everyone made vague noises about keeping in touch, the kind of things you say, knowing fully well that neither party mean it. I sat, sipped at my drink, made all the right noises, then excused myself after a suitable amount of time.

I remember feeling decidedly groggy even as I crawled into bed.

When I woke up the next day, it was afternoon. I was naked from the waist down, and my body ached in ways I had no previous inkling was possible, in ways that left no doubts about what had transpired.

I had no memory beyond getting into bed, alone.

I remember pondering, like an out of body experience, what was worse – what had obviously been done to me or the fact that that I could not, for the life of me, remember anything.

Years later, my therapist would say that I had been in shock. That it was my mind's coping mechanism, allowing me to survive a trauma that violated not only my body, but my will, too. Maybe she was right. Because in those first few weeks, I went about like an automaton. The hardest part had been getting up that first day. I have vague recollections of getting up, dragging myself to the bathroom and scrubbing off nigh a layer of skin.

After that, everything else was a blur.

I slept, a lot. I ate, sometimes. And I saw my friends only when I could not avoid it. I locked myself in my room, venturing out only when I was sure everyone had gone out. And when someone knocked, I feigned sleep. When I was cornered, I was not feeling quite the thing – at times ill, PMSing, or just not in the mood.

School started, and I showed up. My scholarship had a minimum attendance requirement. I sat in the back of the class, never participated. I shrank from eye contact, kept to myself. I lost quite a bit of weight and my clothes hung rather loosely off my new frame. The scarf I wore became an accessory to hide behind. I would draw it as low over my face as I could, trying to be inconspicuous. Trying to disappear.

Two months later, my mother appeared. She never visited me through six years at Noorah, and almost two in Qatar. I should have been surprised when I came out of class and found her standing beside the fountain in the courtyard. Amidst the gaiety of the students surrounding her that brisk fall afternoon, she had stood out with her reserve, her aloofness. Yet all I could do was blink at her, uncomprehendingly, wondering if too little sun was playing tricks on my mind.

'Rekiya, what happened to you?' she launched into speech as soon as I came close enough. 'You have not called home in over two months. Then I called your dorm but was told you did not show up. That you never moved in. And I had no idea… Where have you been?'

'Good Afternoon, Ma. Sorry I did not call. I've been busy. Uh, a couple of girls and I are renting a place in town. Er, when did you get in?'

My voice was husky, my delivery wooden. I had no cause to say so many words since-

'I got in yesterday, as soon as my visa was renewed, and I could catch a flight. And your floor rep has been helpful. Some girls said they had the same classes with you and told me come here.'

She looked me over critically. It was a look that would have had me squirming once upon a time. It was not easy to have a valiantly maintained, exceptionally beautiful woman for a mother. Especially when you bear a *marked resemblance to the slightly-less-than-hideous looking millionaire that broke her heart. Hitherto, I would have mentally followed her gaze, making sure I was at least well turned out. Today, like every day in almost three months, I could not care less.*

'Are you done for today? Can we go to this house of yours, meet your friends?' she asks, still watching me intently.

I pivoted without a word and headed to the bus stop.

'I thought you bought a car.'

I don't stop, don't turn around. 'I did. I just don't drive it much.'

Not after the first few panic attacks. They tend to come on randomly, uncontrollable and sans warning. It had taken two ER trips to accept that my heart was not going to die on top of everything else, and the episodes were indeed panic attacks. I learnt to live with them. They pass, eventually. It was just safer to ride the bus; I did not want to be responsible for anyone else getting hurt. Plus, driving came with its own set of responsibilities that I just did not want to, could not, face.

My mother sat beside me on the bench, and though I could feel the cool assessment of her gaze, I did not turn. We sat in silence till the bus came.

If I could have mustered it, I guess I would have been appalled at the state of my room when we walked in. I have never been particularly house-proud, but this was a whole new level of mess. My clothes were everywhere, in heaps of no discernable order. Some more were piled on the unmade bed.

I had striped it that morning, I think. Books and food remnants peeked from their locations in various corners. Other unidentifiable pieces of junk completed the picture.

I did not care. All I wanted was to crawl on the mountain of rubbish that was my bed, and sleep.

My mother, however, took one look at the room, and pointed to me. 'Pack a bag. You're coming with me.'

Coming with… Where?

I didn't ask the questions. It made no difference to me. I pulled out a small carry on and start stuffing it with some of the pile, just as my mother stepped out of the room. I hear her talking with the girls, lapping up their astonishment and compliments. The cliché compliment is true in this case, my mother could pass for an older sister. Soon, the conversation moved on to let's-bond-over-worrying-about-Rekiya, and I tune them out. I was getting really good at that. Clearing my head, blanking my mind. Hearing, seeing, feeling nothing.

It fit rather well with remembering nothing.

I ended up spending a week in my mother's hotel, where I insisted only on having my own room. I came out of said room once. For my mother, on the other hand, it was a busy week. She arranged with the school for me to take the rest of semester off, she packed up my room and put my things in storage before we flew back to Abuja.

The next semester, I moved into a single-occupant dorm room. A quiet and unassuming Nigerian girl in baggy, ill-fitting clothes. Sans headscarf.

Zaynunah

I was going to take the opportunity of his absence to clean my father's home office when I heard her. It was early morning, hours yet before Ruqqayyah would normally join me downstairs for breakfast, and I had made it a point not to intrude upon her until she did.

But standing in the corridor between the two rooms, I could not ignore this. The sound was primal; a cross between sobs and groans, it was pain in auditory form.

Ya Rabb, I prayed. Undecided. *Please help her. Whatever she's been through, is obviously still going through, please heal her.*

I peek into the room, and my fears are confirmed. This is not physical pain, perhaps it would have been better if it was.

She sat huddled in Mummy's prayer corner, dressed in her old *abaya*. Her knees drawn up, and her arms wrapped tightly about it, making her appear even smaller than she was. Small and defenseless. And very hurt. Her gaze was glazed, blank and staring at nothing. Or at something I could not see. Her body rocked in a front-and-back motion. And from time to time, the sound emitted from her slightly parted lips. Low and frightening, I could almost imagine that it arose, not from her lips, but from the depths of her soul. It sounded… gutted.

In the scant time it took me to catalogue these details, I was crossing the room to her. She did not see me, did not hear me; did not feel me. Even as I sat with her and put my arms around her, shedding tears for her that she probably never did for herself. I knew she had been hurt; she had hinted as much last night. What I hadn't known was that she was *still* hurt. In fact, I – with my staid life, where nothing happens – could never begin to imagine the level of pain she must be feeling.

So, I did what I do every time I was in over my head. I prayed.

> *Ya Allaah, we are Your slaves, daughters of your slaves....*
> *Your control over us is Absolute,*
> *Your judgement upon us is assured,*
> *and Your Decree for us is Just.*
> *I ask You by every Name you have called Yourself,*
> *Or revealed in Your Book,*
> *Or taught to anyone of Your creation,*
> *or kept with Yourself from the knowledge of the unseen,*
> *That You make the Qur'an the spring for our hearts,*
> *and the light for our chests,*
> *the banishment for our sadness,*
> *And the relief for our distress.*

The dua was recommended by the Prophet – Peace Be Upon Him - for the believer in distress, anxiety, and or despair. It was my mother's favorite dua, and I always thought that it was apt – seeing as she was a haafidhah of the Qur'an. I, on the other hand, was too lazy – either to complete my hifdh, or to use the long dua consistently. But crouching beside the vibrating shell of my friend, the words tumble from my lips, bursting from somewhere I never knew had retained it until this moment.

I repeat the Arabic words over and over, asking for solace for her and forgiveness for myself. Because being a witness to her pain make me realize how easy I've had it, and how much I take for granted. The love, security, faith and family I had been given, all through no effort of mine; buffering me from the harsh reality that is life.

I do not know how long we were there, but she eventually quieted down, the rocking stopped, and her eyes focused. She sagged against me, limp.

'Z, I'm so tired.'

In that moment, she was the frailest I ever saw her. And this was a girl who had learnt to mask her vulnerability from a very young age. I had only ever seen her significantly discomfited one other time – when her father paid that visit, during a mid-term break from Noorah. Compared to this…

What am I thinking? Nothing compares to this.

I help her up into Mummy's bed, taking a moment to pull the Abaya off her. She dropped into an exhausted sleep almost as soon as her head touched the pillow. I sit at the foot of the bed, still trying to wrap my mind around what just transpired. The level of emotions I just witnessed, all raw and so real, was such that I wasn't even sure I wanted to know what brought it on.

I think back again to Mummy's assertion that Ruqqayyah was hurt. Well, that was obvious now. But truth is, my mundane life did not give me a frame of reference for something like this. In my life, things had pretty much always gone the way I expected them to – even the challenges and disappointments. The most severe blow I've had to deal with has been Mummy's death, and even in that there's solace in knowing that she was, insha Allaah, in Allaah's Mercy. I couldn't fathom what could possibly cause a person, Ruqqayyah in particular, this much pain.

I look around the room, dazedly noting that we had almost finished our task of clearing it up. We could probably finish it up in one more sitting. Already, the room looked decidedly empty, driving home the fact that I'd lost my mum. And that in a few days, once we were done with this task, Ruqqayyah would be gone. Last night, I thought we'd stay in touch after she leaves this time. Now I'm not so sure. Whatever she's battling, she hadn't wanted me there then and chances are, she wouldn't want me this time either.

I got up.

I had already said my voluntary prayer after sunrise today. For me, it was two rakaa' and I struggled to keep it regular, even amidst the frenzy that was my life. But I needed to pray, again. For Ruqqayyah, mostly – that she finds peace and freedom from whatever is holding her hostage. But also, for myself; in gratitude, asking forgiveness, seeking wisdom and courage…

When Ruqqayyah finally came down, it was past noon. I had checked on her earlier, and she'd still been asleep. Deciding not to wake her, I went through the downstairs rooms, cataloguing anything of Mummy's that I came across. When I heard her go into the kitchen, I sighed. I still wasn't sure how to – or even, if I should – address what happened this morning. Not only would she hate that I had witnessed her in such a vulnerable state, I really did not want to test the fragile strains of whatever new relationship we'd just started building. Also, I feel so out of my depths in the face of such an emotional display, from Ruqqayyah of all people.

'Hey, salaam alayki. Did you sleep well?' I tried to keep my voice level, meeting her gaze openly. I made a snap judgement call. I would not bring it up, unless she gave an indication that she wanted to talk about it. Then I would buck up and be there for her.

She responded to my greetings, and turned back to the fridge she had been busy raiding before I came in.

'I did not make breakfast–'

'It's fine,' she interrupts. 'This will do until lunch. You are planning to make lunch, aren't you?'

I look into her teasing eyes. She's giving off an awfully light vibe for someone who had an emotional breakdown, or whatever it was, this morning. But that had always been her way; hiding behind an enigmatic façade. I momentarily contemplate calling her out on it, then remember what she said yesterday, and what she looked like a few hours ago.

I let it go.

Her sigh reaches me just as I turn away to begin preparation of lunch. 'Z, remember when I said I did not want to talk about what happened to me?'

I gave a non-committal 'hmm-mm'.

'I still don't want to talk about it.' There was a short pause. 'But I'm glad we're friends again.'

I hear the slight raise at the end. I know the mindset that made the statement a question. I smile. 'Me, too.'

The ensuing silence is comfortable. My smile widens. I have missed this, missed her. It feels good to be able to admit that.

'That du'a you were reciting this morning-' I hear Ruqqayyah say.

'I'll show you,' I vowed.

Once lunch was ready, Ruqqayyah dug into it with a gusto while I teased her mercilessly. Afterwards, we headed back up into Mummy's room. As I had envisaged, we were done a few hours later. I shed a few surreptitious tears as we labelled the boxes we had packed. The men would haul the ones marked for charity away tomorrow, when they come over. The rest was for Daddy and the inheritance imam to decide.

Ruqqayyah, looking equally lost, clutched the bag containing all of Mummy's knitting arsenal and our old Noorah graduating yearbook.

'Come on,' I say, wiping the moisture off my face and pulling her along. 'Let's go look through that book and laugh at our teenage selves.'

We've had so much emotional drama in the space of a few days, I figured we needed a break. And standing in the barrenness of Mummy's room would just tip us off again.

My ploy worked and soon, we were in my room, laughing over horrible high school pictures.

'Oh God! These things could be used for blackmail.' I eyed the pictures in mock horror.

Ruqqayyah snickered. 'Do you keep in touch with anyone from Noorah?'

'No. Not really. I was invited to the ten-year reunion, but I did not go.'

I don't mention that without her, I did not feel like I belonged.

'Hmmn.' She scoffed. 'High school reunions! I wonder which genius came up with that idea?'

'*Abi o!*' I chuckle. 'Just an excuse to play the game of my-life-is-better-than-yours.'

'Ewww,' she shuddered theatrically. 'All the smug looks and snide comments as the women show off their catch of a husband and brandish the kids' pictures.'

'What are you talking about?!' I could not believe where her mind went. 'You are the Chief Something Very Important of an international finance house! They'd all be green with envy.'

She smiled wryly. 'Chief Financial Officer, West Africa, thank you very much.' Then she sighed. 'But you know all that means very little in our society without a husband and a couple of kids.'

'Does that bother you?'

'No. Yes. Maybe… I don't know. I mean, not the society part – I never really belonged anywhere, anyway. And I guess I can always return to the US, someday.' She shrugs then, as though corralling her thoughts, continues. 'It just… it bothers me for me. I always assumed I'd get married. And I always wanted kids, you know, a family of my own. And now, I'm almost thirty-three with no possibility for that in sight and must face the reality that it may never be.'

I do not say anything. I, more than anyone, understood her need for a family. I also get her unstated fear that it might be too late. For while women were getting married later in many society, the African and Muslim culture was still not yet caught up on that. It begs the question, then –

'Why did you not get married up till now?' I ask, knowing that I could, and that she'd answer – something I wouldn't have done or known before yesterday.

'I don't know. Life.' She shrugs.

'Er… Use words.' I prod. 'Did you not meet anyone?'

'I had two possibilities but… It never came about, I guess.'

'Qadar,' I say, nodding. 'It was not destined for you.' Then I smiled. 'Tell me about them.'

She giggled and told me about Zeke – the Black-American who'd accepted islaam just before she left New York. She did not sound particularly heart-broken about it, and I, for one, -

'I'm glad you did not marry him. Because then you might never have come back!'

She burst into laughter. Pure, unrestrained twinkles of sounds that I have not heard in years, that I'm sure she hasn't heard in years. Even as a girl, it was a sound she seldom released. I close my eyes and let it wash over me, the twinkles of her mirth tickling joy – hitherto buried under the grief of my mum's death – once more to the surface.

'Well, I'm glad I could oblige you then.' Ruqqayyah stated, tongue-in-cheek.

I open one eye and waited.

'What?' she asks.

'You said two possibilities.'

She smiles again, this time sadly. 'Oh, that was a long time ago. I met him in my final year as an undergrad. Well, not exactly but… Anyway, I thought we had an understanding when he left to return to Nigeria, but I never heard from him again.'

'Really? What happened? Did you try to contact him?'

'No,' she grimaced. 'I didn't know him that well. We'd only been… it had only been a semester. I mean, yes, I sent an email, but he never replied. For all I know, he was just another 419 *Naija* guy, posing as the oldest son of the *Baba Adinni* of Ikorodu.'

There was a tale there. But I could tell she did not want to discuss it. I was fine with that. Something nagged me about the story, though, and not just the way she tried to downplay what had obviously been a big deal for her. But I couldn't place my finger on what it was, exactly, so I let it drop.

Like she said, it was a long time ago.

CHAPTER TEN

Rekiya

Friday afternoon, I woke to the sound of male voices. Plural. It was so alien; I was momentarily disoriented.

Where...? Oh, I am at the Sanusis'.

Mummy is dead, Z and I had been packing up her life over the past few days – amidst drama of our own – and now the family had obviously gathered to continue the family tradition of Friday lunch.

As far back as I knew them, every member of the family tried to be in Ibadan, and at Mummy's table for a late lunch, on Fridays after the *jumu'ah* prayers. These visits often extend until dinner. It was during the Friday lunches that I had any measure of interaction with the men of this family; allowing me to catalogue their personality. Prof. was quiet and reserved, Musa was the broody one and 'Isa was jovial – the one who took time to tease Z and I, taking pains to treat me just as he did his sister.

I waver on whether to join them. Years have passed and sitting down to a meal with three consciously non-mahram males was bound to be uncomfortable. Frankly, I was having problems deciding where to draw the line here. Did honoring Mummy's bequest and staying to help pack her things mean an implicit invitation to the grieving family's tradition of a meal?

Eventually, my stomach drove me downstairs. Dressed in another of Mummy's relics, I dropped a scarf over my head in a manner that provoked a myriad of unwanted memories and follow the scent of food.

I heard feminine chatter before turning into the kitchen doorway, and the women I saw were easily identified based on the male voices that had drifted to me earlier. Jummai, obviously Hausa, was resplendent in her colorful Adire bubu and maroon half-hijab. By contrast, the other woman – I'm guessing Musa's wife – was in black; full-length, one-piece hijab, flipped back niqab and gloves still clutched in one hand.

'As-Salaam alaykum', I mumble, wondering if they thought me as much a fraud as I saw myself.

Jummai, already walking towards me as the customary response rang out, smiled. 'You must be Rekiya. I'm almost surprised to see you all grown up. I think you must be stuck in my husband's mind as your teenage self. He's been regaling us with tales of your antics – yours and Umm 'Abdul-Ghaffar's as girls – since he heard you were here.'

I smile at the affectation. She had no qualms addressing me so familiarly on a first meeting, but no self-respecting Yoruba wife would refer to her sister-in-law by name. It was quaint in this obviously Hausa woman; with her lilting-accented English, bright hijab, and elaborately henna-painted hands.

I feel my smile getting wider, and more genuine as the minutes pass. I find that I like Brother 'Isa's wife. She shamelessly monopolizes me after an off-hand introduction to "Umm Abd-Rahman. Mutmainah. Brother Musa's wife." Her staccato delivery makes the other woman sound like three different women, and I ponder wistfully which -if any - of the three identities she considers her true self. The woman in question smiles and makes polite noises, but no obvious friendly overture. She reminds me of me; of who I could have been; a memory from an alternate reality, poignant despite never having happened.

Jummai carried the conversation on her own steam. She calls to mind a lovely spring morning in a flower garden, with butterflies. Pretty to gaze at, flitting about from one topic to the next, nothing deep or heavy, bestowing joy simply by being.

We eat in the dining room, the thick curtains screening us from the men in the living room. The kids - all of their kids - had been left at 'Isa and Jummai's. They apparently had a host of domestic workers they trusted with the children, and this was the first family meal since Mummy died. While not exactly subdued, there were moments when someone mentioned her and everyone…remembered.

Conversation was quiet, often limited to one side of the curtain. Interestingly, Jummai would sometimes chip in into Isa's tale, and vice versa, but the rest of us kept things pretty low-key.

I mostly listened, feeling a sense of detachment from it all. It seemed after all that has happened within the course of one short week, I was approaching my limit. I felt the familiar nothingness envelope me, a blankness that separated me from my emotions and that of the people around me. I watched myself exist on the fringe of this family, an outsider.

I knew it was time to leave. All the events, all the emotions, all that rousing of ghosts from the past – it was getting to be more than I could, or wanted to, deal with.

'Brother 'Isa, do you remember that *Baba Addinni* of Ikorodu from a few years back?' I hear Zu call out, apropos of nothing.

'Isa's rueful affirmative response of 'Ah, yes. Really sad business,' coincided with his wife's 'who?! What happened?'

'Sad business,' 'Isa repeats. 'Apparently someone tipped off armed robbers that he had a son arriving from the US that day. It was said that when the son denied his having any substantial amount of dollars, they were enraged. The son was shot, and they beat the father so much he died a few days later.'

I watch Zaynunah watch me, as I sat immobile and impassive through the outpouring of indignation and sorrow at the senselessness of it all. There were muttered prayers for the soul of the deceased, desultory comments on the appalling state of security in the country. Then, as though I could possibly have missed the significance of her obvious ploy, she speaks into one of the lulls, those types of silence that follow a people's collective appreciation of man's flimsy mortality.

'It was what… Ten years ago, *abi*? What was his name again *na o*, the Baba Adinni?'

'Owo-something. I don't remember. Yes, almost ten years now. Wait, I remember! It was…'

I don't hear the rest of the conversation. The rest was superfluous anyway. This was what Zaynunah wanted me to hear. The story of what happened to him. Babatunde Owoeye. I never called him that, resenting the name he shared with my father's heir. I secretly preferred the implied intimacy of his official, seldom-used, Arabic first name. 'Abdullaah.

I thought he left me, that he had tricked me. That his promises were bogus, empty utterances he had no intentions of living up to. That reality had prevailed, and my issues had proved too much to confront. Or that his family had baulked, had not wanted an illegitimate taint in their line – even an acknowledged one that came with wealthy antecedents. That…

I had thought so many things, in those early days when I allowed myself to think of him. But I never imagined he had come to this. Killed by misinformed bandits on a quest for foreign currency he did not have. On the very day he returned to the family he had agonized over. He used to say he felt that they needed him back home, and it would have been selfish if he chose to stay behind in the US.

I feel Z snag my wrist before I realize I am on my feet. I see the concern in her face. 'You okay?'

I pause. Shake my head. The quiet 'no' was liberating, admitting when I felt low was not a thing I was accustomed to doing.

She let me go.

I do not make it up the stairs. I sit on the middle landing and allow myself – for the second time in as many hours – travel down memory lane. It is easier this time, not as gut-wrenching. Maybe time does heal hurts. Or my recollections are more honest than my emotions. I examine our shared past with a dispassionate mien that belly this old heartache…

That first meeting, in crowded confines of my favorite coffee shop at the edge of the courtyard. His insistence that we had met before, at the MSA mixer two semesters ago. My inability to remember, compounded by the wariness of all human males. The series of 'accidental' meetings that follow. Me, oblivious but gradually, cautiously responsive to his continued presence. He, the undemanding and devious architect of said accidents. In the time it would take me to appreciate this, we had become friends.

Platonic, meet-in-public-and-daytime-only friends who told each other… everything on his part, nothing on mine. We agreed that I was just not a person who shared. Later, when it all seemed to crumble around me, after he, too, abandoned me, I would question everything.

Why he engineered our initial contacts, the truthfulness behind his dealings with me, the strength of my attachment to him - strongly but reluctantly felt and yet gingerly held apart - and how easily we both moved on from each other. I would mentally deride the evolution of the relationship, seamless and unnoticed, until he was talking about our future as a single entity, and the passivity of my silent acquiescence, barely noticing as someone else took the oars and was fully prepared to allow him paddle the boat of my life.

We spent first semester of my final year in this unspoken, but acknowledged, pseudo-relationship. Then he left for Nigeria – his program was done, and he could not stay on in the US; his family needed him, he said. His last words to me, the day before he left, haunted me a for a long time.

'Something happened to you in the months between our two 'first' meetings. You are so different; you could be someone else entirely. It's like a light went out – something bright, and energy-giving inside you was smothered. Banked. Or covered. Find your light again, Rekiya. You were made to shine.'

Those words stayed with me even when I never heard another from him. They, he, and the tantalizing possibility of a future – of wholeness – that our warped relationship represented were what pushed me through the last leg of college. Through the honors graduation, and a highly coveted fellowship at a major finance company in New York. Through postgrad, and the lucrative job waiting for me in the same company. They resonated within me as I went through the first stages of self-reclamation; changing my name, moving to New York, researching therapists. They were all I had left of him. And even when I thought horrible things about him – or in the years since I refused to think about him – I never let go of those words.

You were made to shine.

I could hear him in my head, as Z's family broke off their first family meal since burying their matriarch. They echoed, distant but persistent peals, even as I hugged Jummai and promised to keep in touch. They comforted me as Z and I, arms intertwined, bade her family goodbye. As we climbed up the stairs – heading, as we had done innumerable times in the past, for her childhood bedroom.

I am suddenly very clear on what I need to do.

It is time.

II

CHAPTER ELEVEN

Rekiya

Abuja is, indisputably, the younger sister and *madame* of Nigerian cities. Blooming late, not necessarily from an ugly duckling status, into a mature beauty further enhanced by a marriage of almost limitless space and a wealth her sister cities could never hope to aspire to, her tree-lined roads, unusually well planned for this country, were framed by the distant majestic mountains, and overlooked arid grounds with its occasional litter of stripped shrubs.

It boasts vast open spaces that held a tinge of dust in its smell, clinging red earth in swatches untouched by man, and stunning edifices in places conquered by our unflagging human greed for more. Her horizon was foggy and though uncluttered by the electric poles and wires dotting her sister cities, had not escape the scourge of giant billboards touting various alcoholic beverages.

The energy of the city is unmistakable; young and dynamic, less frenetic than the hustle of Lagos, unburdened by the history of Ibadan or Benin, Abuja is a place where the young could *make it*. It reminds one daily of this; with its compelling yet slightly garish beauty and an ostentatious display of wealth that yet fails to mask a slightly scandalous past. Abuja would welcome you with coy embrace or jar you with unapologetic brashness but could never quite pull off innocence.

For a city in whose bosom the affairs of the city lie, Abuja must surely be yet another metaphor for the numerous ills besieging the country. And though it was the city of my earliest memories and truncated childhood, I have never called her home, too young to appreciate or value what that word meant until I had none. As a child from a somewhat stable home, it is easy to take for granted that someone will always care for you, welcome you, love you. As a lesson, one only learns it the hard way.

After almost two years of my return, Abuja and I tolerate each other.

I have a small two-bedroom and bath- plus study - apartment in one of the newer serviced estates that dot the city. At a price that would secure palatial mansions in almost any other part of the continent, I consider it an investment. The conveniences – running water and uninterrupted electricity are still, sadly, marketable luxuries, even in this capital city of the nation - round-the-clock security detail, as well as its proximity to the Central Business District were the deciding factors when I opted to buy it. All units were eerily similar, and they displayed about as much character as I must have shown to people I have met in recent years – sleek, modern, almost soulless. Not that it mattered to me, it was just a place to keep my things and crash when I could not avoid sleep. Between the long hours and constant travel my job entailed, I was not in the apartment, or even Abuja, much. It was just another place I was based out of, and no one would notice when I leave.

Not even my mother.

I drive towards her house now, absent-mindedly observing the city she had adopted as hers from her young adult years and acknowledge to myself that I'm scared. Not of any physical danger in this early morning rush when the more diligent workers, or those living at an untenable distance from their place of work, were already heading out. But of unearthing unfriendly ghosts, long ignored into oblivion.

I have been up for hours, a habit borne of the union of my equal parts inability to, and fear of, sleep – and the dreams it may herald. It was still that time of the month where I substituted exercise for *tahajjud*, so I had spent an hour on my treadmill before the wind carried the *adhaan* to me from some far-flung mosque.

It wasn't something that happened often – the estate I lived in was isolated from its environment by design, populated mostly by expatriates, and whatever mosque that sound came from was probably enjoying the rare electric power that allowed the use of a microphone in this instance. After decades in the US, where I avoided any contact with everything that could remind me of a faith I had given up, this had been a major concern for me, contemplating a move to northern Nigeria. But it turned out alarmingly easy to maintain my status quo. Between work, travelling and the apartment I chose, I might have never left New York for how little I encountered any symbols of islaam.

Today though, even the *iqaamah* hadn't cause the niggling anxiety I had come to expect. Maybe the little things I had been unable to avoid in Abuja had de-sensitized me gradually. Or being in Ibadan with Zu and her family had driven home how little meaning I currently find in my life. Could it be that this was the response to that supplication I had got off her? I have recited so much over the past few days, that I've almost committed the words to memory. Perhaps it was just the passage of time, allowing the long-dormant seed I had presumed dead to sprout again so suddenly. Feeble, but still alive.

I listened to the recitations of the imam leading those Muslims devout enough to attend the congregation at the crack of dawn in prayer, feeling the stirring of something I had consciously denied for almost a decade – despite the name, the early morning ritual and therapeutic prayer exercises, the cultural identity I clutched at like a security blanket to get out of situations I was uncomfortable with. Like dating. And drinking.

Those verses - and it was one of the chapters I had memorized at Noorah – felt like they were calling me out, prodding me to admit; to quit hiding, to declare, to live the truth I could no longer escape. Repeated over and over in the course of that one chapter, I could no longer silence my soul.

Which of the favours of your Lord will you deny?

And as the imam finally proclaimed his Lord as Greatest, signaling the end of his recital, I felt Muslim. Probably for the first time in my life, I believed in this Deen – not from parental allegiance, institutional regulation, environmental conformity or cultural affiliation.

I, finally, found my faith. Or, rather, it was bestowed on me.

I acknowledged, unreservedly, that Allaah is my Lord, and in control of all that exists.

I knew what I had to do – all those Tauhid lessons at Noorah stood me in good stead, flashing through my mind as I whispered the Shahada to the stillness of my living room. A simple declaration of faith that re-affirmed to myself and my Lord the truth that I could, quite inexplicably, feel pulsating through my being.

I testify that there is no one worthy of worship than Allaah, alone and without partner, and that Muhammad is His slave and Final messenger.

Almost two hours have passed since my solitary, hopefully life-altering moment, and I am trying hard to hold on to the euphoria that had given me the final impetus to set out on this particular quest. My resolve when I left Ibadan had been to face my past. To own it, so I could – finally – begin to move beyond it. Stoically ignoring the voice that reminded me that was what my former therapist had said all along, I had ridden on a wave of determination to claim my life back.

Well, there's very little of that left now, I acknowledge wryly to myself as I drove into the compound of my mother's house. My feet were decidedly colder than they did when I got on the plane yesterday.

My mother and her family live in an older, somewhat genteel neighborhood. It is populated mainly by government officials who were too honest, or lacked the opportunity, to supplement their income with any of the numerous dubious means of corruption that abound in the federal civil service. When they first got married, the modest three-bedroom bungalow had been several steps down in the life from what my mother had shared with my father. But it had squarely beat being homeless, squatting with friends, or eking out a living on whatever amount of money my provided. Now, decades later, it was just tired.

I walked through the grounds that had never felt welcoming, barely noticing the signs age had wrought, grateful that my stepfather's car was gone from its place of prominence, knowing exactly where to find what, or whom, I sought.

My mother is a creature of habit. She sat, as expected, at the dining table, sipping her tea, and mentally gearing for her day. She had cut out breakfast from her routine sometime during the years I was away, and the tea was no longer sweetened with the single cube of sugar. But this – the early morning reconnaissance at the breakfast table - was a ritual my mother adhered to in all the years I had known her.

She did not notice me as I stopped in the doorway, once again marveling, as always, that this woman had given me life. My mother's beauty is striking. She is fair and willowy, despite her objective lack of height, whereas I am just plain short, curvy and chocolate-y. Not that I am hideous or anything, but my mother's beauty is often the biggest elephant in the room. She was blessed with that rare combination of symmetrical and striking features that have long been associated with beauty. It is a deity she nurtured, pampered, fed, and deferred to. From what she ate, wore, did or did not do, my mother was always cognizant of the fact that she was a beautiful woman.

It was not that she was vain, per se. In fact, she was unfailing gracious and well-mannered. To the point of insincerity, I often thought when I was younger. With the hindsight of age, I have come to see my mother's beauty as less of a weapon, but more of a shield – hiding the woman she could be from everyone around her, maybe even from herself.

Uncomfortable with the similarities that thought provoked, I step forward. 'Good morning, Ma.'

She looks me over, the teacup's halted trajectory the only indication of her surprise. Then she sets it down carefully. 'You look different.'

Unsure if she meant the abaya that I had donned on my way here, out of expediency than anything else - my work out clothes were still under it. Or if some of the upheavals of the past week and half showed on my face.

I shrug. 'I'd like to talk to you.'

She studies my face again before getting up and, without a word, leads the way into her room.

In my early childhood home, my parents shared a room. That room was as much the center of our family life as the living room was the center of their social life. I would spend hours there; playing with my father when he was around and not inundated with guests and visitors, or watching my mother go through the elaborate preparations that preceded the flawless beauty she presented to the world. As a young girl, I was convinced my mother must be the most beautiful woman in the world. And I spent hours basking in the fringes of that beatific aura. In hindsight, I'm filled with sorrow for that little girl now, so starved – even then - of maternal affection that she was content to sit and gaze in silence until perfection was achieved. And when my mother would turn to me and ask how she looked, that little girl would unfailingly reassure her that she was the 'most beautiful Mummy in the whole world!'

Like most aspects of our life, even that bit of mother-daughter interaction was a victim of my father's abandonment. For the first few months after it became obvious that he was not coming back, my mother was too lost in her own private misery to care about beauty. Or me. By the time she finally roused herself, re-joining the social circle with a vengeance that meant I had to continue to fend for myself, I had outgrown my awe of her beauty.

Upon their marriage, she and her husband maintained separate rooms, and I always thought, even as a teenaged girl, that this was my mother's way of keeping a part of herself apart; an insurance against the possibility of being abandoned again. This room was her sanctuary. It was always the least decorated room in the house, except the one I shared with the maid/nanny, back in the day. It is also the only room where my mother exists without her beauty in full armor and no one, not even her husband, ventured inside its sanctum without express invitation.

We assume familiar battle positions from the years of similar interactions past. She sits primly in front of the mirror, while I stand just inside the doorway.

'Did you call your brother?' she begins, but I was not here to discuss Tunde Gbadamosi – who is *not* my brother.

'How could you?!'

My voice is raw and unfamiliar, the weight of emotions it reveals catches even me unawares, but I don't back down. I hold my mother's gaze and let the decade worth of anguish, confusion, powerlessness and unacknowledged anger crash through my soul's window.

She does not pretend ignorance. 'I had to', she says.

I say nothing. This day has been too long coming, and my feelings were too close to the surface.

'You weren't in any frame of mind to make such an important decision, and time was running out.'

I stare at her, aghast. My mother has always been unflappable, more so after picking up her life in the wake of my father's desertion but this cool recitation of her non-answer was jarring. Every word scraped on the exposed nerve endings of my uncharacteristic vulnerability and wrenched what semblance of control from me.

'It wasn't your decision to make! It was my call. My body. My baby!' After screeching through the first sentences, my voice lost both volume and power, wobbling pitifully on the last two phrases.

'A mother reserves the right to act in her child's best interests,' she informs me serenely. 'You'll understand when you have your own children.'

'How?!' The single word was a hiss, a rattling of the cages that held years' worth of emotional baggage as it all seems to be crashing over me in an unending torpedo. 'How am I supposed to get these kids that would enlighten me, and bestow on me, such a pervasive maternal right?'

At this, my mother's calm slipped, her face registering concern. 'What do you mean 'how'? The doctors assured me you could have a normal reproductive life.'

'Normal?' The word was so absurd. I chuckle mirthlessly. 'Nothing about this is normal. Something terrible happened to me, Mother. But before I could process it, you were there – arranging procedures and transcontinental flights, all in a shrouded silence that meant I never moved on from the horror of it all.' I sigh, suddenly weary of this confrontation I'd initiated yet refusing to lower my gaze as I continued. 'How can I have kids when I cannot help but fear the thought of a man's touch? And how normal am I that I cannot let anyone in long enough to build any kind of relationship with?'

The silence drags a while as we regard each other. Her face is less serene that it had been, but I was not familiar with my mother's facial display of emotions enough to know what they signified. I watch in disinterested fascination as they chased themselves across her usually impassive face.

'I know what happened to you…' she started, shaking her head swiftly as I made to protest that she couldn't know. *I* hadn't known for sure until she dragged me to that clinic, and I never told anyone, for years, until it came out during therapy.

'I knew.' Her face was once again a mask. 'I guessed it from the look on your face the moment I saw you. The pregnancy only validated what I already knew. And Rekiya, no child deserves to be a reminder of their mother's darkest memories. Nor did you deserve an even more tangible memento to keep you reliving it. So, I dared. I will dare all over again if I have to. As for being normal, and of relationships, I believe they are within your reach – once you let yourself move past what happened. And I know you can do that; it's been ten years after all. Leave the past behind and build the life you want for yourself.'

'So easily!' I scoffed. 'Just leave it behind! You have no idea…'

'But I do.'

I'm momentarily stunned into silence. 'What?'

'I more than "have an idea." I know it's possible to leave it behind. To walk away from something that shook up your life so much you feel buried under the rubbles. To go on from that and build a new life for yourself. I'm not saying it's easy. But it's possible.'

I feel my ire rising again. 'How could you possibly…?!'

She interrupts me again. 'Because I did it.'

CHAPTER TWELVE

Rekiya

My mother was born Nkechi Joseph to an Ibo lower cadre soldier in the Nigerian Army and his wife, who spent the remaining years of her life following him from one low-cost barracks to another across the nation. An only child, my mother has recollections of her mother being pregnant a number of times – but no siblings were ever brought home. Rather, her mother went off to the hospital, then returned a few days later, noticeably smaller in size. As such occasions – and the temporary reprieve they provided against her husband's fists – got further and further apart, her mother got progressively weaker. Until the day she went in and didn't return.

Nkechi had been thirteen years old.

By then, the family had been somewhat stable in a barracks in Kaduna for a few years. Between his absences for work, and the disappearing for binge drinking spells while on leave, Nkechi managed to simultaneously raise herself through teenage-hood and avoid the worst of her father's ire. She had been seventeen, and a few months into her final year of secondary school when he finally got himself killed on an ill-fated mission in a neighboring country.

Grateful, she had packed up what meager possessions she could lay claim to and accepted her neighbor's offer to move next door. That was a scant day before the new family who had been allocated the flat moved in. The kind neighbor had been friendly with Mrs. Joseph during her last years and had tried to provide what little maternal influence she could in Nkechi's life since her mother's passing. But everyone had their trials, especially hapless women married to men who were paid to protect a country yet were the most malevolent threats to their own families. She had survival – hers and her children's – to contend with most of the time. In the year or so since her own husband had been gone, on the same mission that claimed Nkechi's father, she began a beer parlor business.

Scarcely more than a dinghy wooden shack, the beer parlor nevertheless did brisk business as one of the few places where alcohol was freely served in the Muslim majority state. After moving in with her, Nkechi worked at the parlor on most evenings. Her duties varied between serving drinks to men that grew increasingly raucous as they imbibed, washing used glass cups as needed, and helping with the inventory. Paid a nominal wage which she diligently saved; she had considered it her own contribution to the family that fostered her in her time of need. As no stranger to hard work, she had no problem with working several hours a day in the parlor, after a full day of schoolwork, then helping with the housework before settling down to study. It was a grueling routine, one she maintained for almost three years, as she went on to get a diploma at the local polytechnic located just a few buses' ride from the barracks.

Unlike most girls of her age and station, Nkechi was seriously focused on the goals she set for herself. Growing up the daughter of a functioning alcoholic and his battered wife meant she'd learnt early on the depravity that man was capable of. She was determined to make a better life for herself, knowing she had no one else to depend on. Her severe demeanor and refusal to get involved in a romantic relationships with any of the numerous men who sought her attention – at the beer parlor and through the entire barracks, even the boys at school – soon earned her several snide nicknames.

Nkechi paid no mind to what the men around her did, used as she was to the different forms of posturing they engaged in while trying to impress her. She had grown accustomed to, and often tuned out, the different men and the lengths to which they went to attract her notice. In the end, that obliviousness cost her a lot.

On that fateful night, nothing had seemed out of the ordinary as she went about her routine at the parlor. It was her turn to close the place and she, as usual, hadn't paid much mind to the patrons other than what was necessary for the business. As the night wore on, most of them drifted off to their respective homes – or wherever else caught their drunken fancy – until only three men remained, seemingly solitary drinkers seated at different tables. Nkechi expected that they, too, would leave soon. She'd begun the final wiping down of the table surfaces when one of them suddenly caught hold of her hands in a strong grip that belied his earlier display of drunkenness.

What happened next was a blur. Nkechi always remembered the scene from a detached outside point of view – the place where her soul must have retreated as they took turns unleashing the worst of their beings on her body. She remembered her initial shock and outrage, followed closely by fear when she realized what they meant to do. She saw herself initially fight them and scream, earning nothing but harsher measures and a sickly increased excitement from them, and then the passive detachment from a body that lay limp as those men embraced the vilest elements of their being, with impunity born from centuries of getting away with worse.

When – finally – they were done and gone, she had cleaned herself up as best as she could and dragged her body back to the flat. She never told anyone what happened to her, although she thought her neighbor-turned-benefactress must have known. Her physical state that night, the very long and thorough shower she took – scrubbing her skin until it was raw – and the woman's insistence that she drank a specially brewed herbal concoction every day until her next menses came were all signs that Nkechi did not connect until years after the fact. Plus, she was never again left alone to close the beer parlor after that.

It was a harsh life experience for Nkechi, who had grown up secure in the knowledge of her beauty. As a child, exclamations of admiration had poured forth from adults whenever they saw her. She was showered with token gifts, and endured countless cheek pulling. The former was in supplication for similar features in the bearer's future progeny. The latter, to avert the effects of the evil-eye.

'How fair is her skin!'

'What cherubic features!'

'Oh, and her hair! It's so full, and beautifully woven!'

Nkechi's mother, architect of the much-admired hairstyles, raised her to nurture this beauty. Years before an abusive marriage and reproductive losses turned her into a necessarily strong but invariably bitter woman, she expended time and effort on her daughter's looks. Countless hours of making her hair into flattering styles, after which she loved to declare to the bemused child, 'Nnam, you are surely the prettiest girl born in Iboland!'

Yet she was quick to add that, 'pretty is as pretty does' so Nkechi was brought up to cultivate a character that matched her beauty. In time, she grew up into a kind, well-behaved, and soft-spoken beauty.

Indeed, this was easy for her, for all she knew in her early life was the goodwill of all she encountered.

It would be years later, so insidiously that she couldn't pinpoint exactly when, that she came to perceive this beauty as a weapon. She had watched her mother suffer through her husband's cruelty and disregard, even as the woman slowly killed herself trying to bear him his desired offspring. The oh-so-important male child. Her mother's life had been Nkechi's first life lesson; the place of the females in society.

Stripped of maternal protection after her mother's death, she quickly recognized how precarious even her own place in her father's life was. He was irritable and easily provoked when sober, but content enough to leave her in benign neglect when he'd had his drink. She learnt to read his moods and tiptoe around them long before he started making conscious efforts to restrain his hands from her.

Initially grateful not to be hit as much, a different apprehension soon filled her with dread. The gleam in her father's eyes once her body began to blossom made her uneasy in his presence. Living in army barracks all her life had left her with little innocence and she had agonized over her fears of an even worse, and unspeakable, abuse from her father.

Then she realized what he was about.

Her father, insisting she dressed in somber and sedate outfits that gave off an untouched air, subtly paraded her before men with whom he wished to curry favor. Otherwise over-protective of her and obsessive about what she did, where she went and with whom, he began, on select occasions, to take her along while meeting – or invite to their homes – men who invariably had something he wanted.

She became even more scared of what would happen when his father's games eventually blew up in his face. It appeared glaring, even to her, that she – not he – would have to pay any price of the ultimate fall out. Nkechi had been equal parts trembling and paralyzed with fear during those encounters, grateful that nothing was ever expected of her than to sit and be pretty. Her father's shenanigans, against all odds, taught her another invaluable life lesson.

Beauty, especially vacuous beauty, inspires goodwill.

She would find the secret true for women, too. Females – even high school mean girls – were less unkind, if they found her just slightly pitiful. Combining brains with beauty threatened not only the men. So, Nkechi learned to curb displays of intelligence and worked even harder at good character. And once her father died, mercifully before any of the men forcibly took what he had long taunted them with, she had purposely hidden in plain sight. Drab clothing and pious church program attendance – as well as her aloofness from the opposite sex – had been the shields she employed as deftly as her father had wielded her beauty.

And it had worked… for almost three years.

Refusing to give any power to what had been done to her, Nkechi redoubled on her goals. She moved to Abuja the day after she got her diploma. A classmate from the polytechnic had been going on about her plans to join her elder sister in the new city being built in the center of the country. Her sister, who had moved there the year before, had promised there were a lot of companies who were involved in the planning and development of the city but did not want to relocate their staff. That meant there was plenty of clerical work for hardworking young women who didn't mind the limited comfort available in a city still in its infancy. And, her friend had giggled suggestively, most of the men were either single and ambitious, or rich and lonely, separated as they currently were from their families by the demands of the job.

Nkechi had initially ignored the last part. The idea of better paying jobs combined with moving away somewhere new, where she could finally start her life on her own terms, had appealed greatly to her. She wanted to move away from the city that held painful memories of the loss of her mother, the infuriating ones of her father's abusive neglect and exploitation, and of her own violation.

The closer the final move got, though, she decided she was ready to re-invent herself. If men were going to covet her beauty, she was going to use it to her advantage. She had lived with the curse of it all her life, its effect tainting all her actions and relationships – and maybe even the worst things that happened to her. Now, though, she decided that it would be her weapon rather than her burden. Never would she be taken off guard again, she promised herself.

Disappointingly for her, her final height had stopped just short of five-feet and four-inches. But with a pragmatism with which she had belied her apparent intelligence, she learnt how to make it work for her. Stylish, if second-hand, clothes she invested in soon ensured that she presented the voluptuous figure valued as African beauty; but was careful never to appear overweight. Hair products and make up, new tricks that her friend's older sister had been all too willing to teach her, gave the illusion of a 'natural' look, and she expertly played up the best of her features.

She planned her envisaged life from the moment she arrived in the new, still-under-construction, city in dogged pursuit of one goal. A man. One who'd keep her in the lifestyle she wanted - the lifestyle a beauty, such as she had always been told she was, deserved. She chose a suitably non-demanding job as an office receptionist at one of the better-known firms, became active in one of the new generation Pentecostal churches, maintained her reputation for kindness, and held onto her virtue.

In short, she was the perfect 'wife material' for a Big Man.

And yes, Nkechi was smart. She knew she could get the life she wanted herself; it was the twentieth century after all, and women were supposedly breaking barriers and shattering glass ceilings – at least in places other than Nigeria, anyway. But she also knew, after years of observing life from behind a veneer of vacuous beauty and minimal intelligence, that it was infinitely easier – and faster - to have things given to her than to work for it.

The first time she met Sodiq Gbadamosi, she'd been unimpressed. Although already making a name for himself in business, he was nowhere near as rich as he would become only a couple of years later. It had been at a party she'd attended with some friends, their usual mode of entertainment during the weekends, of which she'd been growing increasingly weary after a few months. The men were either fat, old and married or young, ambitious and not ready to give up bachelorhood. Either way, they were only looking for a good time – unwilling to make any commitment beyond what monetary 'gifts' they would be generous with while their interests lasted.

Nkechi wasn't about to give out any milk for free.

So, when he'd bumped into her that night, spilling his Coca-Cola on her borrowed dress, she'd been much curter than she usually allowed herself to be. But he had been gracious and charming, and the rest of the night passed in a flurry of surprising realizations. For one, he was almost a decade younger than the usual Big Men she met, although his forty to her nineteen would still seem obscene to most people. For another thing, he didn't drink. He said he abstained for religious reasons, but Nkechi could not care less about the reason. Her disdain, understandable given her history, of men who imbibed was probably one of the most defining things about her. Finally, he'd seemed genuinely interested in her as a person; listening to her, asking her opinions, and considering her point of views even when they differed from his. After a lifetime of being seen as her body, and the last few months of men who thought that body was for sale, Nkechi found herself immensely drawn to him, to his interest in her.

What followed had been a whirlwind but cautious courtship. They were no other words to describe it – he took her out to respectable business functions and parties. And asked her, rather sweetly and nervously, to stop attending the raucous ones that served as 'meat market' for the men of his class. Nkechi had been easily persuaded. He had wooed her with sophisticated dates and expensive gifts, but had not pressed his physical attentions on her, touching her only in public and with a gallantry that made her fall even harder for him. She would later learn that Sadiq Gbadamosi was not known as a womanizer. And his name would not be associated with any other woman in Abuja in the years they were together.

Of course, he was married with kids, but his wife was not there, and no man was perfect after all, she had reasoned as she continued to see him.

When matters came to a head, as such matters eventually do, Nkechi's demurring had only been partly calculating. He'd wanted her to come to Lagos with him – he had to be there for a few months and could not bear the thought of not seeing her for so long. He would arrange a flat for her in a place called Surulere and would come see her as much as possible. It wouldn't be as much as he did here, of course, what with his business and family keeping him busy, but… would she come?

Nkechi had been tempted. She had come to care for this man more than she anticipated, more than her avaricious plans should have allowed, and he was offering her more than any man ever had. But if she did this, not only would she be totally dependent upon him, something her experience had taught her was a bad place to be, but she would be at his mercy, with no claims or rights upon his person or property. And, she had realized in dawning clarity, the physical nature of their relationship was bound to change under these new dynamics. In short, she would be giving the cow– not just the milk – away, maybe not for free, but for a whole lot less than she had envisaged.

She had refused him, in a tearful and incoherent speech, and he had left in a huff.

Six miserable weeks later though, he had come back to her. Apologetic and effusive, he had been full of understanding, and of plans for their future. He was sorry, should have been more circumspect of her youth and inexperience – he had also asked around about her, you see, and knew she didn't 'keep the company of men' like the other girls. He would give her time, would do things right, he never wanted to be without her again…

Nkechi saw no reason to tell him about her past. She considered herself as inexperienced about sex and intimacy as he had obviously assumed. As for her past, it made her sufficiently apprehensive enough to justify her demeanor on their wedding night. After a quiet affair of solemnization by the Muslim clerics, followed by a sedate luncheon attended by her envious friends and his sneering ones, her palpable tension over the consummation served to bolster his deduced conviction.

She never told him otherwise.

CHAPTER THIRTEEN

Zaynunah

'Landed in Abuja safely. Glad to have reconnected, even under such sad circumstances. Later.'

That single text had been Ruqqayyah's only contact with me in the three days since she left Ibadan. And she hadn't responded to my reply, not that I'd expected one. Not really. We're making up the rules as we go along, with this new friendship we've just begun to forge. And, of course, the women we are now appreciate the need for individual space, in a way that female teenage angst couldn't.

Except that yesterday, the contents of her father's will had been read. It had been done privately, by the lawyer to the family, yet somehow it made its way into the news. Now, everyone was asking who Rukayat Gbadamosi, the love child of Sodiq Gbadamosi's secret second marriage was. Or so the tabloids claimed. Leaving her a thirty percent of his company, among other assets, Ruqqayyah's father had not just made her one of the wealthiest women in the country, he had thrust her into a very glaring public spotlight.

As yet, no one had connected the heiress with the finance guru that had been making a quiet storm in the insular world of big money over the last year or so. She had told me how she'd changed her surname to her mother's maiden name - or the Arabic version of it - some years back. She had made her first name officially be Rekiya, too. rather than the Rukayat that no one other than her father ever used, anyway. Yet I wonder how long that would protect her.

It would be Noora all over again.

She would hate it; people gawping at her for a name, a father, she'd felt abandoned by. At least he acknowledged her in death as he hadn't done in life, but it all felt so…too little, too late. Too much and not enough all at once.

I wanted to reach out to her, to make sure she was okay. To let her know she had someone. To make sure she didn't disappear into the darkness like she sometimes did, had done in the past.

I wanted to be a better friend than I had been before. I wasn't convinced I had it in me, but I had to try.

Three days of trying to establish a new normal in a life where my mum is not alive, and in which I was reconnected with Rekiya, had made me introspective. As I went about my day, making a life for myself and my family without the woman who had held me up, I took a critical look at myself and my relationships.

I remember being ten and finding out, quite accidentally, that my mum had had a daughter before me. Suddenly I was questioning my certitude of my parents' love. That they had ever wanted me. I began to grapple with the feeling of being a replacement for the child they lost. Or worse, an afterthought, the side effect of failed contraception. I recoiled from the very affection I had hitherto taken for granted, throwing tantrums to express feelings and fears my young mind had been unable to deal with.

It would take the birth of 'Abdul-Malik, my last child; conceived in such tumultuous times in my marriage, but nevertheless loved as fiercely as all my children are, perhaps more poignantly for the knowledge that he would, insha Allaah, be the last; for me to truly understand what my mother had been trying to say to me all those years ago. About the complexities of a parent's love, no matter how unexpected or initially inconvenient a child's conception was. Those short weeks, when I had convinced myself of how insignificant I was to my parents, was the first emotional trauma I would suffer, due primarily to my own anxieties.

When I started mainstream secondary school, my obviously different religious inclinations fed my dormant anxieties that no one wanted me. My grade school years had been spent in the 'homeschool co-op' where my mum and a few other women of similar inclinations had traded subjects to homeschool their daughters and young sons. Each mother was the main backbone of her kids' education, but they all had 'special' classes they taught to all the children. Mummy had taken the Qur'an, Arabic and *Deeni* studies.

Going into secondary school, it had been jarring to find myself in a world where no one dressed, believed or behaved like mine and my friends' families. At that awkward spurt of puberty phase, I was a lot more conscious of the differences between myself and my school peers, so sure the gaps looming so ominously before my awareness were insurmountable, that I was too different – too much a 'stranger'. That no one would want to be my friend. And so, I never let anyone close enough to try.

In Noorah, it was the socio-economic gulf so apparent between myself and the average student, added to my being the only non-boarding one, that I allowed to barricade me from the other girls. By then, I had come to believe the story I told myself – that no one wanted me, that I was okay alone, anyway. So much that I did not even try, never put myself out there, and probably closed myself off to any overtures that might have been made.

All these years later, Rekiya was the only friend I'd ever allowed myself be vulnerable with. I wonder now if we'd have ever been friends if she hadn't caught me at such a pivotal moment. And if she hadn't, then reciprocated with such vulnerability of her own. In the past, I had brushed off such humbling musings, pretending shamefacedly not to know the answer. As though my recurring history of emotional avoidance over the years, or worse, how I allowed myself to be cut off from her when she started pulling away were not my most damning testimony.

I vow to do better this time, but a lifetime worth of anxieties is not miraculously vanquished by insight and good intentions.

'Just call her,' Yu had said yesterday when I picked up my phone for the thousandth time last night, then replaced it without dialing. 'You know you want to. It's the right thing to do. And with all this media circus, she's going to need you, now more than ever.'

'You don't know that!' I retorted. 'She might be busy. She didn't reply…'

'Zaynunah, I love you,' he interrupted, 'but you have to stop treating relationships like a credit transaction – afraid to give too much when the other party isn't making adequate repayment deposits. Sometimes people are busy. Or they have a lot going on. Or they really are just horrible at making deposits, like your brother Musa is horrible at keeping in touch so anyone who's going to have any form of relationship with him has to be the one checking in. But that doesn't mean he's a bad friend, or that they don't care. It definitely does not mean that you stop caring – or stop showing that you care. When someone you care about needs you, you show up. And when they disappear, you check in. That's what relationships mean.'

I hadn't known what to say. That my husband was emotionally aware enough to notice all this and call me up on it while articulating human connections in so profound, yet simple, terms made me overwhelmed.

With shame for my inadequacies, with gratitude that I got to share my life with him, with pride for how much he had grown from that man who couldn't express his emotions when we married, with determination to be purposeful about doing better…

Abruptly, I pull myself away from my reminiscences and switch off the radio – a habit of my mother's that I inexplicably found myself adopting after her death – and make the call.

It was the right decision.

Rekiya was reeling, ironically, not under the revelations of her father's will, but of a conversation with her mum from the day before. Aside from the confirmation that she was indeed legitimate - she's always assumed her parents were never married but the papers were right on that score - she said she'd learned a lot more of her mother's history. And that she was having to reevaluate many of the things she'd spent most of her life believing.

She had not left her apartment since the fated conversation and was still grappling with news of her father's will. I stayed with her while she methodologically planned what to do next. And got yet another surprise. She decided she was going to take a much-needed vacation from work, to allow the media frenzy blow over, and wait for her father's family to contact her. When they did, she would ask her lawyers to look over the terms of the will. She would not make any other decision until then.

After an hour, we ended the phone call. She promised to get back to me on her travel plans, and I reiterated that I was here for her, whatever she needed.

And just like that, I had my friend back.

Rekiya

Awe.

That was all I could identify from the emotional deluge bludgeoning me as I stood, gazing at the totally expected, but wholly unprepared for, sight before me. There were others, of course, but their streams and rivers – powerful and life affirming in their own essences – were trickles swallowed up by the roaring majestic ocean that was my awe. That, and my paradoxical disbelief. After weeks of preparation and hours of travel, I – still -somehow could not believe I was here, staring at arguably the most recognizable unelaborate building in the world.

The inevitable accompanying mass of swarming humanity, making me feel me wholly insignificant and part of something bigger than myself all at once, add a powerful aura to the already compelling vista. This diverse multitude of people, united in the singular pursuit of enduring economic and material sacrifice, just to visit this place, these building, this city.

Modestly draped in cloth of the blackest hues, its adorning calligraphy in a glittering gold shimmer shone blindingly bright, even across the expanse from where I stood. No doubt illumination was multiplied by the gazillion lights from the ginormous building standing in a *high def surround* model of architecture. In this holiest of spaces to an estimated one of six living persons, the cube was much larger than the pictures ever suggested.

In the few seconds it takes me to catalogue these physical details, halting abruptly as I had, and surrounded by the members of my small group of fellow travelers, it was all I could to keep standing. I have never really been one for religious fervor, yet I had an inexplicable urge to fall on my knees. On my face, in prostration. Of praise. Of thanks. For patience. In worship. In servitude…

Nothing prepared me for this; my first sighting of the House of Allaah.

I break out in goose bumps. They come over me as I recall the hosts of invincible ones occupying this space with us. Unburdened by our human concerns, these angels spend their time worshipping, praising, glorifying the Lord of us all.

I'm still in a daze as my group starts moving again, slowly joining the circumambulation around the edifice, inching our way towards the green fluorescent tubes beckoning from their hanging, near distant place. They would mark the beginning of our tawaf, the seven anti-clockwise rounds we would make around the *Ka'abah*, which marks the start of this *Umrah*, the lesser Muslim pilgrimage to the ancient city of Makkah. The green lights, I have read, signify the position of the black stone in the corner of the building.

I wonder absently if I would get to see, touch, or kiss this litmus of humanity's sins at any point during my seven-day trip.

No matter really, I tell myself as I raise my right hand in its general direction and mutter, *"Bismillaah. Allaahu Akbar."*

In the name of God. God is the Greatest.

*

I'm people-watching again.

Before this past week, I never would have guessed it was something I'd enjoy. Most of my life had not been conducive to that particular interest, hiding away as I invariably was – my sordid home life, my sense of abandonment, my shame, my fear, my emotions. Watching people would have been a tacit invitation to similar scrutiny.

I shudder in reactive horror.

This week, though, in this place, I had found a fascination with humans that I never knew. Or maybe it was in the evidence of our dependence on a relationship with God. Allaah. The Transcendent. Whatever you wanted to call it, I could not get enough of watching people praying, worshipping, thronging to and from the *Haram* to offer servitude to the One they consider their creator.

It is beautiful. And maybe it should be private. But with the life I've had, and of all the navel-gazing I've done in the past few weeks, this has been what has given me the most hope, a sense of strength, that I was heading in the right direction.

I watched the elderly Asian man, just one of so many yet completely alone in his realm, kneeling in unrelenting white of the Haram piazza, his lips moving silently. As tears ran freely down his withered cheeks, he was oblivious to the increased flow of traffic that signified the end of this last congregational prayer for the day. The people around him stood and moved in various directions, and I craned my neck this way and that, keeping him in my sight for as long as I could. I didn't wonder what he prayed for, what his life had been, if this communion with God was something he routinely did, or if was borne of the experience of being here. I just watched, and took comfort that he, too, turned his woes over to the One who was Able.

When I left Nigeria in the haze of my father's demise, I'd had no plans.

I'd headed to the US because it was as close to home – after Nigeria - as I could get. I stayed in my NYC apartment for a while, thankful it was free of a tenant just then. I toyed with showing up at my old office but could not bring myself to do it. I prayed. Took more trips down memory lane. Prayed some more. Then went to see my old therapist.

That was a mixed blessing.

I developed some empathy for what kind of a difficult client I must have been for Melissa Barns, LCP. I recognized for the first time, the sincerity beneath her slightly condescending approach, and she gave me copies of my file, a referral. Yes, I had conceded, I still need therapy. We parted on much better terms this time and, on her advice, I went to Houston, to visit my past.

I walked my old campus, and, for the first time, I let myself acknowledge all that had happened here. I mourned the girl that I was, the one that got so lost, the one no one even noticed was gone. I made sure to enter the MSA center and had coffee in the coffee shop where Abdullaah and I had most of our informal 'dates'. I wandered the dorms, my old faculty lecture rooms, the library I hid in during the last few months before graduation. I stood outside the apartment complex where what little innocence I'd viewed the world with was stolen. Across the street from the Planned Parenthood clinic where the truly innocent had paid the price for it all.

And I cried.

I spent so much of that trip crying that the staff at the hotel I stayed in kept asking if there was anything they could do to help. Or maybe that was just their jobs. I was barely functional enough to convince them I was 'fine.'

I let myself remember every emotion I had long since buried, hoping they truly did not, as my therapist always insisted, have the power to bury me - the anguish, the anger, the pain, the loss, the helplessness. There was so much to unpack.

Almost too much sometimes, so I prayed, too.

For the first time in years, I prayed formally and consistently. Five daily salawaat and lengthy duas. Tahajjud that were not just mental health exercises and sent heart-felt pleas to the One who never slumbers. I prayed for peace. Asked for forgiveness. For closure. Solace. Joy. To be able to move on. Faith. Strength. That it would all be over…

But I never once used the emergency number Dr Barns pressed on me.

When I emerged from underneath it all, I was lighter. So, I decided to go to Qatar. Who knows what that trip would unearth? The answer came to me on the flight to Qatar – I was going to perform the Umrah! I called my assistant from the airport, had her research operators that would pass through on their way to Makkah. She had to pick up my Nigerian passport and other required documents from my apartment, deliver it to the agents, and schedule me to join the next available group.

After all that, the rest of my stay in the Gulf country was anti-climactic. Not unlike the girl who barely existed here all those years ago, very little of it impacted me in any meaningful way. The school was as I remembered it; a fancy haven for pampered children of the uber-rich, the academic veneer not quite masking the vapid entitlement. I could see why I was so out of my depths here, the rude contrast it would have been coming here from Noorah and Zaynunah's family home.

I left it behind as easily this time, too.

'There you are!' The chirpy voice pulled me out of my reverie as a teenaged girl materialized in front of me. A small-statured fountain of bubbly good cheer, standing a couple of steps below where I was sitting on the stoop of one of the hotels surrounding the Grand Mosque in Makkah.

'I said you would still be here since we'd agreed to meet here after salaah, but some people,' she sent a cheeky side-eye to the man beside her, who was trying unsuccessfully to stifle his amusement at her theatrics, 'insisted that you would have gone to the hotel.'

'Juwairiyyah, I didn't insist. I suggested that, since you took so long coming out, Rekiya might have headed back to the hotel.' Brother 'Isa responded in the long-suffering voice that must surely be patented for fathers of teenaged daughters.

'Hmmn-hmmn,' the girl scoffed. 'I knew she was still going to be here. Why would someone who came to the Haram, despite not having to pray, want to rush back to the hotel immediately after the salaam? Plus, I told you, she said she'd wait for me here.'

I was so busy following the camaraderie between them, it took me a while to realize what she just said. In fairness to him, Zu's brother did a pretty good impression of impassivity until his daughter caught herself with a belated and blatantly theatrical gasp.

'Oh my God! I didn't mean… SubhanaLlaah! Auntie Rekiya, I'm so sorry!'

She looked so contrite, both palms covering her face, yet somewhat mischievous with her eyes peeking through her fingers that both of us adults met the other's gaze and burst into laughter.

'AsSalaam alaykum, Rekiya. Please forgive Miss Blabbermouth here. Are you ready?'

I returned the greeting and nodded, and we began walking the short distance to our hotel.

I had been pleasantly surprised to find Z's eldest brother among people whose group I joined for the Umrah. He had claimed it was kismet, seeing as – in his words - he had obviously not considered the full ramifications of travelling alone with a teenage girl. I suspect that he had been joking, this was obviously not their first father-daughter bonding trip. And watching them interact over the past week had been yet another joyful thing I only recently discovered. They were a close-knit duo; he an indulgent but firm father, she a loving and only slightly spoiled daughter.

'So…,' Brother 'Isa broke into the companionable silence we all had going as we entered the hotel lobby. 'Dinner?'

'Yes, but I'll meet you guys in a few minutes,' Juwairiyyah said, pressing the button for our floor on the elevator panel. 'I just have to check something with Hamiidah. You guys go ahead. And Daddy, please prepare a plate for me.'

The girl she'd referred to is the only other teenager in our group. She and her mother made up the four in our female room and both girls had formed a fast friendship, despite the obvious difference in their personalities.

The silence was slightly more awkward as we settled at a table in the hotel restaurant, made more so by my slight hesitation before joining him after filling my plate. We had eaten at the same table every night since our arrival, but this seemed different somehow without his daughter's presence.

Oh Rekiya, you ninny! I scold myself as I sat down. This was Brother 'Isa after all, and I grew up having early morning philosophical discussions with him. Plus, it was a public restaurant and the girl was bound to be here soon, spouting inappropriate comments that ended up giving broad hints of my reproductive calendar.

'She reminds me so much of her mother.'

It was my turn to give a gasp and cover my mouth. I didn't realize I had spoken aloud until I heard my own voice. 'I'm sorry. I didn't mean to…'

'Rekiya,' he cut through my blather. 'It's fine. It was a long time ago. And she is uncannily like her mother.' He smiled.

'I'm sorry for your loss,' I whispered.

He nodded, looked away.

'She's growing up so fast,' he mused absently. 'She'll be starting her final year in a few weeks and has been adamant that she won't attend university in Ibadan, Ilorin or Lagos. Too close to home, she says. In fact, she doesn't want to attend university at all.'

'No? What does she want to do?'

'I don't know. She says she wants to cook. I'm not sure if that would be like a restaurant, or catering or what but she's convinced that cooking is her passion and that four years in a university will not prepare her for that.' He sighed. 'I don't disagree with that. I just… I want to give her the best possible start that I can, but I don't know what that looks like without higher education.'

'So, maybe higher education doesn't have to be in a university,' I shrug. 'Maybe a culinary school… Or you could get her to try university for a while. There are courses that would enhance her chosen path – nutrition, food sciences, even business management. And she could balance that with internships at big restaurants or catering services, places in the industry so she knows which way she wants to head out on. That should give her the best of both worlds. She just has to apply to schools in the mega cities, Lagos or Abuja…' My voice trails off.

'Abuja, eh?' There is a familiar teasing note in his voice. I recognize it from his years of tormenting teenage Z and me. 'What about you? Are you in *Naija* to stay or will you be moving back to the US? I read about the work you and your team have been doing in the Business Weekly. You must be proud of yourself.'

I fiddle with the headscarf I'd kept on since Qatar, unaccustomedly shy. Until now, my work has never spilled over into my private life. Who was I kidding? I had no private life. Still, it felt good to have someone, outside of work, praise my accomplishments.

'I'm not sure yet,' I hedge. 'I might stay in Abuja or move to Lagos or another city. The logistics are still being worked out, but I kind of have to be in West Africa for a while.'

'Of course. You are the newly created C.F.O. West Africa.' He was still teasing, but it did not mask the respect in his tone. 'Seriously though. Congratulations for the splendid job you're doing. You must be proud of yourself.' He leaned back in his seat, his food almost all gone. 'Maybe I will encourage Juwairiyyah to apply in Abuja after all. With you as her guardian and role-model…'

I might have spluttered my juice at that. 'Me?! Role-model?'

'Yes?' He drew the word out over a couple of syllables, as though unable to fathom what was objectionable about the idea. 'You are a smart, successful and independent young woman. My daughter could do a lot worse for a role-model.'

I did not have a comeback.

Fortunately, said daughter appeared at that moment. 'Salaam alaykum. Sorry, have you been waiting long? Oh, good, you already got the food! But, Daddy, mine would be cold by now. Why didn't you guys wait for me?!'

Her father met my gaze in mirth for the second time that night, then turned to his daughter. 'Sweetheart, I know this is a hard concept for you to comprehend, but not everything revolves around you.'

CHAPTER FOURTEEN

Zaynunah

'Well, I'm glad you enjoyed your trip, and may Allaah accept your Umrah,' I say into a comfortable lull in the phone conversation. Rekiya had finally returned to the country last week after nearly two months away, although she still plans to spend another week in Lagos before returning to Abuja. I wasn't really sure what the first part of her trip had been about – something about visiting her previous lives in the US and Qatar. I could hear from her voice that she was in a better place than she'd been when she left.

'Ameen.' She sounded calm, well rested. 'But enough about me. What of you, how have you been?'

I smiled ruefully; grateful she couldn't see me across the phone lines. 'Same old. Life, without Mummy. Juggling the kids, work. Trying not to strangle my daughter.'

'I'm sorry. I know it must be hard getting used to her not being here.' She sighed. 'It still hits me hard sometimes so I can't imagine how it must be for you.'

'Yeah…'

'You'll be fine, Z. And you must know Mummy is in a good place.'

'Insha Allaah.'

'Hey,' she interrupts the ensuing silence before it gets too morose. 'What's this about Khawlah?'

'I just don't know what to do with her. I feel like I'm losing her. She never wants to do anything with me or her brothers anymore, we only see her when Yu is around.' I sound like a sitcom mom. Even I could hear it. But the boys were in bed, Khawlah was in her room, as usual, and Saturday nights are the most popular adult classes at the madrassah, so my husband wasn't home. And frankly, motherhood is hard; it felt good to vent.

'She's a teenager, Zu.' Rekiya's voice pull me out of my head. 'She's just beginning to define who she is outside of you all. Give her time. And some space.'

'I never needed time and space when I was a teenager. Or to define myself separate from my family.' I knew I was grumbling but still.

Ruqqayyah's laugh float airily down the phone lines. 'Z, you were never a typical teenager. You genuinely loved and wanted the life your parents lived, the life they'd envisioned for you.'

'What's wrong with that life?'

'Nothing!' She was somber this time. 'But you have to understand that at that age, most kids want to explore the boundaries of their world. They want to try different things than their parents have let them up till that point. And while this can have dangerous consequences occasionally, it is usually a healthy expression of their individuality. You just need to know that you've raised her right; that she will make good choices. And remind her she can always come to you whenever she needs to. You are her anchor.'

'Anchor!' I scoffed. 'That's so …' I couldn't find words. 'And how can you be so sure I raised her right?'

Rekiya just laughed again. 'Don't worry, Baby,' she sounded eerily like Mummy in that instant, the countless times she had said those exact words to me; to us. 'I know you. And your mother before you. I know Khawlah will be fine - she has great antecedents. You'll both be okay.'

I tried to shake my melancholy. 'I wish Mummy was here. She always knew what to tell me, what to do.'

'But she already showed you what to do. Remember Brother 'Isa?'

She had a point. My eldest brother went through a rather long phase of 'defining himself apart from the family'. It lasted my entire life until young adulthood. I shudder to think how much longer it could have lasted, but the death of his wife mellowed him down. Once he climbed out of his immediate spiral that was. And my mum had loved and supported him through it all.

'Perish the thought!' I say now. 'Khawlah is nowhere near that bad. Yet. Plus, I don't know if I have Mummy's fortitude.'

'I do,' she affirms. 'You, Zaynunah Sanusi, do not know your own strength. Trust me, you are every inch your mother's daughter.'

Ya Rabb, I miss that woman!

*

Rekiya

'The doctor will be in to see you soon.'

I smile in acknowledgement as the nurse walked out, closing the door gently behind her.

Taking a deep breath, I looked around again, unsure what to make of the office. On one side were all the trappings of you'd expect in a your GYN's office – an examination couch with attached stirrups, a purring ultrasound machine, and a privacy screen unobtrusively positioned in a discreet corner. On the other side, there was your quintessential living room, all warm tones and welcoming sofas, albeit done on a mini scale. Both sides were oddly tied together with the ultra-modern office setting in the middle of the office, its gleaming wood desk and inviting leather chairs adding to the overall ambience of a room that shouldn't have worked, but somehow did.

Unsure of where to seat, I headed toward the living room section, concluding it was the most welcoming part of the room.

The list I had been sent by my old therapist was woefully short; apparently, Nigerians had yet to catch up to the idea of seeking professional mental health help. My choice had been a no-brainer; Dr. Aisha Ayooade had been the only female, and a Muslim at that. I always suspected that what stagnated my progress with Dr Barnes had been a cultural gap that the therapist had either not recognized or had not known how to breach.

That first telephone contact and, initial consultation yesterday had reassured me on the validity of my choice. We had, in her words, 'outlined our goals for working together', deciding on an initial daily session for this week, to be followed by remote twice weekly sessions once I return to Abuja. Yesterday had been largely painless. We went through my very short medical history; she performed the most thorough examination I'd ever been subjected to, all the while giving me a run-down of her credentials and how her practice runs.

I think she had felt compelled to explain to me that her medical qualification was in obstetrics and gynecology, and that her own brush with postpartum depression and the disillusionment that accompanied residency had led her to begin studying counselling psychology, long distance. She eventually pursued a graduate degree and completed the hours required for licensing in the US. She currently runs her 'well-woman' clinics as a combination of physical and mental wellbeing, she'd said, smiling wryly that most of her patients were more comfortable with that model than if she had been 'just a therapist'.

I am withholding my judgement until after today's ordeal.

'AsSalaam alaykum, Rekiya.'

I sat straighter as I responded, watching her come in and settle on the sofa across from me. We had discussed greetings, form of address, and if I wanted Islam and its teachings as part of our sessions yesterday. Apparently, it was important in a therapeutic relationship not to take anything for granted.

'So, I have been through the notes your previous therapist sent along with your referral,' she began once we'd both settled in. 'But I want to hear from you, why are you here and what do you hope to achieve?'

Dr Aisha was a petite woman with a ginormous presence, something that caught me unawares when I met her. She had a cool serene visage that, for all that she was probably only a couple of years older than me, hinted at an uncommon understanding. And a direct approach I had appreciated immensely. Until now.

'Well,' I hedged. 'I might be suffering from PTSD, and possible from some other issues from my childhood. I really just want to get over them, live my life.'

'Okay. We'll come back to that as we gain clarity.' She paused. 'What's the worst thing that ever happened to you?'

I recoiled. Literally.

I understand direct but that… That was… I had no words.

Except I did.

And she didn't stop.

We went over my life as a narrative; me haltingly stumbling through the telling. She, gently but firmly, prodding me through it. She listened actively, spoke only to clarify or redirect, but did not make notes or betray any emotions.

Two hours later, I was so wrung out I couldn't identify any emotions of my own. It was all I could do to return to my hotel instead of booking the next available flight out of Lagos. I had never talked about everything that brought me here, probably not to any one person, and certainly not in one sitting. It had taken Dr Barnes a couple of weeks just to get the barest facts about my parents and our family growing up. And I don't think I ever mentioned Z and her family to her.

Still, I showed up the next day. And the day after. And the one after that.

We explored everything. How I felt, as a child, when my father left, and my mother fell apart. My days at Noorah; both pre and post Zaynunah. What that friendship meant to me, and how lost I felt when I was wrenched away from the acceptance I had found with that family. We talked about Qatar and Houston, and the significance each place played in my development. We even talked 'Abdullaah and I almost lost it, telling her about finding out what happened to him over a decade later, unexpectedly grieving for the man I never allowed myself to love. We talked death; Mummy's, my father's, and how I have sometimes thought that mine would be better than its pointless existence.

And of course, we talked about the rape – she insisted I named it. She wanted to go over what I knew of it, for all that I still did not remember it. The players of it; my college friends and roommates, the guys from Europe, the particular one I suspected did it – the one I had flirted so naively with. Inexplicably, I found myself telling her about the abortion – I had never mentioned it before. And of my mother's role in its orchestration, her own past of violent sexual abuse and how she, also, had never mentioned it to anyone.

She made me go through a ton of questionnaires, which she called assessments. IQ tests, personality tests, depression scales, so many that I stopped trying to remember what they were for after a while.

Then we talked religion; what it meant to me, and how I'd lost faith all those years ago. What I really believed now, and how I suppose it impacted on my life so far. My recent Umrah and how I saw myself delving into the realm of the spiritual moving forward.

On the day of our last session, she asked permission, hugged me, then briskly went about the business of giving me her professional assessment.

'I do not believe you have a schizoid personality disorder. But you do appear to have an attachment disorder carried over from your childhood. You have suffered from major depression in the past, but you have largely come out of that, although I cannot rule out a possible dysthymic disorder. You do, however, have PTSD, but that is something we can work on. You have maintained a high level of functioning over the years, despite it, but you have avoided forming any attachments as a result. And I believe that is what you want the most, to form healthy relationships, and with people who love you, who belong to you, and to whom you belong. I also believe that you are already on the way. So, we will work together, you and I, we'll pray together. And insha Allaah, you will be better.'

In that moment, even though I didn't understand some of the terms she used, and I was unsure how I really felt about her spiel, somehow, I believed her.

*

Zaynunah

I listened to the sounds of the night as the phone rang on futilely on the other end. There was a rhythm to this cacophony of sounds, something one never hears in the city, and most of which I could never hope to identify. I have lived in Ibadan all my life; born, bred and buttered, as we say in this country. I did have the childhood jaunts to the village during school vacations and festivals to visit my grandmother but those were too fleeting and far-flung to have any significant impact. The city girl in me cannot tell a grasshopper from a grasscutter, and certainly not by their sounds.

I could understand the appeal of country life, though, sitting here as I am in a rocking chair on Jummai and Brother 'Isa's screened porch. Everything is so peaceful. I berate myself yet again that I have spent so little time out here in all the years since they built this house on his farm, a measly fifteen-minute drive from the city limits. I am ashamed to remember how many of Jummai's invitations I blew off over the years, amazed at how they never stopped being extended, and humbled by the kind heartedness of this woman I have long since pigeon-holed as "my brother's wife". Looking back, I am unsure why I rebuffed all her obvious overtures of friendship over the years. Was it my usual reticence, left over from an adolescent girl's fear of not being accepted? Or did I take one look at my much-older brother's teen-aged bride all those years ago at their very festive, very Hausa wedding and decide our characters would not gel, pre-judging her sunny nature and brightly coloured hijabs?

AstagfiruLlaah ya Rabb!

This introspection since mummy's death, and Ruqqayyah's reappearance in my life, was showing me in poor light indeed. A woman who was so comfortable, almost smug, in her life – her family, her business, her Deen – that she was nearly inaccessible to anyone else. I have a very strong network of women – like-minded Muslim women – that I have met over the years, from Noorah and U.I., through my husband and brothers, in the various neighborhoods we have lived in and through the activities of our kids. But I cannot name a single one I count on as a friend. I know this is mostly due to my aloofness. Like the Yoruba proverb, *a mother will lift the child who raises its arms*. I realize I have singed a lot of bridges in the past, turned down so many overtures that could have led to deeper connections. I only hope they hadn't totally burnt down and that some of them, at least, could be repaired.

Jummai had been the easiest choice to begin with because she has always been so giving, and she never stopped trying, in all the years we've known each other. So, when she invited me again, I accepted. Then reciprocated. And now, weeks later, we're slowly building a relationship outside of Brother 'Isa, on our way to a friendship that's teaching me we don't have to be alike to be friends, just accepting of each other. In truth, the more I learn about her, the more layers I discover about someone most people probably dismiss as a flighty 'Rich Man's Wife' – like her postgraduate studies, her charity work, and the playful, energetic mother that she is, that my own boys adore. Even Khawlah seems to be enjoying this increased contact we are cultivating, following Juwairiyyah about like a little sister she's never been. I suppose her older cousin, stylish under Jummai's influence yet appropriately covered by Deeni and her father's standards, provides her with someone to look up to.

I remember when that was me.

The phone vibrating on my thigh pulls me out of my maternal self-pity.

'Hey, AsSalaam alayki. I called you earlier.'

'I know,' Ruqqayyah says after retuning my salaam. 'I went to the park and time got away from me. I was just praying maghrib when you called.'

I felt a glow at how naturally the words rolled off her tongue. *AlhamduliLlaah.* But – 'You went to a park?'

She chuckled. 'I know. But my therapist has me doing this thing where I have to make non work-related conversations with people every day. I've been cheating - and confusing my staff - the entire week by throwing random conversation starters at them. But there was no work today, so…' I can almost hear her shrug. 'I went to the park.'

'And made random, non work-related conversation with… strangers?' My confusion registers so loudly in my voice that she begins to laugh.

'I know! I swear my staff must think I'm having some sort of psychotic break, between my behavior, my odd dressing, my secret father's death and not to forget my very powerful and now very rich brother descended on the office, leaving the males awe-struck and the females swooning.'

Did she think she was making any sense?

'Are you?' I ask quietly.

'Am I what?' It is her turn with the confused voice.

'Having a psychotic break?' My voice is as gentle as I can make it, scared.

She bursts into another bout of laughter. This one is so long I find myself thinking of who I need to call. I mean, I hadn't seen Ruqqayyah in over ten years before Mummy died, who knows-

'Z. Seriously?!' She's still chuckling. 'Of course not! Although I don't suppose I'd realize it if I was having a psychotic break, would I?' she muses.

I do not know what to do with all this. 'Rekiya,' I started – and I *never* call her that – 'You are scaring me. Have you ever had a psychotic break before?'

There was a moment of silence, I think she was waiting to see if I was joking. Then,

'Z! No, I have never had a psychotic break before.' She paused. 'At least, I don't think so. I mean, I had to take anti-depressants for some time, but that was years ago. And I feel better now than I have in years. Plus, I spent the whole of last week being worked over by my new therapist and I still spoke to her this afternoon, so if I was having some kind of break, she would have caught it, right?'

Okay. That sounded fair enough. 'But I'm still so confused,' I mutter.

'Just ask,' she replies.

'Okay.' I take a deep breath, then rush in. 'Therapist? Anti-depressants? Are you okay?'

'I'm fine,' she reassures me softly. 'The anti-depressant was years ago, remember those stuff I didn't want to talk about? A lot happened over the years, but Mummy's death and being with you all made me realize I needed to deal with it, hence the new therapist. That was why I was in Lagos for a week.' She pauses. 'It was very intense but I'm hopeful for the first time in a really long time.'

Huh. 'So, you just have to talk about non work-related stuff?' I ask. *How does that help anything?*

'Yeah. That, and say something personal to someone who's not a stranger. That's you – and this conversation - for today, in case you hadn't already figured that one out.' Her laughter peels down the phone waves again. 'Apparently, I have – over the years – developed a pattern of not engaging with my surrounding beyond what is absolutely necessary, which for me meant work. So, these exercises are designed to push me out of those cages, metaphorically speaking.'

'You meant to tell me that you, Rekiya Gbadamosi,' I stressed her teenage name for emphasis, 'have spent the past week or so telling people these type of deeply personal stuff about yourself?'

'Oh God, no!' I could hear the horror in her voice. 'Of course not! She said it didn't have to be very personal, just random things that other people would normally share, but that I had become accustomed to keeping to myself.'

'Like what?'

'Well,' her voice trails off, then rises. 'On the first day, I arranged a video call with HR at the head office to talk about my hijab, and made sure to mention that it was something I used to wear until I moved to the states. Then I told my assistant my mum was Ibo. And that I grew up in Abuja. Oh, and that I was in Ibadan for secondary school. Stuff like that.'

Okay, that wasn't so bad... There were so many things I wanted to unpack from this conversation, but I went with - 'So Tunde Gbadamosi came to see you. How did that go, by the way?'

'Surprisingly well,' she responds. 'He'd made an appointment to see me two days after I returned to work, and I wasn't sure what to expect but he was pleasant. He apologized for his behavior all those years ago – something about his mother's hurt and his not knowing the entire story.'

'But what did he want?' I persisted. 'After all these years, why was he suddenly reaching out to you now?'

'He says he wants to be friends.' She chuckles at my disbelieving snort. 'I'm not sure yet whether he's sincere or trying to butter me up for the shares our father left me. I haven't read the lawyer's report. but I know we all got equal share, which must be hard on him after pouring his life into that company. But he didn't say anything about it yet so, we'll see… We have a lunch date for next Wednesday before he leaves Abuja.'

'Maybe he really just wants to get to know you. It will be good for you to finally get to know each other. You are siblings, after all.'

Her 'Hmmn' was non-comital but, figuring it was better than her previous vehemence of being an only child, I let it slide.

'So…' I tease, 'what did you say to the strangers in the park?'

'Urgh! It was awkward. I finally sat beside a young woman who was watching a little girl play on the slide and complimented her on how pretty her daughter was.' Her voice made it obvious the story did not end there.

'That sounds good.,' I prodded. 'Mothers usually love talking about their kids.'

'Yeah…' she chuckled. 'Except she smiled faintly then told me she was the nanny.'

It was my turn to send peals of laughter over the airwaves.

CHAPTER FIFTEEN

Rekiya

The Lagos-Ibadan expressway is a trial, even on the best of days.

At over one hundred and twenty kilometers long, it is the major road connecting Lagos, Nigeria to… anywhere. The busiest inter-state route in the country, it is said to be one of the largest road network on the continent. Unfortunately, it has started showing its age years ago, as the country's oldest expressway; with crater-sized potholes and erosion nipping at both edges of the asphalt.

Today was one of the not-best days.

There had been a grid lock traffic on two different sections of the road. One was caused by a congregation of one of the religious bodies that decided to make their home along the road with no regard to the suffering of other road users. The other had been due to two goods-laden trailers breaking down, absurdly, side by side to each other. This was compounded by the manic style of driving adopted by otherwise seemingly sane Nigerian drivers in such conditions. I am understandably thankful I managed to get through the ordeal without being killed, maimed or dissolving into a homicidal rage. In fact, I was feeling quite proud of myself for not railing at the *danfo* driver who broke my passenger-side mirror just as we pulled free of the last bit of chaos. Rather, I had calmly deposited the dislodged appendage on the passenger seat and continued driving, much to his consternation.

Now, as I turn at the gates marked MUSLIM ESTATE just a few kilometers from the Ibadan city limits, I regret not accepting the offer of a driver that came with this car, courtesy of my mother's husband. Sighing wearily, I promised myself a chocolate bar as reward for the ordeal of the past four hours.

At least Z had stopped calling every fifteen minute. After the last call – almost an hour ago – it had been obvious I wouldn't make it to her place in time so she decided to join Jummai and Brother 'Isa. Thank goodness I had left so early because we'd planned to go together. I am now only about a half-hour late for the mysterious gathering.

Idling in front of the gate I believe to be my destination, I call her.

'Yeah. AsSalaam alayki. We see you. The gates...' her voice trailed off as the gates pull open.

I drive in, nodding my gratitude to the gateman, and park beside the cluster of cars just off what was obviously the entrance of the white stately building within the massive compound.

'Come in, come in!' Zu's voice beckons me from the shadowed depths. 'I've been so worried!'

I smile at the young lady holding the door open, obviously the staff member whose job it was to usher me in. She, in turn, watches in bemusement as Z proceeds to hug me as though I had just returned from war.

'Z, get off me! Seriously, I can't breathe.' An exaggeration, but physical displays of affections still make my skin, well not crawl, but break out in... something.

'Don't mind her,' Jummai is smirking as she joins us. 'SH flayed her when he learnt she 'let' you drive from Lagos alone. Apparently, Lagos-Ibadan is a fly trap today. *Pele*. Was it so bad, how are you?'

'SH?! Who-'

'Her husband.' Zu interjects, rolling her eyes. 'Don't ask – they're sickening!'

'Oh, and you and Yu aren't?' Jummai volleys back.

Okay, this was weird – this camaraderie they not only shared but appeared to expect me to join in. Maybe it was the circumstances; I had only met the other woman at the time of Mummy's death; but I don't remember them being this…friendly then.

I clear my throat to interrupt the bantering they had going on. 'Z, what's going on? What is this place, and what are we doing here?'

Zu hadn't given me any details. When I mentioned coming to Lagos for work this week and coming out to see her today, she had promptly invited me to a gathering she had to attend, brushing off my attempts to backtrack.

'Come on,' she says now, pulling on my arm. 'Come meet everyone. I suppose we'll all find out together.'

The room we enter is large but well appointed, with a sizeable oval conference table at one end and a more informal sitting area at the other end, from where a woman had separated from the others, and was currently walking towards us.

'This is Habeebah Ayoade, our hostess,' Z introduces. 'And this is Ruqqayyah Sodiq-Gbadamosi, my best friend from way back.'

I smile at the cryptic introduction and accept the woman's handshake of salaam. 'Wa alayki salaam warahmah. Nice to meet you, too. And I go by Rekiya Yusuf now,' I give Z a side-eye.

'Noted. And my condolences on your dad. Please, come. Let me introduce you to the others.' Habeebah Ayoade was…soulful was the only word I can think of – as if her thoughts were concerned with matters not of this ephemeral world.

Mentally shaking my head at my own flights of fancy, I decline her offer to have my abaya hung in a corner that boasted Jummai's lilac hijab very prominently obvious in a cluster of other somber coloured outer garments. With Jummai in what must be customary-for-her Ankara, and both Zu and our hostess in regal thobes that I would have easily worn as abayas - scarves loosely draped about their faces – I figured it suffices just to loosen the pin holding my own scarf together.

We reach the women sitting and chatting quietly in the corner and the introductions commenced. Interestingly, I know of almost every woman in the gathering – a national media personality, a small-and-medium business owner and entrepreneurial powerhouse, a former minister of state in the present cabinet, the proprietress of an elite Muslim school in the FCT, and…wasn't Habeebah Ayoade the daughter of that industrialist that died a couple of years back, making her one of the "Richest 30 under 30" for that year?

'And this,' the woman was saying, 'is my sister-in-law, Dr. Aisha Ayoade.'

I freeze for a moment, unsure of how to react, but Dr. Aisha only extends her hands, giving salaam like the other women had done. Her gaze is intense, but steady – it was up to me to mention our previous association.

Oh, well, it had gotten easier over the past few weeks, this business of telling strangers my business.

'Fancy meeting you here, Dr. Aisha. We could have car-pooled.' This was my very weak attempt at humour, but her smile took on an appreciative gleam as she nodded at the acknowledgement.

'You guys know each other?'

I'm sure Z didn't mean to sound so incredulous that I might conceivably have a previous acquittance with a woman of similar age and social status as ours, so I just shrug. 'She's my therapist. Remember? I told you about her.'

'She is? I thought you were ObGyn, Aisha.' She gamely directed her question to Dr Aisha, even though I could almost see her bite back the curiosity.

Jummai and I hover at the edges of their conversation as Z and the good doctor discuss her service model, and not long afterwards, our hostess ushers us to the conference table where each seat placement had a folder placed on the table.

'Thank you all for coming,' Habeebah Ayoade begins, her voice ringing with a steady determination that had not been evident in our earlier socialization. It was a tone I recognized; this was a woman who meant business. I sat up and eyed her warily.

What is going on here?

'I know most of you are wondering what you're doing here. And I must say, I appreciate your taking time out of your busy schedule to meet us, especially since the purpose of this meeting has been left purposely vague.' She makes sure to meet all of our gazes one by one before proceeding. 'If you will please go through the proposal before you, that purpose will become clearer. Then we can address any concerns or clarifications you may raise.'

I look her over again, this woman whose very presence seems to suggest more questions than it answers. She's the epitome of still waters running unbelievably deep, her eyes unwavering when they meet mine. All around me papers are shuffled while I try to decipher what lays behind her placid expression. She gives nothing away, just a single nod as she sits back in her seat and waits.

With no other option, I begin to read.

Years of business negotiation have taught me the art of keeping a blank face, but I couldn't help the incredulity I felt as I raise my head. I find Habeebah still watching me.

Is she for real?

Zaynunah

'Okay, I'm just going to say it,' Jummai declares. 'Zaynunah, you know I liked this your Habeebah Ayoade well enough when you mentioned her, but… she's crazy! The woman wants to rule the world!'

Ruqqayyah, who is driving, and I laugh along with the observation as the car navigated through the sluggish late evening traffic towards Jummai and Brother 'Isa's farm. It is almost maghrib, hours later than I envisaged our return, and both my husband and brother have taken to blowing up their respective wives' phones in the past hour.

'Not the entire world,' Ruqqayyah corrected. 'Just our corner of it. And I must say, I'm intrigued. What if she's right, what if we can change lives for Muslim women in Nigeria, with no one the wiser?'

'By pulling the strings in the background like puppet masters?' Jummai was still understandably skeptical.

'By using our not inconsiderable resources,' Ruqqayyah levelled an admonishing gaze on Jummai, who was riding short-gun and had begun giggling, as she continues to quote Habeebah almost verbatim, 'to influence the lot of as many as we can of our fellow sisters.'

'Hmmn. I don't know, *fa*! It's still all a bit cloak and dagger for my taste,' I was thinking aloud. 'All this secret meeting and working in stealth…'

'But' Ruqqayyah's eyes challenge mine in the rearview mirror, 'isn't that the only exception for cloak and dagger meetings? To bring about good, and to engage in charity. I seem to remember a verse?' She leaves it as a question.

'Is it?' Jummai turns to me.

'Yeah,' I mutter, as the verse in surah *Nisa'* pops up behind my lids.

'We can pool our collective knowledge and clout in the different sectors, make impact where it is most significant, and the fact that we'd not be publicly associated with it makes it the best form of charity.' Ruqqayyah's smile was part admiration, part smugness. 'I like this your friend, Z!'

I scoff at her. 'Of course, you do. Is this what having too much money does to people?'

'What do you mean?'

I recognize the note in her voice – this was the Rekiya from Noorah, the girl who thought she was accepted only for her father's wealth. 'I mean Habeebah. She was a normal girl when I knew her in U.I. Or at least, a normal rich girl with a mouthful of silver spoons but still, you know what I mean. Now she's all mysterious master planner of Machiavellian proportions. So, I'm wondering if it's what being unimaginably wealthy does to you?'

This time, Jummai turns to assess Ruqqqayyah, who eyes us both before chuckling. 'I wouldn't know yet. I have yet to take control of my newest assets, although I'm not sure even that would put me in the "unimaginably wealthy" category. Tell you what,' she jokingly concluded, 'ask me in a year or two!'

'What's her deal, anyway?' It was Jummai who broke the silence that followed our shared mirth. 'This Habeebah woman. Rich people rarely care enough to do stuff like this, and when they do, they usually just give the money. And they want recognition for it'

'As opposed to playing Godfather?' I smile at Ruqqayyah's head shaking and continue, 'who knows? Maybe she's just looking to make a difference. I've known her since our university days, and what I know of her is good, *masha Allaah*. We weren't really friends, just friendly acquittances until recently, but I know she's had some challenges.'

Ruqqayyah's muttered 'Haven't we all?!' was almost swallowed by Jummai's inquisitive 'Really?!'

'Yeah.' I shake my head as I recall Habeebah's matter of fact recanting of the details of her life when we'd been catching up recently. 'She has some medical issues which means she can't have kids. Ever. And, though they are childhood friends, I can't imagine it can be easy watching her co-wife having one kid after the next.'

'Allaah seriki!'

Most other times, Jummai's expressions make me smile, but –

'Wait, that pregnant lady - the lawyer, Tawa – that can't be her co-wife, is she?' Ruqqayyah breaks in.

'Yup! She is. Married their husband just over two years ago, and that is their second pregnancy. I didn't know her then, but she was in U.I., too. Apparently, they all went to the same boarding school in Lagos;

Habeebah, Tawa and Aisha. I only met the others through Habeebah, a while back.'

'And now,' Ruqqayyah mused. 'They are all related by marriage.'

Jummai's puzzled face pings between Ruqqayyah and I a couple of times before she huffs derisively. 'I cannot understand you Yoruba women and your insistence on viewing polygamy as evil. I mean, I can't imagine not being able to have kids at all. But you say it as if her husband marrying her childhood friend was a trial. As if that is the bigger trial here. For all you know, it was her idea. Personally, I would prefer someone I already know and like to share my husband with!'

'Okay o, Hausa woman, *kulu temper*!' I tease. This was not a new topic for me and her. Brought up in a largely polygamous culture, and family, Jummai was unable to appreciate the reticence displayed by us southern Muslim women toward the institution.

Eni de ba lo mo, as Mummy would say. Some things are best experienced to be appreciated.

'So,' Ruqqayyah interrupts our resultant banter. 'You not only won't mind your husband marrying someone, you would prefer if you knew her before?' She eyes Jummai measuredly before turning back to the road. 'I mean, how will that work – would he have told you before asking her? Because won't you feel betrayed otherwise? And would she talk to you before accepting, because how else would she know you were cool with it, and not calling her a home wrecker?'

'*Auzubillaah!*' Jummai exclaims dramatically. 'That's what I mean with you Yoruba women. You consider a man your own. *Ta che*, home wrecker! I think if a man wants to marry again, he should be courteous enough to inform the wife at home. That's just common-sense courtesy! As for the lady outside, she has the right to consider the man and his proposal on its own merit and not based on the expectedly touchy feeling of the current wife.'

'Dat wan na grammar! We're talking of someone you know. Like, say if Brother 'Isa wanted to marry Ruqayyah, for example,' I widen my eyes at her in the rearview mirror, so she knows I'm joking. *She is the only unmarried woman we know!* 'How will she know you won't go all *crazy Mallama* on her next time she sees you? Or are you going to be doing the proposal for your man?'

'*Gaskiya*, I don't know that one o,' Jummai admits. 'I mean, for your friend and her friend, I'm sure the man must have discussed it with his wife first and she found a way to communicate to her friend – after the fact – that she didn't mind. But if it was someone I knew, maybe not that well of course, but I liked… I don't know, maybe I'll buy her a gift or something so that she'll know there's no hard feelings.'

'And that's not weird at all!' I hear Ruqqayyah mutter sarcastically under her breath just as a Zain Bikha song rents the silence.

'Speaking of husbands…,' Jummai sighs.

'Oh, please tell him to chill out! We're literally at your gate.' I scoff in exaggerated exasperation.

Brother 'Isa is second only to Musa in his protectiveness towards his womenfolk. He had been very vocal earlier about my 'making the poor girl drive by herself' when he heard Ruqqayyah was meeting us. As if I – or worse, he – had any say in the choices she makes. Case in point, she refused to come inside to wait while I prayed maghrib, preferring to sit in the car and catch up on some emails.

Workaholic.

When I exit his house a few minutes later, my overbearing brother was trying to browbeat Ruqqayyah into letting him drive us to my place. I lean against the car and prepare to be entertained.

'Seriously, Abu J,' Ruqqayyah was trying hard to sound reasonable. 'It's less than twenty minutes from here, as I understand it. If you cease delaying us, we would be at Z's before it gets completely dark.'

'It is already dark,' he rejoins. This is his imposing voice, which means he must have already tried logic and negotiation. 'I will take you girls home, and that's final. I don't know what Yusuf was thinking letting you both drive alone at night!'

Uh-oh. This ought to be good.

Ruqqayyah visibly takes a deep breath, then meets his gaze. 'First, we are not "girls", we're grown women! And if you mean Zaynunah's husband, he doesn't "let" me anything, seeing as he has no authority over what I do, or do not do.'

She breaks their eye contact and fiddles with her hijab before continuing. 'Neither, for that matter, do you. Z, get in!'

I watch my brother's silhouette as we drive off into the twilight, imagining the look on his face; the stern visage and narrowed eyes that never fully masks the concern behind his autocratic displays.

'You know he means well.' It wasn't a question.

'Yeah,' she sighs wearily. 'I know. But Z…'

'You've been on your own a long time, and you don't need a man telling you what to do,' I finish.

She is quiet a moment. 'I do not have the luxury of a man telling me what to do.' Her delivery is in a monotone; poignant, yet factual.

'Do you want that?' I ask.

'Yeah,' she sighs again. Another beat of quiet. 'I mean, not the telling me what to do bit. Just, you know, someday… A man who has the right to *think* he can tell me what to do.'

'They all think they can tell us what to do,' I chuckle in agreement. 'So, someday… soon?'

She honks impatiently at the bus driver discharging his passengers right in the middle of the road.

Typical of Ibadan.

'I don't know, Z. I'm just now beginning to feel like it's possible for me. I know I still have work to do on myself yet, before I would consider adding a relationship to it. But marriage, family… I don't have the best role models for that, even without my own issues. So, who am I kidding? I'd probably be terrible at it.'

Her laughter is derisive and self-depreciating and I take a hold of her hand as it lay idly on the gear stick. 'Ruqqayyah, when the time comes, just say the word and we'll find you a man. Between my brothers and Yu, I'm sure we'll come up with someone worthy of you.'

Hmmm, did that sound as weird to her as it did to me?

'Z, despite the actions of your other eccentric, rich friend,' I could see her trying valiantly to maintain a straight face when she pulled up in front of my house, 'I will not share your husband!'

She ignores my gasp of mock outrage and climbs out, waiting until I had done likewise before sticking her tongue out at me over the roof of the car.

Touché.

'And does Jummai know that you are volunteering her husband to desperate, ageing spinsters?!'

Wretch. Beautiful, funny wretch.

CHAPTER SIXTEEN

Zaynunah

The next few months passed in a reel of…living.

I felt newly awakened, like I had been sleepwalking through most of my adult life. I'm not sure if it was the reality of Mummy's death, Ruqqayyah's reappearance and our reinvented friendship, or connecting with Habeebah Ayoade and her grandiose ideas, but I couldn't shake the urge to do more, live more….*be more* than I had been before.

It wasn't that I was dissatisfied with the life I had lived up to now. It was more that I realize that I had cruised through life until then. For the most part of my life – comfortable, wary of being boxed in, but unwilling to step out of my comfort zone. I never really had to fight for anything and so did not give myself wholly to anything either.

If the lone tree falls and there's no forest to hear the sound it makes, did it exist?

I know, intellectually, that my life is in no way different than millions of people the world over – work, home, family, religious observations. I am grateful for that; really. For life, Deen, security and wellbeing that meant I could take care of my family and go about the daily routine of my mundane living. But it had been a jarring to awaken to the consciousness that my fear of being boxed in, of being labelled, of losing my individuality to my identity, had done just that to me.

I was unsure of who I am outside my roles – wife, mother, daughter, sister.

It was a slow awakening, and I wasn't always sure what I was hoping for. But I was eager to find where this process would lead, this resolution to live each moment to the fullest.

My *salaah* became more involved and my *khushoo'* soared, my *dhikr* tugged more insistently at my heart strings. The words of the Qur'an more expressively ministered to my soul, reminiscent of all those hours spent memorizing and revising with Mummy. I found the push to finish the last few *juz* I had been 'too busy' to do for an embarrassing number of the past few years. I threw myself into my revision, and I rediscovered joy sharing similar hours with my children, correcting their *tajweed*, listening to their *hifdh*, encouraging them in *muraaja'a*.

My home life blossomed even more, and our homeschooling gained more pizzazz. Even Khawlah and I found a healthy balance for our relationship. Yu and I agreed to let her enroll at Noorah for Senior Secondary, and she found that enough motivation to study for her Junior Secondary Certificate Examination. I gradually learnt to give in, let her self-study and direct her learning and, in turn, she relaxed back into a semblance of the sweet daughter I had before the teenage monster invasion.

I cut my work hours in half, bringing in my first employee as a partner. He had started working for me when I first began making serious money at freelancing. Then a student at the polytechnic, he has become the public face of the company over the years – doing most of the travelling and client schmoozing I was unable to. The new partnership is a win for both of us; I get more time to devote to my life's new direction, and he could finally resign from his corporate job in Lagos, with the attendant hassles, to concentrate on his own thing. Our business, and his dream of becoming a writer.

My blog, which I'd begun two years back as a way to explore the challenges of being a woman running an I.T. company had somehow morphed to include a mentoring program for women in Tech. Giving it more attention and promotion, it soon became the fulcrum of my newfound determination to make an impact, my way of giving back to women who were trying to make their way in the male-dominated field. Quite unexpectedly, this resulted in our business gaining more visibility and success.

Between Ruqqayyah and Habeebah, I was brought around on their Machiavellian plan and soon harnessed my vast network of women in I.T. Between them and my business contacts, I began to see that it was possible – as they had predicted – to positively impact the women in the industry. Sometimes it was being asked to put forward candidates for a position, at times it was offering material and technical support on a start-up; other times, it was just the knowledge of a community of like-minded women that gave someone the impetus to reach for her dreams.

Locally, Yu was enthusiastic about my community outreach. I began running basic computer skills at the Madrassah a couple of times a week. They were free and began at the most rudimentary, but soon we had to have different levels on different days. Every segment of the community was represented; from older retirees, housewives and small business owners, to teenagers and young adults looking to acquire skills that might give them the needed edge in the job market. Immensely popular from the start, I was rather pleased to give logistic and material support when a group of sisters had the idea to float a business that catered to those seeking more advanced skills, leaving the free classes accessible for the most disadvantaged in our community – who needed it the most.

Yet as the months progressed, bringing with it Ramadhaan then 'Eid, I came to the recognition that who I was wasn't radically different from the roles I fulfil. And I, no apologies, am okay with that.

I am a woman who looks to serve her Lord in the meaning I bring to the lives of others.

I could not even begin to imagine a life with Habeebah's riches, would probably never have the influence she could wield with the amount of wealth at her disposal. I don't want a career like Ruqqayyah's, would be lost in her world of corporate ladders and the big businesses that shape our world in more ways than people like me could ever comprehend. I wasn't sociable and friendly like Jummai, whose sunny disposition could open doors no one even realized were there, allowing her into the lives of people to whom she invariably brings her light. I was not a media personality, a powerful government official, the owner of a prestigious school or…

What I am is a mother, wife, daughter, sister, friend, neighbor, mentor, community advocate. A Muslim woman with rather belated appreciation of her blessings – her relationship with God, family and friends, a near genius intelligence, a proven record in a field women still navigated with trepidation and a previously dormant resolve to give back, to live mindfully. Meaningfully.

Like my Mummy before me, I found my contentment in making my home a haven for anyone who comes in contact with it and its occupants. And my meaning in service to as many as I encounter. I do not need to change the world, just do my best to serve my corner of it.

And with that sense of peace, of all being right in my world, that undefinable feeling that I was right where I was supposed to be, I finally found the courage to discuss with Yu, the only elephant in the room of our marriage.

It had not gone as expected. Not with him, nor with Ruqqayyah, now, on our weekly phone call. I had just told her of my conversation with Yu.

'You did what?!'

I winced at her aberrant screech. 'I told Yu that I was open to the idea of him marrying a subsequent wife.'

I know, totally non-sequitur.

'Why would you do that?' she shouted. 'You know what? Don't answer that. I don't want to hear it. I'm sure you have some asinine reason you've cooked up, and you are telling yourself this is the right thing. You are just so…' She trails off on a huff.

I don't say anything. In the nearly a year since Mummy's death, Ruqqayyah and my relationship with her have evolved. If I have been awakened from sleepwalking, she had suddenly burst to life from a coma. And we were open and honest with each other in ways our even teenage selves could never have been. She was my mirror, reflecting me back to myself; flaws and all. So, when she is being brutal, I listen.

She sighs after almost a minute of silence. 'Why do you do this, Z?'

'Do what?' I genuinely want to know.

'You sabotage relationships. You tell yourself you couldn't possibly be good enough, that things must be too good to be true. And you pull back. Or worse, you wait for the other shoe to drop. You never let things just be right. You poke until it gives. Isn't that what you're doing now?'

Is she right? I mean, I may have done that in the past, but –

'That was why you stopped reaching out to me all those years ago, wasn't it? You decided my distance was about you, something you had or hadn't done that made you, and our friendship, irrelevant to me.' she persisted, sighing.

'Yeah,' I mumbled. 'I mean, kind of. But this isn't that. I just… I see Habeebah and Tawa, and they are good together. Habeebah is content with her lot in life. I am ashamed that I ever pitied her – and all because I assumed that not being able to have a child, or her husband marrying her friend somehow made her pitiable. Yet she is so…serene. I remember myself, how churlish I was when Yu raised the subject years ago, and I feel small. Like I let jealousy make me smaller than I was, than we were. Our marriage, our love, our Deen. And I am in such a good place in my life right now, we are in such a good place, I had to rise above all of that.' I concluded, not sure if she – if anyone – could understand my reasoning.

Yu hadn't.

'What did he say?' her voice was calmer.

It was my turn to sigh. 'He said he was happy I felt confident enough to say that to him. But that he was happy with our life and family right now, and he wasn't looking to add to it.'

I could hear her whoosh of exhale. 'Zaynunah, listen to me. I know you have convinced yourself you mean well. And I hear you about feeling small for letting your insecurities getting the better of you way back then. But like you said yourself, you are in a good place now. Don't blow it. Maybe your husband will end up taking a second wife down the line. And maybe it will turn out all flowers and roses. Or maybe it would be a trial for you all. What it shouldn't be is laden with your own sense of regret for not letting sleeping dogs lie. Remember once when you explained to me what that Yoruba term meant, *afowofa, abi* what it's called?'

I smile ruefully. Causing one's downfall, metaphorically speaking, with one's own hands is a cautionary Yoruba tale. Maybe she is right. While I do not necessarily agree with her assessment of my motivations, at least not on this occasion, I could not deny that I had a history of – unwittingly – sabotaging relationships due to my anxieties. And even though I believe that I have, for the most part, overcome that issue in my marriage, maybe it was a good idea to leave this up to the man. If he ever chooses to toe the line of polygyny, I have to trust that my husband will do it right and that our marriage – our love, my faith – would be strong enough to weather any trials that may arise.

'Speaking of marriages and unexpected, questionable choices…'

I chortle at Ruqqayyah's teasing, grateful for the change of subject I could hear coming. 'Is that what we were doing?'

Her response rushed by in a mix of excitement and apprehension. 'Zeke is here. In Nigeria. And he wants to marry me.'

What the –

'Who is Zeke?!'

'You know,' she mumbled. 'I told you about him. My colleague from New York, remember?'

'Oh. Yeah,' I do remember something in our earlier conversations after Mummy's death. 'But how- Wait, he came all the way to Nigeria to marry you?!'

'No, silly.' She chuckled. 'He's been in the country for about two months now. He's heading the Lagos branch kick off, and we've been working closely together on that.'

'Obviously! You are, after all, the C.F.O.' I snorted. 'But *Omoluabi*, you need slow doing, *fa*! I'm not quite making the leap from "working closely together" to a marriage proposal. And how come I'm just now hearing about this?'

'Well,' her voice is light and lilting, 'there wasn't really anything to tell until now. I mean, I thought he might have been hinting at something a couple of times, but I'm a proper sister now,' we both chuckle at the reference to her hijab, 'so I knew he had to be thinking matrimony if anything. But I didn't want to say anything because what if he wasn't? But today, he asked.'

'Just like that, he asked?'

'Yup,' her *p* popped loudly in my ear. 'We finished work and he walked me to my car, and just like that, he asked if I'd be willing to get to know each other better for the purpose of marriage.'

'Really smooth,' I sneered. 'What did you say?'

'I panicked, Zee!' she exclaimed. 'I didn't know what to say. I don't even know what the proper etiquette is, so I said he had to meet my *Waliyy* first – Professor Sanusi.'

I laughed at the imagery. Ruqqayyah all awkward and flustered, is not a sight a lot of people get to see.

'Do you think he'll mind?' she asked now, quietly.

'Who, Daddy? Of course not. Muslim men love marriage, don't you know? Nothing warms their hearts than another Muslim woman finally under the 'care' of a man, unless maybe when they are the lucky man in question. I'm sure he'll be tickled to be your *waliyy*. And frankly, he needs something to cheer him up. I'll call him tomorrow to warn him, then I'll send you his number. Insha Allaah. As for Zeke,' I continue. *Is it me or is that a weird name?* 'He definitely shouldn't mind meeting your Waliyy if he wants to marry you.'

'Okay. Thanks.'

There is a small silence, then I ask. 'So… is it someday now?'

'I don't know, Zu,' she confesses. 'I think it could be. At the very least, I suppose I should at least try to find out.'

Rekiya

I am having a panic attack!

Unbelievable. It has been years since I had one. I thought they were under control! That one at Z's parent's after Mummy's death didn't count, not really. I had woken up from sleep in the middle of what could have been a panic attack, but I was never quite sure if it was one, because for the first time in years, I had been crying actual tears. That was enough to confuse a girl!

But this. And now, of all times!

I lower myself slowly unto the sofa, yanking off the hijab I had been wrapping before the panic hit me, ripped open my abaya, all the while forcing myself to focus on my breathing. In. Out. In again. Out. I continued this for an indeterminate length of time, purposefully keeping my mind blank. This is not my first rodeo and I had learnt my tricks the hard way. Eventually, I felt the panic receding; the air came back and my breaths were almost effortless again, my heart slowed its pounding into a somewhat steady beat, and my vision cleared sufficiently for me to look into the hallway mirror across from me.

I saw a broken mess of a woman.

It took me a while, but I got up. Found my phone and sent Zeke a text. Made wudhu and prayed two *naafil raka'a*. Started repeating the du'a for distress, again. By now, it had become my favourite, and most common du'a to make. I tried, and failed, to cry a bunch of tears while making the *du'a*.

Ultimately, I dialed Dr Aisha's emergency number. It was the first time I would use it in the months since she gave it to me, in the months since our sessions started.

'Rekiya? AsSalaam alayki. Are you okay?' Her concern rang over the lines, clear and comforting.

'I had a panic attack,' was all I said.

'When was this? Where were you, and what were you doing?'

I let out a deep breath. 'Maybe half an hour ago. I am in my apartment. I was preparing to go meet Zeke at the park.'

His name had come up quite a bit in our sessions, as I tried to figure out if I was ready to plunge into matrimony and, if that, with him.

'Is this the meeting where you were supposed to give him your response to his marriage proposal?' the concern is muted now, and she is in her usual therapist mode.

She had withdrawn from Habeebah Ayoade's secret charity board after that first meeting, putting forward another woman doctor. That woman is a consultant in one of the leading teaching hospitals with a husband in the national government, and she fit the group dynamics. But it meant I never get to see Aisha Ayoade socially. I never got to ascertain if this was her regular demeanor or if she put it on for her clients.

I close my eyes and visualize us in her eclectically decorated office. It was my own way of staying in therapy mode.

'Yeah,' I mumbled.

'What do you think triggered the attack?' she asks me now.

I am quiet. I don't know.

It had been a strangely anti-climactic two months. Zeke had gone to Ibadan to meet Prof. Sanusi, who had done whatever interrogating and vetting he needed to before deeming him a suitable possible match. He had suggested we get to know each other, and urged us both to persist in making *istikhara*, before I give my response. What followed was a series of emails spanning the past couple of weeks where we'd asked questions and clarifications of each other, established boundaries, and hashed out any issues. Under Prof.'s largely silent moderation – we cc'ed him on every mail - we found out we were categorically compatible. We were both career-oriented introverts who wanted to learn more about the religion we practice, but do not see ourselves as especially passionate about any specific thing. Neither of us had any defining hobbies outside work. We were both looking for long term companionship, were both still ambivalent about whether or not kids would be a part of this relationship. If we choose to get married, that is.

The only issue I'd had was that he hadn't told his wife, who was still in the US, about me and I refused to consider his proposal any further until she had, at least, been informed. Last week, he said he had finally done that, and she had taken it about as well as could be expected, given that they were currently estranged.

I had asked for this meeting. I'd thought I was ready. It seemed like a good match, and I didn't want to keep dragging it out. Plus, he has to be here in Abuja for work, anyway, so I thought…

And then, the scary fangs of panic descended on me just as I was almost ready. Was there a parallel?

'I'm not sure,' I confess presently. 'One minute I'm fine, thinking I would finally have a family of my own, and the next minute, I'm struggling to find air.'

'Is that what this marriage, to Zeke specifically, would mean to you – a chance to have a family of your own?'

I don't have to think about it. 'Yes. I've always wanted a family, and for years, I thought I had lost that chance. With my issues, then my age… even at the back of my mind somewhere, my religion, too. I guess I always wanted a man who was purposefully Muslim, you know. And all of that wasn't possible for so long. But now…' My voice trails off.

'Now…?' She prompts when I don't continue. 'Do you feel that is or is not possible with Zeke?'

'I don't know.' My voice is small as I abruptly stop the pacing I'd been doing and sink onto the sofa once more, faced with a dawning, petrifying realization.

There's a brief silence where neither of us speaks. I recognize this tactic of hers by now – she was letting me sit with what she had known but I was just coming to recognize.

'Okay. Home-work.' she says brusquely. 'Write down what your family looks like, this future family that you hope to have someday. Make sure to include every possible definition of family that matters to you, from a religious point of view, social, cultural, even ideological. Whatever and whoever family means to you should go there. Don't forget those you want to keep from your present, existent family. Once you are done, re-evaluate Zeke's proposal with that in mind. After that, whatever you decide will be fine, insha Allaah. You've prayed long and hard about this. Trust in Allaah.'

She says that last part in Arabic. Tawwakkal ala LLaah. And, quite unbidden, I remember the verses I had read just this morning, bizarre to me that they were placed in the chapter on divorce.

And whoever puts his trust in Allaah, He will suffice him.

I thank her, absentmindedly, answer some questions where she checks my coping strategies, taking care to reassure me often. We confirm our next appointment and ring off, with her reminder that asking for help when needed is a sign of tremendous progress.

There is a familiar sensation of steely determination settling over me like a well-loved mantle. I grab a pen and pad from my coffee table.

It is time to meet my family.

Z is understandably perturbed the next time we speak on the phone, on the following Saturday, just minutes after I return from meeting with Zeke.

'You rejected him?! I thought…' She trails off, there was no need to vocalize what she thought. It was what I'd thought, too, until Dr. Aisha made me reflect on my family.

Well, until that panic attack, if I was being studiously honest.

'Z, I couldn't.' My voice does not display the calm certainty I felt when I had finally acknowledged I had been contemplating marriage for the wrong reasons, that Zeke could not give me what I need. Rather, I hear the insecurities and fears that have plagued me since I decided to refuse him. That I was being rash and ungrateful, that I was letting my past sabotage any chance I had for a future, that no one else would want me.

'I mean, he wasn't even going to tell his wife! If I hadn't insisted, he'd have married me without informing the woman he promised to love and protect, the woman who bore him two children! He says they're estranged but… If he does that to her, what can he do to me in the future, if we got married? Especially if we don't have kids. And that is another thing. I'm still unsure if I should have kids but I need a man who is a bit more open to the idea than I am. How am I going to have the family I dreamed of if it's just me and him – part-time and possibly across different continents, or far away from the family I have only just now found again? If anything went wrong, would I be all alone, all over again? I can't become my mother, Z!'

By this time, I am almost wailing. Beset by emotions I had not dared express to Zeke, knowing he could never get it. Not without me sharing the ugly details of my past and life with him. And I had come to accept that the tepid companionship a marriage to him offered was not enough to induce that amount of openness. So, I had just told him that I did not think either of us was in a good place to contemplate marriage. He needs to fix things with his current wife before acquiring another one, and I need to focus on renewing my relationships with myself, my Lord and my family before adding another one. Plus, I pointed out, our circumstances would not make for the most convenient marriage of convenience – we could not expect to do a long-distance form once his two-year contract in Africa was up, and I was unlikely to ever move back to the US.

His hemming and hawing over the last point, and the relative ease with which he accepted my rejection afterwards was another score for my certainty that this was the right decision.

Still the fears… 'I couldn't do it, Zee.' I sigh now, weary. 'Not even if that was my last chance.'

'*AstagfiruLlaah*, don't say that!' she admonishes me. 'You don't know what Allaah has in store for you. *Khayr, insha Allaah*, everything will be fine. I just… It sounded like you guys were compatible and… I want you to be happy, Rekiya.'

Her uncharacteristic use of that name makes me smile softly. 'I know.'

And she had tried very hard to be supportive while the whole business was going on, with a chirpy enthusiasm that was more Jummai than her, the friend I know well enough to spot the fakeness. I am not sure if it was fake because she had reservations about the whole thing, or just because she was trying so hard. Zaynunah Sanusi does not do chirpy enthusiasm or giddy excitement. I mean, even her romance novel habit was more Jane Austen, Georgette Heyer and the rather ancient Mills and Boon paperbacks!

'I know, Z.' I say now, thankful once again for that long-ago book I forgot in a high school classroom. 'And I want that, too. In fact, I am happy now. I mean, I think my someday has finally come and I do want to be married. But not to Zeke. He's a good man, don't get me wrong. But I'd have been miserable with him. The parallels to my early life, you know, my parents and everything…it was too close for comfort. Plus, I realized that any family I make now will have to be in addition to the one I already have – you and your million relatives, my mother and her family. Even Tunde Gbadamosi is beginning to grow on me. He's asked me to spend the next 'Eid with him and his family. So, you see, I was alone for so long, I could never let anything, or anyone, tear me away from you all again. It may not be conventional, and yes, they are fragmented and not always related, and even I am just acknowledging it, but I already have a family. And I am not giving it up!'

CHAPTER SEVENTEEN

Zaynunah

The meal was poignant. Fitting, seeing as it was the last of its kind.

It is a few days to the 'Eid Al-Adha, and a Friday. My family had helped us move the last of our belongings from our rented apartment to my parents' house. Ours now, I suppose. Daddy had come to see Yu and I a few weeks back and offered to transfer the property to my name. He was spending most of his time at one of the guest chalets on Brother 'Isa's farm anyway, he'd said, and didn't think he'd ever be comfortable in Mummy's house again, by himself. Those were his exact words.

And since the boys both owned their own homes already, he'd said, he decided to give it to me.

On one hand, I was happy my childhood home was going to stay in the family, and that Yu did not raise much of a fuss over the matter, other than insisting he would continue to pay rent to me.

On the other hand, Mummy was dead, and I was moving into her house!

I spent the past few weeks renovating and finding out that the crying bouts and spontaneous burst of tears I had suffered when she died weren't quite as behind me as I'd thought. It had been hard, but cathartic at the same time, converting my parents' room into the home office and homeschooling room. My childhood bedroom became one for Yu and me, and I turned the boys' bedrooms into one each for Khawlah and my boys. I even changed the living room décor, bringing in my own furniture, and turned the dining room into a second living room. I've always wanted that!

Now, we all sat in the living rooms, my father, his children and the respective spouses, and their own children. We had eaten dinner after the males came back from *'Isha*, but no one was in a hurry to leave. To close this chapter that felt very much like saying goodbye to Mummy all over again. The next Friday lunch would be at the farm and, although unsaid, so would subsequent ones after that.

Jummai was taking over Mummy's role as the matriarch of the family.

She's not even thirty yet!

As though she had an inkling of the emotions I was battling with, Jummai squeezed my hand that lay between us on the sofa we shared.

'So, Rekiya refused that man?' she asks. 'I thought for sure she would accept. Too bad, he seemed like a nice man. And imagine how romantic that story would have been to tell their children someday.'

I smiled ruefully at Jummai's need to find romance everywhere. I'm not sure if it was an age thing, her natural optimism, or the many sisters and cousins she has back home who are still in the finding-love-and-getting-married phase. She is always giggling and dreaming about possible love matches. Of course, it could be all the Hausa movies she loves watching so much.

'Yeah. No, she refused.' I shrugged.

Seeing that her subject ploy worked, she slid closer and attempted to lower her voice. 'Are you *sure* it wasn't because he already had a wife? Rekiya seemed so *strange* that day we were talking about polygamy in the car.'

I am sure. I am also sure that I'd told Jummai this. Quite a number of times in the weeks since Ruqqayyah rejected Zeke's proposal. I narrow my eyes.

What is up with her?!

'Jummai, I told you already. It wasn't because he had a wife. If anything, she refused to even consider the proposal until he had informed his wife. She just didn't think she fit into his family, nor he into hers. They weren't a good fit,' I nodded emphatically as I finished the last bit, thinking to myself that was a logical way of presenting Ruqqayyah's reasons for refusing without mentioning any of her private issues.

What failed to grab my notice until I stopped talking was how much higher my voice had risen from our initial near whisper. Not that I was shouting or anything. Just that no one else was talking on either side of the curtain and I got the distinct impression that my last proclamations had been heard by the entire family.

Ouch. Way to protect her privacy.

Other than myself and Daddy, and Yu of course because I continuously bent his ears on the topic, no one talked about Ruqqayyah's possible marriage. We all knew about it, though. Zeke stayed overnight at the farm on two occasions and got to meet both my brothers at some point during those visits. But after she declined his offer, everyone just moved on and went about their business as usual.

Except Jummai.

I know she's always aflutter over romance and can be a bit of a harmless gossip but even so, she seems to be having an especially hard time letting it go, and I couldn't imagine why. I only hope she won't still be hung up on it when Ruqqayyah gets here for 'Eid next week. She plans to spend the day with her brother and his family, then coming out here early the next morning for three days.

My mind lingers on how long it's been since I saw Ruqqayyah as everyone finally begins to leave. I have missed her. I would have loved to have her here, on this first night of moving into Mummy's house, and I know we'd hash it out tomorrow on the phone – my night, my feelings, the house, everything. But I really wish she was here with me right now. As my honorary sister, she is the only one who could possibly understand my jumble of emotions over this move. It would also allay my worries over how she's been doing since the whole marriage proposal debacle. Although she keeps insisting that she's fine, I hear the uncertainty in her voice when we mention issues of marriage and family. I agree with her that this had not been right for her, but I try not to share her worry that she might have somehow missed her chance.

Ya Rabb, please bless my friend with a loving husband and a wonderful family.

Sunday morning, an unexpected visitor disturbs the tranquility of my alone time. Yu had the kids at Madrassah, and I had just decided that what was left over from the feast Jummai brought in on Friday would do nicely as lunch, freeing me to take an indulgent soak in the tub when I hear the gates creak open.

From the vantage position behind my bedroom window curtains, I spy my visitor. And could not banish the stray thought that took home in my brain as I descended the stairs to admit my eldest brother into the house. A house I still had problem accepting was mine.

We hugged, gave salaams, eased on to the living room sofa and caught up.

Brother 'Isa is, undoubtedly, my favorite brother. Musa is way too stuffy and rigid, always has been. But life and its vagaries mean we rarely have time to be together like this, just the two of us, spending quality time together. With his previous work in a multinational firm, and now the farm, my own business and both our families, there was always something else to do, someone else around. So, this was nice. And since I was pretty sure I had an idea why he was here, I was content to let him get there at his pace.

After half an hour of "checking that I was well settled in" into the house where we both grew up, he got up to leave. I was about to call his bluff when he turned back to face me, hesitant, with his hand on the doorknob.

'So, Rekiya.'

I smiled. And waited.

He scowled gruffly at my taunting silence but continued. 'She really didn't reject that Zeke guy because he has a wife already?'

'No, Brother, she did not.' I assured him. 'She rejected him because she feared becoming her mother. Or at least, what she believed her mother had been to her father, all through her life until recently – a glorified side-chick.'

He pondered the words for a moment then shook his head. 'I don't even know what that means.'

'And I can't tell you more than that. It's not my story. Not my place. Just,' I sighed, 'any man who wants to marry Ruqqayyah will have to claim her, publicly and without reservations, and commit to building a family with her, however messy that might get.'

I saw his disconcertion increase and decided, *Forget it!* I drop all façade of ignorance and give my brother a stern look. 'Truthfully, I don't think she's ready for marriage. She just started considering the idea seriously very recently. I think she needs to sit with it for a few months. To gain clarity on what she wants. And then, maybe. Do you understand?'

He nods. *Abo oro la n so fun omoluabi*. The discerning man needs only pertinent facts. He turns back to the door, his grin wide, bashful, and altogether too cute for a man his age.

'*Boda m*i,' I stop him again, just as he twists the knob. 'When the time is right, Jummai's gift will be indispensable.'

'What?!'

I wave off his confused face and shoo him out, laughing with joyful abandon as I locked the door and went to take that much delayed bath. So, this is what joy, hope and anticipation – rolled together into one huge emotional high – feels like.

Rekiya

'Eid ul-Adha was even more bittersweet than 'Eid al-Fitr had been.

I spent the first day of 'Eid in Lagos with Tunde Gbadamosi and his family and had a surprisingly nice enough time of it. The family, initially of five, along with their staff of domestic workers, live in a sprawling mansion in Lekki, a ginormous edifice with towering fences that kept the outside world away. Arriving late on the day before the 'Eid, I did not appreciate the beauty of the place until after fajr the next morning. Housed in one of the guestrooms downstairs, I had a leisurely tour of the grounds that got me out of the way of the staff, who were trying to go about their chores unobtrusively. I spent over an hour just walking through the compound. I absently registered the chirping of the birds, the fleeting dance of the butterflies and the spectra of colors in the flora as day bloomed over the inspiring canvas of nature.

It was a bit disconcerting to become an aunt, so suddenly, at this juncture in my life. And to bond quite effortlessly with a nephew whose existence had never registered in my consciousness before now. Wale Gbadamosi was Tunde's youngest child, at twenty-one years of age, and was the only one still at home, such as it were. Home for 'Eid from the US where he is a final year student at a North Carolina University, he's rapidly becoming the highlight of my trip. He had jokingly informed me that, '*ileya* is not the same unless you are in Naija o. And getting to meet my other Aunt is simply an awesome bonus!' Even the initial cautious greeting between his parents and I upon my arrival yesterday had not fazed him. He had been at ease with 'meeting his long-lost aunt after all this time', and in a short while, his relaxed attitude had set the tone for the evening.

I understood his proclamation about the 'Eid the next day. My brother and his family celebrated the occasion with a zest that, surely, should have waned over the years. We drove all the way to the National Stadium to join thousands of other gaily dressed and joyously-mood Lagosians for the prayers. Apparently, my brother – as had been our father before him – was an important member of the national board, or whatever, of the Ansar-ud-Deen society of Nigeria. Even I, with my unconventional upbringing had heard of the group, usually in the context of their resistance to the British legacy of forced conversion of the Muslim child to Christianity before enrolment in school. They had pioneered establishment of Muslim schools in southwest Nigeria. Their activities were a lot less visible and circumspect these days, but they undeniably still held a clout in the Yoruba-majority states.

Looking at the mass of people, all festive in their attires and their attitude on that expansive land of a National monument, I concluded that it was worth it. Even having to leave so early and driving the considerable distance to another part of the state, surely bypassing many other praying grounds in the process, was worth it. There is undeniably a feeling of belonging from praying in such a large, joyful congregation. It was the *Ileya* I have always heard, but never been part, of.

When we returned to the house, Tunde's wife bustled about, supervising the catering staff hired for the day to supplement her regular workers, while her husband and I watched the news channel on a loop. Wale kept us company, scrolling through his phone, and asking me details of my life and volunteering that of his entire family.

It was a surprisingly restful morning.

Soon, the first batch of meat was ready, and we had an unorthodox breakfast of fried meat and whatever caught your fancy from the array of food served buffet style. I went with pancakes and orange juice to accompany my meat, laughing with astonishment as Wale packed away an impossible amount of food, much to his mother's consternation.

My brother's wife was nice enough, reserved and a bit awkward around me, which I suppose was to be expected, all things considered. She did go out of her way to be a gracious hostess, asking multiple times if I was okay, if I needed anything. Her daughters, both in their late twenties and married, paid quick visits to the house with their spouses in the early evening. I later find that this had been for my benefit, and that they usually come on the second day but wanted to meet me since I was leaving the next morning. The first daughter had a little girl of her own, a shy and adorably cute three-year-old who refused to greet me, and the second had been married just a few weeks when our father -their grandfather - died. We didn't quite hit off as with Wale, but everyone was trying.

They all had been perfectly welcoming, but I could not help but breathe a sigh of relief as I drove away early the next morning. There was only so much family togetherness I could handle! Hopefully, over time, as I meet them in more manageable chunks, it'll get easier. Apparently, they all had reasons to come to Abuja several times a year, so we had promised to keep in touch, exchanging numbers and what not.

Enjoying the pleasantly light traffic, I could finally admit to myself that the trip had gone better than I dared hope for. Even the ambush by Tunde Gbadamosi that I was convinced was behind this sudden quest for sibling bonding never came. Rather, other than a curiosity over what my life was like growing up as an only child, we did not talk about the past at all.

There was that one awkward moment when Wale let it slip that his grandmother had been less than happy about my being invited, refusing to come to her son's for 'Eid as was her custom, until the next day – when I would be gone – but even that didn't bother me. I was okay with building a family of my own from scratch, made up of people who want me, those who want to be in my life and vice versa. If that did not include my late father's wife, for whom he abandoned my mother and I, it was no hair off my back!

I arrived at Brother 'Isa and Jummai's farmhouse just minutes after Zee and her brood. Prof. Sanusi's move to the farm evidently meant it had become the de-facto venue for family gatherings, a fact that made me hesitate over the invite. But Z was a pro at disregarding my excuses and thrusting me into the midst of her family, so, here we are.

Like bygone Sanusi family gathering in my experience, this one, too, was relaxed, segregated, and had only grown louder with the addition of almost a dozen kids. The men gathered at Prof.'s place – he had moved into one of the visitors' chalets on the farm, saying he preferred a place of his own. It is just a few minutes-walk from the five bedroom home his son's family occupies, which was where the women held fort.

Jummai's home was lovely; spacious and airy, with an abundance of light from the huge windows that had only the sheerest lace for curtains. In this expanse of land that was their farm, even the fence that demarcated the house yard from the rest of the farm was superfluous. There were no peeping toms or neighbors to be concerned about. And the house radiated that kind of joyful warmth that comes only to those who take for granted that no one is watching.

The kids, of course, had a blast running between both gatherings, outdoor activities and innocent frolicking must have been just an additional benefit.

The day passed uneventfully. We nibbled on 'Eid meat, chatted about how we'd spent our respective first day of 'Eid and other insignificant nothings, monitored the staff and ensured food was sent to the men at somewhat regular intervals. The family received the few visitors that braved the distance to the farm, we settled quibbles between the kids, all the while breaking up at the appointed times for *salaah*.

By *maghrib*, I had had enough. Enough of 'Eid, and meat, and family, and people.

I sat down on the praying mat, watching as the other women finished their *nawaafil* and *duas* and left, pondering the sad realization that this year was my first family 'Eid celebration.

Ever.

As a child, I never knew why my father was never around. I'm not even sure if I noticed those particular absences as peculiar until much later. And my mother, with her customary indifference to anything once he wasn't around, never got into the celebration beyond the obligatory ram that was slaughtered and invariably eaten by her friends in a party-like atmosphere. The few times I attended the 'Eid *salaah* had been in the company of the domestic staff and I stopped doing even that after my mother re-married. In her new Christian household, 'Eid would have been yet another reminder of how I did not belong.

So, today, though I enjoyed this 'Eid with the Gbadamosis and the Sanusis, I was essentially alone. Yet again questioning where I fit into the dynamics of these families that I called mine – but weren't.

'There you are,' Juwayriyyah stepped into the room. 'Mama J wants to know if you want dinner. She's sending some to the men.'

I grimace as I get up, grasping gratefully at the hand she extends to me. 'No, please. I don't think I should eat anything for at least three days,' I say as we move to join the others in the living room. I suppose I can't hide out here forever, anyway.

'Aunty Rekiya,' she begins, biting her lower lip in indecision before finally rushing out her words in a theatrical whisper. 'Did you really reject that American man because he already had a wife? I thought he was a Muslim, *shebi* he can marry more than one wife?'

I smile at Brother 'Isa and Tope's daughter, a wave of emotion washing over me. In the months since we returned from our inadvertent joint Umrah, I had come to care for the teenager a lot. She was a perfect mix of all the people who made and raised her -her parents, Mummy, and even Jummai.

'Sweetheart, marriage is a complex contact. I didn't think either Zeke or myself was in a good place to enter into such a life-altering arrangement at that point.'

She cocks her head to a side like her father was wont to. 'So, you didn't love him?' she asks.

I gasp in mock outrage. 'And what do you know about love, Missy?!'

'I know enough,' she sniffs and turns up her nose, and we both burst out into laughter.

The other women look at us in enquiry as we make our entrance into the living room. I place a hand on her shoulder before she could turn away. 'I think love is a verb, something you do. A choice. And choosing to love a man you know cannot fulfill your needs just so you can be in a relationship is asking for misery. And I've had enough of that to last me a lifetime.'

I see the confusion swirling behind her eyes, another question brewing, but hold her off with a smile. 'You'll understand someday,' I promise her, turning to join the company and endure a few more hours of human interaction.

Being alone is such an underrated experience!

*

'It sounds like it was a good 'Eid.' Her inflection goes up at the end, and I hear the question.

'Yes, it was.' I admit. I knew, even then, that I would not get away with that prevarication.

'Yet you didn't have a good 'Eid.' This time, it wasn't a question.

'I did. It was just… I did. I just…' I sigh. Inhaled. Exhaled. Aimed for clarity. 'It was a good celebration. And I did have a good time. I met my brother's family and we took the first tentative steps towards building a relationship, and I'm cautiously optimistic about it. I spent time with the Sanusis and realized that while they have multiplied in the decade since I was last there, I am still as welcome within their fold as I've always been. But it also made me sad.'

I knew the next question before she asked. 'Why?'

This answer is not quite as pat. 'Emmm. I'm sad for all the 'Eids I never got to have as a child. For the family togetherness that never shaped my life experiences. I mourn the years I missed out on, even as an adult, because I had isolated myself, choosing to simply exist rather than have to deal with all that life threw at me. I despair that I would ever have what they all so blithely take for granted, a sense of rightness in the world that comes from knowing that someone, some people, think that you matter.'

The expected silence is much shorter than it used to be months ago, when we first started these sessions.

'You know what I'm about to ask you to do now, don't you?'

I smile wryly at Dr Aisha's dry sense of humor. 'Yeah, I do. You are going to ask me to re-examine all that I have just said. To deconstruct it with the objectiveness and clarity that I have gained so far. And yes, I realize that the peculiarities of my upbringing were not of my doing. That while my parents may have made mistakes, they did the best they knew how. It is however up to me to take control of my narrative from here on out, to quit letting their inadequacies define me. I am not the little girl they abandoned all those years ago, not anymore. I am a smart, educated, and independently successful woman who can choose to make her own way through life, on her terms.'

'Go on.' Her voice is carefully neutral.

'I appreciate that things that have happened to me in the past have not always been good, nor within my power. And that, as a result of that, I have sometimes made choices, including sometimes refusing to choose, that led to an unhealthy patterns of living. It is however up to me to decide where I go from now, and I choose to live. Freely and unashamed, unencumbered by regrets over the past and unlimited over fears of the future. I am more than all that happened to me. I choose to be grateful for what I have now – my Deen, my career, my life, including the families I have made. I choose to accept that Allaah's decree is always

Just, and I can only position myself to be ready for the future, whatever that is and whenever it shows up.'

'Now, how much of that do you *really* believe?' There is an unusual teasing quality to the question this time.

I am floored by it for moment, then I hear myself bellow out a peal of joyful laughter. 'Everything!'

It's true. It has taken us months. Hours of therapy over phone calls and several office visits whenever I was in Lagos. It had been a regimen of homework and assignments, recommended texts and acts of *ibaadaat*. Of building and cultivating my relationships; with Z, my mother and siblings, my brother and his family, my staff at work, even Jummai, Habeebah and the other women on our super-secret charity board. Of taking long walks and talking to perfect strangers. Learning to be open, vulnerable, flawed. Human.

I did not realize it until this moment, but I had been learning to live again.

'Thank you.' I say now, tremulously.

'No. Thank you,' she says, and the silence is a moment in glory.

'Now,' she clears her throat, and continues brusquely. 'Time to prepare for the future, if and when it shows up. What do you want from life?'

We would spend the next few months of therapy defining and re-defining the things I hope for myself, and she would push me beyond where I assumed my limits should be. Beyond passively hoping for the future, into actively living in the moment. Dr. Aisha would be there to remind me when I slip up, but never in my face or obstructing my path as I found my own way.

She would also progressively reduce my therapy hours, and we would finally overcome the professional barriers to meet up at Habeebah's instigations from time to time.

She would push me to become a mentor, even as I thought myself an inauspicious role model for women in the world of finance, and the many Muslim women who had no one to share their traumatic experiences with.

I would turn away a couple more marriage proposals, finding it easier to laugh with Z over the more preposterous of them.

In time, I would become a woman comfortable in my own skin; flaws, issues and all.

Of course, I did not know all this then. But on that fateful day, sitting on the floor of my apartment, lonely and decrying my sadness at the most memorable 'Eid I'd ever celebrated, I had turned the most important corner.

CHAPTER EIGHTEEN

Rekiya

The number was unregistered.

'Hello?'

It is a question, a prayer, a hope unarticulated, a culmination of three days in which I was *not* waiting for a call.

'AsSalaam alaykum warahmah, Rekiya.'

My stupid heart actually skips a couple of beats.

I do not want it to. I had steeled myself, insisting that the day was just another normal one. In fact, it has been a perfectly ordinary three days - I made sure of it - since Z and Prof. Sanusi left Abuja. Z had attended some tech conference and he, her mahram, had come with her.

'You are so spoilt,' I'd told her as she pouted in protest. She stuck out her tongue at me, we all fell laughing at the obvious protrusion beneath her niqab, and she and I hugged goodbye before she walked away. I was dropping them off at the airport, and Prof. had just asked her to go on and check them in while he has 'a few words with Rekiya.'

What he then said, I could never have envisaged in a million years.

And now, it is three days, during which I steadfastly refused to 'think about anything until I had something to think about', later. And I'm gaping like a fish on dry land, as though unexpectedly drowning in air.

'Wa alayka salaam warahmatullaah wabarakah.' Yes! My voice is so crisp, I could have fooled myself. Cellphones don't pick up on racing heartbeats, do they?

'So... I'm not sure why you asked me to call you. I would have preferred to take this up with your *waliyy* first.'

Oh God, has his voice always been so smooth and beckoning?

'You know my *waliyy*. You already discussed with him.' I manage to keep my voice still somewhat level.

Get a grip, Rekiya you are too old – and too damaged, remember – to be so flustered.

'Yes,' I could hear the smile in his voice. *Urgh, why did I have to know him so well?* 'But he says, given the circumstances, I should approach your brother. Tunde Gbadamosi. That you guys now have a good relationship?'

I am speechless, mentally calling myself all sort of names for dumb right now. Why didn't I use the past three days to prepare for this, at least to figure out what I would say? There was living in the moment, not letting hopes and fears for the future limit me, and there is just plain, stupid unpreparedness. I didn't even mention it to Dr Aisha for God's sake!

'Rekiya?' The higher octave of his voice alerts me to the fact that this might not have been his first time calling my name.

'Huh, what?' *Oh my God! I sound so silly.*

'Do you have any objections to me approaching your brother for your hand in marriage?' This time I swear I can hear the strain in his voice. It calms me a bit. *Maybe I am not the only one in this quicksand.*

'Em… No?' My voice seems to have all its pretentions toward crisp levelness. I cringe.

'You don't sound so sure.'

Because I am not sure what is going on! My mind is screeching.

'I meant no.' I catch myself after a beat of awkward pause. 'I have no objections to you speaking to my brother.' I clarify superfluously.

'Right. *Alhamdulillaah*,' his smile is more audible this time. 'Oh, Jummai said to tell you to expect her gift in the mail. I'm not really sure what that means but she assures me you'll understand.'

'Oh, Okay.' *I am a horrible person! I had forgotten about Jummai.*

'Wa salaam alaykum warahmatuLlaah wabarakah,' Brother 'Isa bids me, ending the call.

***

'Ruqqayyah, salaam alayki. *Ki lo n sele*?' Zaynunah's voice came across the lines, displaying her anxiety over my out of norm call to her, mid-week.

'Wa alayki salaam, Z. Nothing! I mean, it's not nothing… I don't… Your brother just asked to marry me,' I blurt.

'And what did you say?'

'I didn't… Wait,' I pull back suddenly and eye the phone in suspicion, wishing I had made a video call. *She didn't ask which brother! That sneaky, little* – 'You knew about this!'

She giggled. 'Not knew, no. Suspected. I have for a while now.'

'How long is "a while"?'

'Hmmn,' she dithered, but I could still hear her smugness. 'Not long after Zeke.'

And the hits just keep coming! 'And you didn't tell me?! What if I had married Salihu?'

'Oh, please, Ruqqayyah! As if you would ever have. Frankly, you were not in a good place then. You didn't need the hassle. Also, like I said, I didn't know anything for sure. And his situation is, well, what it is. He probably had some things to work out. You all do. Plus, it really wasn't my place.'

'Yeah.' I let that one word, and my heartfelt sigh, convey my acknowledgement of all the truth she just spewed. 'What should I do?'

Her sigh was smaller, but no less burdened. 'What did you say? To him, when he asked you?'

'Well. Technically he asked if he could speak to my brother. I guess your dad thought it was judicious that he should not be the one to act for me in this case, all things considered. Which is understandable, of course.' I clamp my mouth shut. I was in danger of rambling. And I, Rekiya Yusuf Gbadamosi, did not ramble.

'Aaaand, you said…?' she prompted me.

'I said yes! To him talking to Tunde, I mean. But now. What do I do now?'

I am not sure myself why this feels so different. I had received a handful of proposals in the past year – and what is with that, anyway? It was as if donning a wardrobe of abaya and scarf somehow sent out a signal decode-able only to marriage minded men. Of these, only two had made it through whatever stringent measures Prof Sanusi applied. I had declined Salihu, the rising, young Hausa politician. Our first meeting had been a disaster. He constantly he spoke over me as we shared a very public lunch under the watchful gaze of about half a dozen of his 'most trusted men'. And even during that close call with Zeke, I had not felt this baffling mix of anxiety and… something I cannot name.

This might be *it. But, oh, God, what if my it doesn't work out?!*

'You pray.' Z's voice yanks me out of the spiral and thank God for that. Her no-nonsense tone grounds me a bit. 'Make your *istikhara* and trust that Allaah will not steer you wrong. Then make a list of questions, concerns or any issues you may have going forward. The thing that most matter to you. You will need to talk to him, to address your list and assess him, so to speak. I'm sure there are a lot of issues you both need to work out. And if you need it, we – my family - are here to answer any more questions. Of course, we're biased because we love him. But don't forget we love you, too.'

'Speak for yourself,' I grumbled in discomfort. 'Jummai probably hates me right now!'

She is silent for a beat. 'I mean, well, probably. But that's not personal. I would hate you, too. Maybe. But as far as co-wives go, Jummai is probably one of the best a woman could get. And she's always been vocal in her acceptance of polygamy, although I expect the actuality might just now be hitting rather close to home. I think, though, if you choose to go ahead with it, you will all find a way to make it work as painlessly as possible.'

'She did say to expect a gift in the mail. Do you think-?'

'Yes, I do. That is her, letting you know that she doesn't hate you. Remember that conversation we had in your car. Just… Give her time.'

'Okay.' I look around office, still dazed, arranging the stack of papers on my desk on autopilot. There is no way I am doing any more work today, anyway. 'I have to go. Talk to you on Saturday?'

We ring off and I prepare to take off at an uncharacteristically early hour that is bound to have the entire office in a tizzy.

Whatever, I had a private freaking out to do. Oh, and istikhara!

*

'AsSalaam alayk.'

This time, my voice was flinty hard. I know exactly who was calling - I had saved his number the last time.

'Wa alaykissalaam warahmah,' he sighed. 'You are angry.'

Well, duh! 'How could you? What were you all thinking?'

'Rekiya, I…,' he paused, probably searching for the words to explain this gaffe. 'My dad brought it up. He convinced your brother, after that phone call to you, that we should make the *nikkah* official there and then.'

My incredulity grew. 'The phone call in which if he asked me whether I had any objections to your suit? That was all I was consenting to. Your suit! Not the actual marriage!' My voice had risen now, never mind that I'd already had this screaming match with Tunde Gbadamosi when he called to inform me that he had 'married you off.' *Oh, the gall!*

'I suspected as much,' he begins.

'Then why didn't you stop it?' I interrupt, unwilling to let him display belated concern for my wishes now, after the fact. 'Why would you go ahead with such a scheme knowing I couldn't have meant to be married to you yet, if ever? I mean I'm just beginning the wrap my head around the thoughts that you want to marry me. I thought you always saw me as Zaynunah's slightly pitiful friend.'

His words, when they came, were without the slightly conciliatory notes they had held until now. And his stern tone had me picturing him in his protective big brother mode – God knows I've seen him in such a mode plenty times over the years.

'You are not, in any way, pitiful. I don't know why you'd say that. And I did see you as an extension of my sister for several years – after all, you were all of thirteen or fourteen the first time we met you. But then you came back after Mummy died and you were a different Rekiya, all grown up and a successful boss lady. Although it wasn't until that Umrah before the thought of a different relationship occurred to me. I don't know why, but there was something about you on that trip, it called out to me. And don't think I didn't try to fight it. I did. I even thought I had won the fight and was prepared to leave you alone. Then, Zeke... It was harrowing watching everyone think that your marriage to Zeke was inevitable. It forced me to acknowledge how I felt about you, and that I did not want to lose my chance with you.'

'How do you feel about me?' I whisper.

He chuckles. 'And this is why I didn't try too hard to stop the nikkah. I know we have a lot to talk about, things to figure out. Being legally married in the shariah means we can take our time doing that, with as much honesty as we choose, without the restrictions of a *ghair-mahram* relationship.'

Unwilling to let him side-step my question so easily, I pull a Mummy, and wait him out.

'Fine!' He caves quite easily. 'I care about you a great deal. Obviously, I have for a long time, as you are an honorary member of my family. But there has been a more personal component to it in recent times, and I would love to share my life with you, as my wife. And that is all you are getting out of me for now.'

It is quite a lot more than I expected.

'Hmmmn,' I scoff, not quite willing to be mollified just yet. 'So, how will this work? We try getting to know each other better, like a halaal boyfriend-girlfriend thingy until we decide? Because, let me tell you – if I am to marry you, I would want a proper nikkah; with papers, witnesses and a *walimah* with all the fanfare.'

'You deserve no less,' he concedes. 'And, well, yes. I guess for lack of a better way to put it, that is kind of the relationship we can have until *you* decide.'

I ignore his inflection. 'But what if it doesn't work? You would just pronounce a verbal talaq and no one would be any wiser? I hope you did not tell anybody yet. God, everything would be so awkward. And your family! Your family has been the only family I have, for a long time.'

I always come back here. If a marriage between us doesn't materialize, or breaks down, I could lose the Sanusi family. That singular anxiety had taken over my mind that I haven't had mental energy to devote to evaluating the proposal on its own merit.

'Whatever happens, you will always be part of our family. Zaynunah wouldn't have it any other way. But don't worry,' he assures me, 'it's going to work out. You are my wife. You just need time accepting it.'

Infuriating male.

*

'So, are you any clearer on your marriage?' Dr Aisha asked.

Our phone sessions have become fortnightly now, and I haven't gone to see her in well over three months. But of course, we're talking 'Isa and his infernal marriage proposal – I refuse to acknowledge that sham of a nikkah! In the two weeks since the whole thing erupted, it was all I could fret about.

'No.' I sigh. 'I have been handling the anxiety, though, and I think that's getting better. Every time I start thinking about it, my mind goes immediately to what would happen if I messed this up, reminding me that I stood the chance of losing a husband, a marriage, and my family in one fell swoop. When I get there, to that place, I remind myself of the facts. That marriage to a good man who cares about me is a good thing, not something bad. That marriage is hard work for everyone, not just for someone with issues like mine. That I have been working on said issues and am doing better. I shouldn't let that stand in the way of my future. That whatever happens, the people who love me will be there for me.'

'Masha Allaah, that sounds like you have been coping quite well,' she says. 'Is it helping? With the anxiety a bit more manageable,' – she would know because our last session two weeks ago had been in those early days of swirling emotions – 'do you feel more confident of making a decision?'

'I don't know. I have made the lists and we talk on the phone almost every day. And I haven't really found any cons from his side but-' I falter.

A few seconds of silence pass before she prompts me. 'But?'

'I don't even know if I want to marry him!' I finally wail. 'What if I just want the idea of him? He's a good man who takes care of his people. And he has this amazing family that have saved my sanity more than once. But is that enough a reason to marry him? Am I deceiving him?

And him, too, what does he really know about me? I mean, yeah, he's known me since I was a girl, has some idea about my parents, but he doesn't know me. Not really. Not the scars that teenage me hid nor the ugliness that has shaped the adult woman I am now. Can he handle all of that? Do I want to expose myself enough to allow him to?' I finish on a deep inhale. That felt surprisingly good to get off my chest.

I had not been able to say that aloud in two weeks, not even to myself, so scared was I of messing up. Not that I had anyone to talk to about it, anyway. Z was trying so valiantly to thread the fine line between her own giddiness, over the thought of her brother marrying her best friend, and trying to stand back supportively while I made the decision that was right for me.

'Why not take it one step at a time?' Dr. Aisha's voice drags me back to the present. 'First, you need to decide if you want to be married to him, aside from his family. Do you want him, the man? You need to remember that people get married for all sorts of reasons, Rekiya, and no one has any rights to question the validity of your motives. Except you. If you decide to remain married to him, you can tell him what you want on your own timeline. Obviously, some things I'll advice you to disclose upfront, in view of your past PTSD from the assault and how that may affect your intimate relationship. But, ultimately, that's up to you.'

'That sounds reasonable, I suppose.' I muse. 'Thank you. We'll see how that goes.'

'Right. So,' she continues. 'Any dreams lately?'

I haven't had any in over half a year. No symptoms, either, after the panic attack that ousted the flaws in my plans to marry Zeke. As we go through the motions of examining my lack of symptoms of psychological distress, my relationships, my mental wellbeing and my internal dialogue, I acknowledge the fact that my time with this woman is limited. While I wasn't looking, she has seen me to a safe place where, though not cured, I am no longer "suffering from" anything.

I still have my issues, probably always will. But I know what they are now, can recognize them when they act up, and I have learnt to deal with them.

I am finally free to live my life, issues and all.

*

'Aunty Rekiya!' Juwairiyah hurtled herself at me, then pulled back and peered into my face. 'I can still call you that, can't I?

I am puzzled. 'Of course, you can! Why wouldn't you?'

'Well, Daddy said you guys got married so I wasn't sure if you would want to be called something else, like Mama J. Maybe Mama R?' She wrinkled her nose theatrically, conveying her distaste for the idea.

'Did he now?' I murmur, shooting a glare at her errant 'Daddy', I step back to admit them into my apartment. 'Never mind all that. I will always be your "Aunty Rekiya".'

'Don't be too angry with him,' she says, walking around the room, curious eyes probably taking in the rather few personal touches in the stark space. 'I know it's all secret till you decide if you want to keep him or not. I think he only told me, and that when we were already on the plane to Abuja, so I would not think you and he were dating. As if!'

I smile at her retreating back, then turn to face her father.

'AsSalaam alaykum,' I mutter, inexplicably shy.

'Wa alayki salaam warahmah.' His gaze is disconcertingly direct. Appreciative. 'You look beautiful.'

If I wasn't black, I reckon I would have blushed, like the simpering miss I wasn't. I look away, trying to find something to say. I had requested this meeting to gauge if I was physically attracted to him and now that he is here, I couldn't even look him in the eye or accept a simple complement. I never appreciated how liberating his lowered gazes were until now.

'Thank you,' was all I could muster. I fidget with my abaya scarf.

'Okay, I get that you guys are newly-wed and everything,' the teenage girl broke into the moment, compounding the already embarrassing encounter. 'But this was supposed to be my university trip. I don't even mind that Daddy hijacked it to come see you. But I refuse to spend the entire weekend watching you both making googly eyes at each other. Yuck! Get it together people!'

From the mouth of babes!

Once we all got over that initial uncomfortable beginning, the weekend passed in relative ease. Juwairiyyah insisted I tag along for her 'college tour'. It was her father's compromise to her insistence to moving away – that they'd both tour the school before a final decision was made. Going by how excited the girl was, and how indulgent I've seen her father, I knew her chances of being back in the capital next year was pretty high.

We did the few tourist spots. The teenager was shocked to find I had grown up here – for the most part – and I had been back almost three years, but I hadn't been to most of the places she pulled up on her phone. Not having an appropriate response to her bafflement, I had shrugged it away. How does one explain my life over the last few years?

We went on a date, too, 'Isa and I, leaving his daughter to the delight of room service and cable TV in their hotel suite. It turned out to be a greatly successful night, equal parts romance and fun, much more than I expected.

I felt I was suddenly privy to a different facet of this man I thought I had known so well. He was smooth and sophisticated, considerate and gentlemanly, the quintessential perfect date. At least, as perfect a date as an African Muslim man in full beard and native dress could appear, only to his Nigerian Muslim Wife-he-still-has-to-woo.

He was thoughtful and attentive, flirty but straightforward, and the hours flew by unnoticed while we sat in that small but classy halaal food and no-alcohol restaurant that I would never have stumbled upon even if I lived in Abuja till I was a hundred years old.

The conversation was effortless. We had more in common than I'd have ever guessed and I had my private confirmation of physical attraction over multiple meeting of gazes, accidental touching of hands and the hordes of butterflies that refused to quit flapping about in my belly.

The next day, once I knew their plane would be in the air and his phone turned off, I send him Dr. Aisha's number.

*

'AsSalaam alaykum,' I answer the phone on its first ring. 'I wasn't sure you would call.' It had been three agonizing days since I sent him the number, two endless ones since she confirmed what was okay to tell him. *Everything.*

'Wa alakissalaam warahmah,' his voice, unsurprisingly and unusually serious, reflects my tentativeness. 'I was always going to call. I just wanted to take time and think about everything I was told. It deserved due consideration.'

'So…?' I prompt.

'So, I spoke to your doctor. First, I'm humbled that you shared your story with me. You didn't have to. Second, I'm sorry that you've had to go through all of that. But I'm glad you are getting the help you need. Finally, I hope this means you have decided to stay married to me. And I promise to try my hardest to be the man you need – loving you, standing by you, supporting you and protecting you – as you navigate your way through life's journey.'

I let out the breath I wasn't even aware I was holding. Slowly. 'You still want to marry me?'

'Well, yes. Of course, I want to remain married to you.' He sounds so genuinely baffled that I could have possibly thought anything else. 'Rekiya, what I learnt has only made me care for you even more, not less.'

'But… I might not… I don't know yet if intimacy will be a problem for me.' I am not sure if my mumbling is a warning to him, or myself.

'And if it is, darling, we will face it together,' he reassures me gently. 'As long as we are open and honest with each other, and willing to put in the work, we can face any problems that arises.'

I feel myself tumble down the cliff whose edge I had clung so tenuously to in the past weeks. The doubts that held me up were suddenly giving way under the weight of his reassuring care. I grasp at what flimsy tendrils I could still reach.

'I… I am not a particularly domestic or submissive woman. And I have a career, a big job. Plus, I live here, and you are there. What kind of marriage can we possibly have?'

He laughs, loud and exuberant, as if he already knows what and why I am fighting so hard. 'Your career is one of the things I most admire you for, Rekiya. You forget I had one, too, once. And even though I chose to get off that tract relatively early, I know how phenomenal you must be to get to where you are now, being a young woman your age.

And I would never ask you to give it up. I mean, I hope we would make major decisions together, or at least, we'd consider the effects on our life together when you make career decisions, but what direction you chose to go with it is up to you.'

I wait, pondering.

'Now let me see…' he continues in an altogether too jovial a tone. 'Yes, domestic and submissive. I don't even… You know my mother and sister, probably a lot more than you know me. And while I suppose they are domestic enough, no one could ever have called them submissive. And you met both my wives, I am sure you will agree that they do not possess a submissive bone between them. Yes, Tope did housework enough, and I guess we'll never know if she would have kept it up. But Jummai's idea of domestic is to direct an army of domestic staff. Rekiya, with the women in my life so far, I don't think I'd know what to do with a submissive, domestic wife!'

'What about kids?'

'What about them?' For the first time, I hear uncertainty in his question.

'I don't know… I'm not sure if I'll ever be ready for that.'

There is a long silence. 'Children are the expected conclusion of an intimate relationship. For people like us, at least. But I have lived long enough to know that life is a lot more varied than we give it credit for. With your history, it's understandable that you harbour some… hesitation about having kids. I hope that changes, someday. I would love to have children with you. But I have four beautiful ones already. We can wait until you are ready.'

'What if I'm never ready?' I push.

'Then it was never meant to be. We are Muslims, Rekiya. We believe in Qadar. So, if Allaah decrees kids for us, together, we'll have them. If not, then we don't.' There is a small chuckle with his next words. 'It's not a deal breaker, if that's what you are asking.'

It is my turn to be silent. I consciously let go of the tendrils I had been clinging to, letting myself take the final steps toward the life I had been too afraid to want. 'Well, I suppose we can do a long distance-and-commute thing until we figure out something else. It's not like I have to be in Abuja.'

'Only somewhere in West Africa,' he completes, and we share a low, infinitely intimate laugh. That umrah trip seems like yesterday and another lifetime ago, all at once, one more of time's vagaries.

Then I hear, transmitted over the phone waves, a sound that would be called a gasp, normally. But in such a manly man, I decide it must have been a surprised, sharp suction of inhaled air.

'Do you mean…? Are you saying…? You will marry me?'

'Abu J, you have spent the past few weeks insisting that we are already married,' I tease. 'But yes, I do. I am. I will. Here, in Abuja. At the National Mosque, I think. I'll leave the official arrangements to you. But not earlier than three weeks from this Friday, please.'

'Thank you.' His words are solemn, his voice beloved, a promise.

We end the call, rather abruptly, on that note. I think we both needed to absorb the magnitude of what just happened. I wait for the anxiety, the fear. I catalogue my emotions - poking them for indication that something might be not as it ought.

What I find is joy. Gratitude. Excitement.

I am ready.

Alhamdulillaah.

'You look beautiful.'

Zu is leaning over me as I sit in front of my dresser. We are both perusing the handiwork of the make-up artist who had finally permitted me to look into the mirror.

I smile in agreement and turned to the University of Abuja student who had just achieved the miraculous transformation. When my assistant assured me that she was the best kept secret in Abuja fashionable society currently, I had, admittedly, been skeptical. Especially when I met the plain-faced, Ankara-and-Pashmina clad young woman. But I am a convert now. She had somehow spent one hour applying make-up that was barely visible, yet made me look like a more radiant, effortlessly beautiful and totally natural looking version of me.

'Thank you.' I say to her, making a mental note to add a generous tip to her bill.

'Wow, Aunty Rekiya. You look gorgeous!' Juwairiyyah blew into my bedroom, all good cheer and no boundaries. Khawlah was at her heels, as always. 'Do you have a business card or something?' she asks the woman who was heading out of the room. 'I will be in Abuja next year and might need your services.'

'And why, dear niece, would you need a make-up artist, hmmn? Her real aunt asked. 'Or have you decided to join us munaqabahs?'

I chuckle at the girl's theatrical shudder of horror. 'Ju, will you please show Rabia to the food so she can eat before she leaves?'

'No problem,' she jumps at the save. 'Actually, that's why I came to get you. Blessing says people are about to leave so, you should come say goodbye.'

'Alright. Tell her I'll be out soon.' I turn and take another look at myself, absently spritzing the perfume I had bought especially for tonight.

I look good, I decide. I had chosen an ivory silk gown with classy flowing lines that fit my figure, molding but not clinging to my curves. It had sheer three-quarters lace sleeves and the hem fell just above my ankles. Paired with a silver strappy sandals that had heels almost as impractically steep as its price, seeing as I might never wear it again, and some tasteful white gold accessories, I look the part.

'You make a lovely bride.'

This time, it is my mother's face looming beside mine in the mirror. Even now, at her age, and on my wedding day when I am looking my best, my mother's beauty is still… overpowering.

I turn away from the mirror. 'Thank you, Ma.'

'I like him,' she tells me, hesitant. 'Isa had gone to see her yesterday, spending well over an hour at her place. Neither of them has told me what transpired during the visit.

She holds out her arms now. 'I hope you will be especially happy,' she whispers into my ears, squeezes me tightly once more, and steps back.

It is the first hug I received from my mother in recent memory, short but freely given. It is… nice.

I spy Mary, my half-sister standing just inside the door with Z. We have gotten to know each other somewhat over the past year, developing an uncomplicated friendship untainted by the baggage of the barely overlapping years of our childhoods.

I hug her, longer and a lot less loaded with past issues, she teases me and wishes me well. Then we all head back to the living room. It is time to thank, and bid farewell to, the women who had come to celebrate my nuptials.

It is exactly the sixth Friday from that fateful telephone call. The day had started blessedly quiet, with only Z and I in my apartment. As my self-appointed matron of honour, she had arrived the weekend before and driven Blessing, me crazy going over the plans for the wedding. She had been a worse bridezilla than me, insisting we shop for a mountain of things I did not even know I needed. Like new placemats and a slew of kitchen utensils, lingerie and a man's bathrobe. And fretting over minute details I was more than happy to leave to Blessing's discretion - she is an extremely capable assistant.

Considering the simplicity of the event, private ceremony at the mosque followed by small segregated luncheons/receptions, I couldn't understand how Z found so many things to fuss about. Tunde, or more specifically the people he hired, was in charge of the male celebration; a 3pm to 6pm late luncheon at the halaal restaurant where 'Isa and I had our first date.

The women – my office staff and the wives of male staffers, some wives of Tunde's and 'Isa's associates who were brave enough to attend the wedding celebration for a woman they hadn't met, and the women I met through Habeebah Ayoade and her Super-secret charity work – got to be hosted to an informal, catered buffet in my apartment between 4pm and 8pm.

It had all seemed painless enough a plan, until Zaynunah Sanusi blew into town.

This morning, fortunately, the only thing on her agenda had been a bridal package spa – manicure, pedicure, massage and henna – one my assistant said she'd insisted on paying for. I endured three hours of more pampering than I'd ever had in my life, then we rushed to the National mosque for Jum'ah, arriving just at the nick of time for the *khutbah* to commence.

After the prayer, we crowded into the Chief Imam's office for the Nikkah ceremony – me, Z, 'Isa and their Dad, and Tunde Gbadamosi. It was a short service, I floated through most of it. But as I signed my name beside his on the marriage register, I felt it rather keenly when 'Isa's hand grasped mine. I put the pen down, letting him pull me to the sides. The others had to sign, anyway, my mahram and our witnesses.

He caught both my hands in his.

'How are you feeling? Any regrets?' his voice was a low murmur. With our entwined hand and his forehead resting lightly against mine, we were wrapped in a cocoon of our own.

'No. No regrets,' I tell him, our gazes clinging to each other's. 'I'm feeling…lucky. A lot of things have happened to me and, as you are aware, not all of them have been good. But they brought me here, to being this woman – the one you chose to marry. And I just keep thinking it must be a sign of better things to come, bi ithniLlaah.'

He grinned, wide and so happily. 'Insha Allaah. But if anyone is lucky here, it's me. I can't imagine that you agreed to marry me. You are so-'

Of course, my bridezilla of honour chose that moment to interrupt and drag me away. We had a lot to do before the guests start showing up apparently. Shrugging helplessly and throwing a rueful smile his way, I allowed myself to be pulled away again. Privately pondering the irony that even at his third marriage, and with my plans for a very low-key celebration, the wedding was still more of a hassle for the bride than the groom.

Almost six hours and two change of clothes later, I am close to wishing I was a guest, too, so I could escape with the women taking their leave from my apartment. I smiled, thanked them, *"aameen"*ed to their *du'as*, and heaved a sigh of relief as the last of them finally left.

'So, there's three portions of food in the fridge,' Z informs me as she emerges from the kitchen following her third, hopefully final, check of the place. 'In case you and your husband are hungry. The rest have been taken away for distribution to the poor, as requested. Don't forget the cleaning people are coming at noon tomorrow. We'll go now and send your groom up. They just texted that they are downstairs. Girls, let's go!'

My new stepdaughter and niece-by-marriage were finally beginning to flag. They had appointed themselves hostesses and had spent the afternoon getting in the way of the wait staff with their helpfulness. But they had been so excited that I hadn't the heart to tell them to leave the job to the professionals.

Juwairiyya, resplendent in the sky-blue head abaya Z made her to match with her cousin's, hugged me for the millionth time that day.

'Aunty Rekiya, welcome to the family. Again. I know you and my daddy, and Mama J, will be very happy. Insha Allaah.'

Awww, I love this girl.

'Insha Allaah. And thank you for everything you did today. It would not have been the same without you. You too, Khawlah,' I turned to Zee's daughter. She was still awkward and shy around me and she mumbled a '*BarakaLlaahu feeki*' just as her mum swept me into the black swaddles of her own abaya.

She repeated the du'a for marriage, again, and held me close, whispering into my ears. 'Be happy, Rekiya. You deserve it. I love you.'

I hear the tears in her voice. And pull back to see the short tracks they make running into the lower layer of her niqab. I smile through the realization that Z's tears, from our first meeting, have brought me all of the greatest loves of my life. Her. Her mother. Her family. Her brother. Me.

'Me too,' was all I say.

I was still standing there when 'Isa comes up. He takes in the tears flowing down my face, happily and unashamedly for the first time in my life, and he holds me, just as his sister had done. For a long time, we stand there, me in the circle of his arms. Unhurried, we do not say a word.

I sigh, happy. His embrace is welcoming and non-constraining. His lips move against my ears, unfamiliar, barely audible. Erotic.

'You are so special.'

*

Today is the first day of the rest of my life.

And yes, I realize how cliché that thought sounds, even in my head, but I can't help it. That is how I feel.

In the four months since my marriage, I have often felt like I was living in a limbo. Like the explosion of joy that characterizes my life was a manifestation of the un-realness of it all.

'Isa and I continue to build our relationship. He came to Abuja for a long weekend twice a month, and I had been to Ibadan once to meet Jummai and the kids.

It hadn't been a particularly painful meeting. Jummai went out of her way to be welcoming, and her kids were either too young or too sheltered from the possible implications of polygamy to be bothered. I stayed in the one of the guest chalets, unconcerned, even though 'Isa was very profuse with his apology, very earnest in his plans to build me a house on the farm.

It hadn't seemed worth the expenses to me, seeing I was in Abuja and would only be there for the occasional flying visits. But then, in an unexpected turn of events, the company had a sensitive opening in the Lagos office. Zeke had refused to renew his contract for the job, opting to take a pay cut and return to the New York office to work things out with his estranged wife.

With the Abuja office thriving, they had asked me to take over in Lagos. It would mean a significant pay rise because even though my job title is unchanged, my responsibilities have grown. I also negotiated a remote working clause for the two days every fortnight when I am supposed to be covering the Abuja office. Meaning I could live in Lagos and take a long weekend every other weekend to be with my family in Ibadan.

Hence why I felt like my life was finally beginning anew.

'You okay?'

I turn a quizzing glance toward the source of the question that broke into my ruminations.

Joseph, my stepbrother from my mum, was driving me to the airport on this, my final trip out of Abuja. Our new relationship is not as effortless as the one I had with Mary. We were both too old, too busy with our careers – he is twenty-five, with a soul sucking marketing job at one of the new generation banks in the country – and too used to the lifetime of apathy that characterized our relationship, to make much of an effort.

Still, we met up for the occasional lunches, had spirited debates about how business and finance is done in Nigeria, and internationally. So, when I accepted this move, I offered him my car.

'Why wouldn't I be?' I ask him now.

'Well,' he hedged. 'You seem to be making an awful lot of life-altering decisions in the past few months. I wonder…'

When he doesn't continue, I prompt him. 'What?'

He regards me steadily for a few seconds before returning his regard to the road. 'Just last year, you were this aloof older stepsister I barely remember who was too focused on her career for anything else. Then, all of a sudden, you are turning religious, getting married, moving cities. And you are nice! Nicer than I ever thought. So, I wonder… You are okay, right? You didn't find out you're dying or anything like that?'

I smile wryly, touched by his badly worded concern, rueful over his assessment of my previous self.

'No, I am not dying,' I assure him. 'Not that I am aware of anyway. And before. It wasn't all career focus, you know.'

'Yeah, I know.' He answers, his voice older than his years. 'It hardly ever is.'

We finish the rest of the trip in silence and are soon at the car park of the airport. It is an ordinary June afternoon in Abuja, not too hot, with clear skies hanging far above the earth. I spy Wale, my nephew, waiting for me close to the domestic terminal entrance. His father must have sent him with a peace offering, the traitor. We were all supposed to be taking this flight together, that was why 'Isa did not come to Abuja to make the trip with me. But my brother had pulled out late last night, claiming his business in Abuja was going to require a few more days. Rather than waiting, I am flying solo, opting to face the music when my husband finds out, rather than live through the delay. I have to report in the Lagos office for a few days before heading to Ibadan for the *Walima*h the Sanusis have planned for us next weekend.

There is an awkward moment after my bags are loaded on the trolley. My other brother and I decide pause, unsure of the protocol for saying farewell to the sibling you have only started getting to know.

I hug him lightly. 'Thank you. Goodbye.'

'No, thank you,' he smiles, gesturing at the car. 'All the best in your new life. And sis? Don't be a stranger.'

I laughed my promise as I walk towards my nephew, the terminal and my future. My steps are brisk, my heart is light.

Today *is* the first day of the rest of my life.

EPILOGUE

It is incongruous how innocuous the most devastating days of one's life starts.

An ordinary weekend day, the dawn had risen as innocently as ever, hours after my day began, bringing with it the bustle that is universal to mothers of multiple school-aged children anywhere. Presumably, the sun was shining, but one hardly notices such details anymore, we take even that singular source of light for granted in the never-ending hamster-trek that is our life.

I had driven Khawlah to Noora, where she had been a weekly boarder since the beginning of the school year. It had been our compromise, she got to go to a traditional school that offered her the art lessons and peer interaction she 'needs for an all-round psychosocial development' – her words. Her father got her on the weekends to ensure she was still keeping up with her hifdh and madrassah studies. And I had to do unidirectional school runs only on Sundays and Fridays.

As usual, I watched her walk away from me, with a mixture of pride over the not-so-little-anymore human I've raised, and nostalgia for the little cheeky girl that thought I was "the best Mummy in the whole world!" I muttered a prayer that she was 'adjusting' better than I did at the beginning of my time there, and that she'll find at least one meaningful friendship in these formative years of her existence.

I remember thinking then that I should call Rekiya as soon as I got home. Before she left….

Then I dropped the boys at the madrassah. Their father had decided they needed a more structured study of their Deeni sciences, so weekend mornings was dedicated to that, and I found myself having several hours to myself several days a week.

Bliss.

And so, on that fateful day, I puttered about my house. Cleaning, and then taking a gloriously indulgent soak in the bathtub, putting final touches on a contract I was working on and checking in on the people who worked remotely for me. I was aware of a feeling of contentment – of rightness in my world as I finished praying 'asr and awaited the return of my sons.

Then the news broke all over the radio waves.

For a second, even as a cold wave of premonition washed over me, my brain refused to compute why information, certainly devastating in its own right, was catastrophic for me personally. But my body must have retained this knowledge because I found myself reaching for my phone and dialing. Then re-dialing.

And dialing again.

Is there anything worse than an unanswered or 'unavailable' phone when your anxiety is already spiraling?

I hit another speed dial. Same response. Again.

A third one.

She answers on the third ring, but I have no words.

'Umm AbdGhaffar, he's here. He didn't make the trip yesterday so he's here...,' Jummai's voice trails off and my brother's harried one comes on the line.

'Zaynunah. Tunde Gbadamosi was in Abuja and we decided they should travel together. You know how close they've become. As of last night, he wasn't ready to leave because his business wasn't finished, so there was some talk of staying a few more days. Right now, I'm not sure… I don't know if any of them are on this flight. I'm going to keep calling him. You keep calling her. We'll check in with each other as soon as we have any news. Ok? Insha Allaah, khayr.'

We ring off with Jummai's admonition to keep praying and holding unto hope.

I call the same phone number back to back. I am hoping for an innocuous reason like the phone's been stolen. Or even a somewhat sad one, like she's depressed she couldn't come 'start her life' yet – that's all she's talked about recently – and has turned off all electronics to wallow. That anything else was responsible for the obnoxious voice telling me the phone number is not available and imploring me to 'try again later.'

Her mum's call come in just as I was about to hit yet another re-dial. Or I call her. I don't remember. Neither of us know more than the other. She had called us individually early yesterday, before Tunde Gbadamosi was even in the plans. We both hoped that the change in plans had somehow kept her safe. We promised to keep each other updated…

I don't know how many minutes or centuries passed.

I prayed, and I kept calling. Futilely.

Then I hear Yusuf come in. He's on the phone, too, but he hugs me fiercely before settling us both on the sofa and handing me his phone. He does not say a word, his arms remain around me.

And I knew.

Even before Brother 'Isa's voice, distant and disembodied, informed me, I knew.

That on this fateful June afternoon in 2012, when the ill-fated flight from Abuja crashed just a couple of miles from its destination in Lagos, killing all aboard and six innocent by-standers, Ruqqayah Sodiq-Gbadamosi was one of its victims.

It's been almost three years since that fateful day, and the grief lingers.

Yes, we stopped mourning after three days, and didn't allow any transgressions of the limits of the religion Rekiya was re-discovering towards her very end. It helped that her mum and her brother, as representatives of their respective families, deferred to her new husband. Her burial was as swift as we could manage under the circumstances, and devoid of fanfare that might be expected of someone of Ruqqayyah's background and accomplishments.

And even I was unprepared for the extent of said accomplishments.

Aside from the media frenzy over this little-known daughter of Sodiq Gbadamosi, the international finance world mourned and celebrated the life of one of its *'rising stars, sunk too soon'*. There were accolades, testimonies and articles from all angles. And when Tunde Gbadamosi put out a press statement asking that the family be given space to grieve in peace, and that all condolence messages be sent to his head office in written form, or as a donation to a charity project his sister was involved in, the response was overwhelming.

He brought the personal messages to us in Ibadan, and we spent days reading, laughing, crying and marveling at this newest member of our family who had for so long given the impression of being so aloof yet had done so much, touched so many. And continues to do so, even in death…

Her will, typical of Rekiya, was a revelation.

Written while she was finalizing her move from Abuja, she directed a third of her assets to a trust to maintain the charity she'd founded. All existing charitable commitments she had made would be honored from that trust, and I was named managing trustee, along with her husband and brother in largely advisory but silent roles. The rest of her assets she trusted will be distributed by her husband to her rightful heirs in accordance with the Shari'ah. Both men, and the sister she'd never met, had promptly given up their shares to the charity and I found myself sole administrator of a charity fund worth millions.

That also helped, I supposed.

I had to hit the ground running, making sure the legacy Rekiya worked so hard to line up didn't die with her. She had secured an expanse of property close to Brother Isa's farm which we continued building as per her specification, and the House of Ruqqayyah became operational nine months after her death. It was the headquarters of the similarly named charity and housed a refuge of sorts for women who need help getting on, or getting back on, their feet. Aside from offering them a place to stay, if needed, we had programs to teach skills for economic empowerment, a network of people who were willing to employ our ladies, and a startup loan for those with viable business ideas.

It was a truly daunting task for me, at first, but time, nigh unlimited resources and constant support had helped me to somewhat get a handle on this legacy entrusted to me.

My grip on the grief accompanying the loss of my friend was more difficult to attain and is still tenuous at best. I suffered crying jags that left my husband so bewildered that I started to hide in the shower after the first couple of months. I couldn't explain to him, to anyone really, how pervasive the loss was. One minute I seemed to be fine and the next I was a blubbering mess of emotions, most of which I had difficulty deciphering myself.

I was bereft at losing my best friend, especially since we had just found each other again after so long. Yet I was grateful that we did find each other again, that I knew her at all, that she was able to make such tremendous changes in her life towards her end. I was hopeful that she was at peace now, that she found acceptance with her Lord from all that troubled her in this Dunya, that the testimonies of all she had done and all she had reached would weigh heavy on the scale of her good deeds. But then I would marvel at how much of me was wrapped up in our friendship, gasp at the void her absence would leave – a void that was never even glossed over in the years of our estrangement. And I would be overcome with regret and remorse for those years, for the time wasted – our blighted ignorance of how little of it she, we, had. I was humbled by how little I knew of this woman I thought I knew so well, awed by the extent her quiet generosity and innate goodness reached without any aggrandizing, humbled by how trifling my own life – and the concerns that dominated it daily – seemed in comparison.

All these and many more emotions rode me in varying combinations in the period following her demise, indiscriminate of any order or precedence. And my triggers were as innocent as they were ubiquitous. School girls in uniform, the sight of my brother, some random memory, the quiet of the night time prayer – anything and everything could set of an almost physical sensation of pain in my chest that could cause me to weep, drop a tear, smile, clutch my chest while gasping for breath, or pray. I found my solace in making du'a for her whenever I was once again confronted with the knowledge that she was no more. That, and taking a morbid comfort in the fact that Mummy died first, and I had survived that. I knew I would survive this too, I just had to be patient.

It took me a while to appreciate when I stopped spontaneously bursting into tears. And I had to re-learn what I knew from my experience with Mummy – that while it is true, the pain does not go away; time does blunt the edges. The sharp lances become dull aches, they scab over, and we heal the best we can. The invisible scars, occasional twinges and aches that remain are the lasting reminders of all we have lost. The hard-won gains we will always treasure.

GLOSSARY OF TERMS

Rekiya/ Rukayat – Hausa/Yoruba variations of the same Arabic name, Ruqqayyah.

As-Salaam alayki/um warahmtullaah wabarakah – Lit. 'May Peace, and Allaah's mercy and Blessings, be with you' is the customary greeting among Muslims. There are various diminutive forms, all generally referred to as giving/replying the salaam.

Amala – a staple starchy meal made from yam flour, usually eaten with a form of vegetable soup.

Insha Allaah – Lit. 'God willing.' The phrase Muslims are encouraged to use while making plans, an acknowledgement of the fact that only God knows and controls the events of the future.

Pele – Lit. 'Sorry', it is a phrase wielded with deft power by the Yoruba, in different ways under different circumstances.

Halaal/Haraam – permitted/forbidden under Islaamic law.

Abaya – a flowing outer garment traditionally worn by Muslim women in public.

Salaah – pl. *salawaat*. Any of the five obligatory prayers prescribed at fixed daily times. *Fajr, Zuhr, Asr, Maghrib, 'Isha* are the names of the dawn, noon, afternoon, sunset and evening prayers.

Dua – supplication, the act of asking God for something.

Takbir – the act of saying 'Allaahu Akbar' i.e. 'God is the Greatest'

Ankara and Adire – local African prints

Iro and Buba – Traditional garb of Yoruba woman, consisting of a loose blouse and a wrapper worn around the waist.

Tahajjud – an optional prayer offered at the pre-dawn period.

Ileya – Yoruba term for 'Eid ul-Adha, the major Muslim festival celebrated at the culmination of the annual pilgrimage. The other 'eid, 'Eid al-fitr, is called *itunnu awe* – lit. 'breaking of the fast', a reflection of the fact that it is held at the end of Ramadhaan, the month of fasting.

Alakowe – a Yoruba term for an educated person/ their mannerisms, sometimes used derisively.

Abula- A combination of two soups; gbegiri, bean soup, and ewedu, parsley soup.

Buka – dinghy local eateries that are better experienced than explained.

Haafidh/Haafidhah – a male/female who has committed the entire text of the Qur'an to memory. Hifdh is the process/act of memorizing.

MSSN- Muslim Students' Society of Nigeria

JAMB – Joint Admission Matriculation Board. The body that regulates admission into higher educational institutions in Nigeria.

Adhkaar – Plural of Dhikr, i.e. remembrance of Allaah. It often involves chanting/repeating/meditating on phrases that reminds one of God and our reliance on Him.

Sunnah – a term loosely used to encompass the ways and life of the Prophet.

Jumu'ah – The Friday noon prayer is a weekly congregational one that is said in select mosques and consists of a religious talk, *Khutbah*, before the prayer units.

MSA – Muslim Students Association.

Zina – Pre-/Extra- marital sex. Sex outside of wedlock.

Qadar – Destiny/ predestination. It is one of the six articles that a Muslim must believe in.

419 – Fraudulent/ related to fraud.

Naija – What Nigerians call their country in informal exasperation.

Baba Adinni – A totally weightless title conferred upon prominent, usually rich, Nigerians in the South-West region.

Iqaamah – The last 'call to prayer' said to indicate the start of the prayer.

Deen – Religion. Deeni is used for 'related to religion.'

Subhanallaah – Glory be to Allaah. Sometimes used as an exclamation.

Astagfirullaah – 'I ask for God's forgiveness'

AlhamduliLlaah – 'Praise be to Allaah'

Auzabillaah – 'I seek refuge in Allaah'. It's said as a supplication for protection

Dat wan na grammar – Nigerian Pidgin English for 'That's just semantics.'

Khushoo' – Mindfulness in prayer

Juz – the parts, 30 in all, of the Qur'an.

Tajweed – rules about the proper pronunciation and recitation of the Qur'an

Kulu temper – The Nigerian Yoruba take on 'cool your temper'

Muraaja' – Revision. In context of the memorization of the Qur'an, it means revising the parts already memorized.

Naafil/ Nawafil – Supererogatory acts of worship, as opposed to the obligatory ones.

Rakaa' – prayer units. Each prayer has between 2-4 units of prayer.

Istikhara – A special prayer asking for guidance when faced with a major decision.

Ibaadat – Acts of worship. It's plural for Ibadah, singular.

Waliyy – Guardian. In Islam, a woman is married with the permission of her closest male relative – father, brother, uncle, son etc. In absence of a Muslim relative in this capacity, a trusted Muslim man of authority can stand in.

Nikkah – marriage, the solemnization, the contract

Munnaqqabah – a woman who covers her face in presence of non-related males.

Dunya - The worldly life, as opposed to the life of the hereafter.

BarakaLlaahu feek – May Allaah bless you/it. Usually said as a congratulatory prayer.

Walimah – A feast to celebrate an occasion, usually marriage.

Ingram Content Group UK Ltd.
Milton Keynes UK
UKHW011830270423
420877UK00001B/97